Murder Ahoy!

A Bella Tyson Mystery

By Fiona Leitch

Copyright © 2020 Fiona Leitch

The right of Fiona Leitch to be identified as the Author of the Work has been asserted by her in accordance with the Copyright, Designs and Patents Act 1998.

Published in 2020 by Fiona Leitch

Apart from any use permitted under copyright law, this publication may only be reproduced, stored, or transmitted, in any form or by any means, with prior permission in writing of the publisher or, in the case of reprographic production, in accordance with the terms of licences issued by the Copyright Licensing Agency.

All characters in this publication are fictitious and any resemblance to real persons, living or dead, is purely coincidental.

PROLOGUE

"Where do you get your ideas from?"

I've been asked that question so many times in interviews over the years that these days I have a stock reply. People don't really want to know the answer, because in reality it's pretty boring. They'd rather you came up with some mystical old codswallop about Art and Truth and Unleashing Your Inner Creativity. I was interviewed by this New Age women's journal once, and I managed to convince them that I go and sit in my garden at midnight in just my pants, listening to the susurration of the wind in the trees and the hoot of the barn owl as it hunted for sustenance, in the same way that I was spiritually hunting for my Vision. I would enjoy the evening breeze on my nipples, engage my Inner Core, and commune with the Earth Goddess until I felt the tingle of inspiration (or maybe cramp, due to engaging my Inner Core a bit too strenuously).

This is - and I can not stress this enough - bollocks. For starters, I live in London, and the only thing I'd be listening to if I sat in my garden at midnight would be the mange-ridden neighbourhood fox rifling through my bins; plus it's really bloody difficult communing with the goddess when you're under the Heathrow flightpath and your nipples are being nibbled (not in a sexy way) by gnats. And anyway, I'm normally in my jammies by 9, in bed by 10 and (if Will's not too tired) rolling over to go to sleep by 11. Okay, 10.30. 10.15, at least.

"Where do you get your ideas from?" - like it's a secret. Like there's some clandestine, exclusive Writers' Club where you're inducted into The Ways of the Wordsmith. That way, if you're one of these people who could *definitely* write a bestseller but don't, it's not because you're not good enough, it's because you don't know the right people and you're not part of the club. (There are myriad reasons why your book isn't a bestseller, usually very little to do with you not being good enough and mostly to do with marketing, but definitely nothing to do with this mythical Writer's Club. Which, by the way, if it existed, I definitely wouldn't be invited to join.)

I get my ideas from the same place everyone else does. I see things on the telly or in the paper. Items on the news. This is how you get a slew of books and movies all on the same subject; everyone gets inspired by the same thing. NASA sends up a rover to explore Mars, and all of a sudden you get four thousand books and movies about trips to the red planet. Are they all the same? Not exactly. They won't all have the protagonist surviving on potatoes grown in their own faecal matter (pootatoes?). Some will be more similar than others (there are only so many plots), but that doesn't mean that they've copied or are even aware of each other.

Other times, of course, it'll be something that happens to me on my travels. Like going to Venice and getting embroiled in a gruesome murder investigation. Or getting stuck on a boat in the middle of the Atlantic with the person you hate most in the entire world, and watching as the bodies start to pile up.

That sort of thing…

Some people say that the worst thing you can accuse a writer of is plagiarism, of purposely stealing someone else's ideas and passing them off as their own.

This is also bollocks.

CHAPTER 1

It sometimes seems to me that the more successful I get as a writer, the less people actually want me to write. There are book tours and signings, of course, and some of the crime writing festivals are fun. I love meeting my readers. But then I get asked to do after dinner speeches at corporate Christmas parties (rubbish like 'Harnessing the Killer Instinct in Business'); or give talks about 'How to Write the Perfect Crime' (there is no such thing as a 'perfect' crime, or if there is I don't want to hear about it, because my characters always have to be able to solve them). I even got asked to do Celebrity Masterchef once and turned it down because quite frankly, God would not have invented Waitrose OR Uber Eats if She'd intended people to cook stuff from scratch. They got one of the Chuckle Brothers instead.

When people first started asking me to do stuff like that I always said yes. I didn't particularly want to do any of it, but I thought it would be arrogant to turn people down when they were nice enough to think of little old me. I've got a lot better at saying 'no' over the years, but there are some things you just don't turn down.

And this was one of them. A whole week on a fancy cruise liner, leading a team of amateur detectives in a murder mystery game every night, and being pampered in the luxurious surroundings during the day. I wasn't sure how I would possibly manage…

"There you are! Thank God!" Susie waved and rushed over to me and Will. She had our tickets in her hand and a harassed expression on her face. Being my agent does that to you, apparently.

"We're not late, are we?" asked Will, watching as the taxi driver took our suitcases from the boot of the car. Susie gestured over to a porter who was hovering nearby, who hurriedly loaded the luggage onto a trolley and disappeared into the cruise terminal at speed.

"Not quite," said Susie, corralling us in the porter's wake. "You're cutting it fine as usual, though."

"I just like to make an entrance," I said, stopping to look up at the cruise ship in awe. The biggest ship I'd been on up to now was the Isle of Wight ferry, and the longest sea journey I'd had was a memorable (for all the wrong reasons) school trip to Dieppe in the 5th year of high school, when Sarah Wells had somehow managed to get her hands on some duty free vodka and puked up spectacularly all over the lower deck, and Miss Rogers the history teacher had had a nervous breakdown, thinking she'd left Lynda Benson behind in France when she was actually just hiding in the toilets having a fag. As you can probably tell, I didn't go to Cheltenham Girls' College.

"Holy shi - " I started, gazing upwards at the architecturally impressive, gleaming white and basically fecking massive ship next to us. Will looked at me and smiled. I bit off the end of the word. "No swearing on the posh boat, I remember."

"Come *on*!" said Susie, exasperated. Will and I exchanged amused looks and legged it after her.

We breezed through check-in and made our way through the terminal, onto the glass-covered gangway that led us up and onto the ship. Smiling crew members in spotless white uniforms lined the entrance, checking tickets and showing passengers where to go; despite Susie's attack of the vapours, we weren't the last people to board by any stretch of the imagination.

A sturdy but smartly dressed woman, whose gold pips on the shoulder of her white suit suggested a higher rank than that of her colleagues, stepped forward to greet us.

"Ms Tyson?" She spoke at a professionally discreet volume in a soft, Scottish burr, and I immediately warmed to her. She held her hand out to shake. "I'm Maureen O'Connor, the Chief Purser. Let me show you to your room."

"Thank you," I said, smiling. She gestured along the corridor in front of her and stood back to let us go first.

We made our way along the hallway. Everything was plush and opulent; the carpets were thick and soft under our feet, muffling the sounds of the passengers behind us, and the walls were lined with artwork and mirrors on a large scale. The ship had an almost 1930s, Art Deco feel of decadence about it, despite being less than 20 years old. It gleamed warmly, with walnut panelling and gilded statues. Even some of the crew were bronzed. A young man in an immaculate white polo shirt and trousers smiled at me with teeth that matched his clothing as he quietly rapped his knuckles on a door off the corridor; no one here would be so uncouth as to actually make a loud noise. I felt Susie's earlier panic subside slightly; you couldn't be stressed on a ship like this.

We took the lift up to deck 10, and made our way to the back of the ship (or aft or whatever you call it when you're on a boat - the fat end, as opposed to the pointy bit at the front. I dunno, you look it up). We reached the end of the corridor and stopped as the Chief Purser took a key card from her pocket and swiped it. I turned and looked back along the corridor, surprised at how far it stretched ahead of me. This really was a fu - flipping big ship.

Behind me the door softly clicked open - everything on this ship was soft and discreet, it seemed, and I suspected I would stand out like a sore thumb - and again, the Purser stood back to let us in.

"Holy shi - shiz balls!" I cried, looking around at our home for the next week. It was bigger than half the places I'd lived in, let alone holidayed in. The flat I'd rented when I first left home, where I'd written my first novel on my nan's ancient typewriter balanced on a couple of old milk crates, had been half the size of this cabin. The carpet was deep enough to lose a small child in. A soft, cream coloured sofa and armchair sat in front of a glass topped coffee table, laid with an ice bucket and bottle of champagne, glasses and a crystal-handled corkscrew. I was relieved to see that to one side of the room was a small kitchenette and dining area; I do like a nice cup of tea first thing in the morning - and last thing at night - and several times during the day - so I *hate* staying anywhere without a kettle and a fridge. The room was divided by a tall bookcase, with a large TV set in it, giving access either side to the bedroom. The bed was big enough for an entire harem - shame I hadn't brought one with me - and the bedlinen was as crisp and white as newly-fallen snow. A padded gold silk headboard, studded with crystal buttons, and a matching gold and crystal chandelier gave it a feeling of expensive, tasteful luxury.

"Bloody hell!" said Will. I looked at him. He shrugged. "That's not really a swear word, is it?"

The Chief Purser followed us into the room and drew back the gold shot taffeta curtains at the big glass doors to let in some more light, then turned and placed the key card on the coffee table.

"I think you'll be comfortable in here," she said. I laughed.

"We'll manage, we're used to roughing it," I said. "It's lovely, thank you so much."

"You're very welcome," said the Purser. "And may I say it's a pleasure to have you and Mr Tyson on board. I'm a big fan of your work."

I could hear Will muttering under his breath as he investigated the bathroom. "Mr Tyson my ars - armpit…"

I ignored him. "Thank you. We're really looking forward to murdering someone on this cruise."

The Purser laughed. "Between you and me, I've felt like that a few times on this ship myself! Please, take some time to settle in and then join us at the bar when you're ready, I know the Captain would like to say hello before dinner. The steward will bring your luggage up presently."

Susie grabbed the bottle of champagne and had already poured out three glasses before the Purser had finished closing the door behind her. "It would be rude not to," she pointed out, noticing my expression. I laughed.

"And you're never rude. There's a drink for you here, Mr Tyson!" I called. Will joined us.

"Thank you, *Mrs Carmichael*." I handed him the champagne flute and kissed him.

"I'm sorry. This is work, innit? Our next holiday will be as Mr and Mrs Carmichael, I promise."

We looked around the beautiful, richly but tastefully decorated cabin again. I prodded the bed experimentally.

"Nice work," said Susie, enviously. "*Some* of us have to go back to a tiny office in London for *their* work."

"Yeah, it's a hard life, innit?" I said, flopping (carefully, so as not to spill my drink) onto the bed. It was perfect; not too hard, but not too soft either - like floating on an orthopaedic cloud. "It's a - " I frowned and reached under the pillow, drawing out a slightly squashed but thankfully wrapped chocolate truffle. "It's a shame you're not coming with us. I'll tell Peter and Mark that you said hello."

"Peter and Mark?" asked Will.

"My fellow crime writers," I said, my cheek bulging with chocolate (I can unwrap a truffle in less than 5 seconds. Years of practice). "Peter James and Mark Billingham. I told you, they're hosting the cruise with us."

Susie looked at me, guiltily. "Ah, yes, about that…" She took a gulp of champagne. The harassed expression was back, and clearly had nothing to do with us running late. "There's been a bit of a change to the line up. Mark had to pull out at the very last minute. Family emergency."

'Oh, that's a shame!" I said. "I haven't seen him since Harrogate, two, maybe three years ago. Never mind. Peter - "

"Yes, and so did Peter." Susie knocked back her drink and set the glass down on the table, looking at her watch. "Look at the time, you'll be sailing soon. I'd better go."

"Not Peter too?" I was really disappointed now. I'd been looking forward to catching up with old friends. "Who's taken their places?"

There was a knock on the cabin door. Will opened it to find the tanned young man with the ridiculously white teeth outside.

"The ship is getting ready to sail," he said. He may have looked like a bronzed Adonis, but his accent was pure Liverpudlian scally. "Anyone not sailing needs to make their way back onto shore. Sorry."

"That's fine," said Susie hastily, heading for the door. "I was just leaving."

I followed her and gave her a hug before she could escape. "Thank you for getting me into this," I said. "And Will, too. You are officially the best agent and friend a writer could have, ever. It'll be like our honeymoon, only with a few murders thrown in for good measure. It'll be fun!" I said lightly. Susie looked unconvinced.

"Hmm, yes, well we'll see about that," she said, then made a quick exit before I could ask her what she meant.

The steward with the white teeth came back five minutes later, accompanied by a porter with our luggage. He introduced himself as Karl and said that if we needed anything at all on the voyage, to let him know. As he shut the door behind him, Will pulled me into his arms and kissed me long and hard.

"Steady now, Mr Tyson," I said. He laughed.

"I suppose I can put up with being a kept man if it means we get to go on trips like this," he said, letting go and looking around the cabin again. I grabbed him and pulled him towards me.

"Now don't you go thinking you don't have to earn your keep," I said, reaching down to squeeze his bottom. He looked shocked.

"Mrs Carmichael! What would the Captain say?"

"I dunno, I wasn't planning on telling him…"

CHAPTER 2

The ship sailed at 6.30pm. We did the whole standing-on-the-deck-waving-goodbye thing, even though there was no one seeing us off (Susie hadn't waited, having a three hour drive back to London). We stood on our private balcony and waved at a group of people on the docks, who stared back at us clearly wondering who the hell we were and why we were waving at them.

We went back inside and threw ourselves on the bed in a fit of giggles. That's one of the things I love so much about Will: his laugh. He's got quite a deep, manly voice, and is so nicely spoken that he could read out the telephone directory and make it sound sexy (I do have a bit of a thing about posh boys, though), but when he really gets the giggles he goes all high pitched and sounds like a 14 year old whose testicles haven't quite dropped yet. It's not exactly a turn on, but it is really sweet and endearing and always makes me sigh and think, *everything is just fine with my life.* Sigh.

"How the - heck - did we end up here?" I said, still giggling. "I'm a university dropout from Croydon, but here I am in the penthouse cabin of the fanciest ship in the world, *and* I'm getting paid to be here!"

"You do have to work," pointed out Will. He can be so sensible at times. I find that quite sexy, too. Sue me, I'm a weirdo. "Not that it'll be particularly hard. The most difficult thing for you will be - "

"Not swearing in front of the paying guests, I know!" I rolled over and propped myself up on an elbow to look at him. "I'm not a child, I can f-fudging well behave myself."

"I *was* going to say, to not give the game away," he said, rolling his eyes.

"I can't give it away, can I? I don't know whodunnit," I said. He looked surprised.

"I thought Susie gave you a pack, with the story and all the characters - "

"She did, but I'm only supposed to look at it if my group are completely useless and we don't get any of the clues," I explained. "I don't *want* to know. It's more fun if we don't, innit?"

"True..." Will laughed. "You can tell which one of us works in law enforcement, can't you? I don't want to test my detective skills, I just want to know who the murderer is." He frowned suddenly, narrowing his eyes and reaching out to pluck something from behind my ear. "I just found that other pillow chocolate..."

I laughed as he managed to unwrap the extremely squashed truffle and held it out to me, teasing me with it, then popped it in his own mouth.

"It tastes strangely warm..." he said, chewing.

"Serves you right. Anyway, the important question now is..." I draped myself languidly across the hopefully chocolate-free pillow, pouting in what I hoped was a seductive fashion but probably looked like someone sucking a lemon. "...have you ever had sex on a boat?"

Will raised an eyebrow. "No, but I thought about it in Venice... I thought about getting a sign for *La Sirena*, that night we had dinner on her." Will and I had met in Italy, when I was trying to find inspiration for a new book, and he'd certainly provided that. "Something like, 'if my boat is a-rocking, don't come a-knocking.'"

"Classy. You'd definitely have got my knickers off with that line."

We managed to contain ourselves and instead of ripping each other's clothes off (which, not having been married that long, we were still in the habit of doing), we changed into more formal outfits and headed for the bar. I had to restrain myself from wriggling, as the dress I was wearing kept riding up over my knees and I was worried about giving the other passengers an eyeful of my massive Harvest Festival pants (so called because 'everything is safely gathered in'). As I would be hosting a table at dinner every night, when the murder mystery game would be played out, I couldn't get away with skulking about in the cabin in my jeans and trainers, and would have to dress like a grown-ass, sophisticated woman for a whole week. It really would be murder.

The bar looked like something out of the Great Gatsby, beautifully decorated in warm wood tones with gold and bronze accents, lots of geometric-shaped mirrors and plush red velvet seating. Waiters did the rounds with glasses of champagne and wafted past with trays of delicate, delicious canapés. Guests came and went, some watching from the sidelines until they were imbued with enough Dutch courage to join the melée, others confidently diving straight in, clearly old hands at cruising. Will grabbed two glasses of Bucks Fizz and led me over to a seat. I'm not shy, but the thought of just going over and talking to someone I didn't know - no thank you. I'm a writer, and most of the people I talk to are in my head or on a page.

"I should probably mingle…" I said weakly, but Will shook his head.

"Let them come to you," he said. "They will."

He was right. They did. I'd barely taken a sip when a woman of around 60 with bright blue eye shadow and a hairstyle so heavily lacquered you could probably have cracked open a coconut on it nervously approached me.

"I'm sorry to bother you," she said, "but you are Annabelle Tyson, aren't you?"

After that, it was Game On. The passengers had found out whose teams they were on when they'd checked into their cabins, and my team were quick to introduce themselves. Helmet Hair lady's actual name was Sylvia, and she was on the cruise with her best friend Heather. They were from Derbyshire and were officially Off Men, but from the way the two of them were looking around at all the single males in the room (particularly young Karl, who was helping to entertain some of the quieter guests), I got the impression they would both be back On (or possibly Under) Men by the end of the week. There was a married German couple, whose names I instantly forgot but who seemed nice enough, and Harvey and Michael, who were on their honeymoon and so clearly madly in love that I fell for the two of them straight away. Will watched them too, smiling, and when they left to get drinks we both looked at each other and said, "Aaah!!"

There were several more team members who hadn't come along for the welcome drinks, but I was quite pleased about that; meeting loads of new people at once can be overwhelming.

But I still didn't know who the other team leaders were. The guests that I spoke to had all been under the same impression as me, that my old crime writing friends Peter and Mark would be hosting the other tables, but apparently the line up had changed right at the last minute. During a respite in the bombardment I looked around to see if there was anyone I recognised; after all, the tickets had been expensive enough for the guests to expect crime writing hosts of a certain calibre, and I thought I knew most of my contemporaries, certainly all the European ones, anyway, from the annual Smoking Gun awards or festivals like Harrogate and Bloody Scotland.

The room was full and bustling, with guests and crew alike - I'd read somewhere that this ship could accommodate around 2,000 passengers, not that they would all be taking part in the murder mystery - and from my seat it was impossible to see through the crowd by the bar. The moment I thought that, the crowd parted and I gasped. A figure leant insouciantly against the polished wood and chrome counter, tall, slim but in a muscular kind of way, dark haired. They did not talk to anyone, just lifted the pint glass in their hand to their lips and looked around, coolly observing the room.

"Oh fu -" I breathed.

"Language!" muttered Will, warningly. I shook my head.

"No, no… It's Joel," I said.

"Joel? Not - "

"Yes, Joel. My ex-husband. He's at the bar. He must be one of the other hosts."

As we watched, Joel, the bastard unfaithful ex-husband, he of the third rate but inexplicably successful crime novels and the string of affairs, turned and caught my eye, and gave me The Look.

If you're a woman, you'll know The Look. It's the one that turns your knees to jelly and involuntarily loosens your knicker elastic, the one that starts a fire in your nether regions and travels all the way up to your cheeks (the facial ones). Not all men have The Look - Will has A Look, which I love, but it's not the same thing. The Look comes in different variations - it can be a knowing smile, a twinkle in the eye, even an arrogant, slightly disdainful sneer (Joel's Look was definitely closest to the latter). But the one thing that all Looks have in common is that the only men who really have them are the ones who have already broken your heart at least once.

So there stood my bastard unfaithful ex-husband, the one who had already broken my heart several times, giving me The Look. And I'm ashamed to admit that for one moment, it worked. I wasn't sure if I wanted to smack him so hard in the mouth that his teeth landed in someone's drink on the other side of the room, or rip his shirt off and lick him like a testosterone-flavoured lollipop.

"Are you alright?" said Will next to me, and I flushed with shame this time rather than lust. I was disgusted with myself for giving into carnal thoughts of Joel for even one second when my wonderful, loving and sexy new husband stood beside me.

"Absolutely fine," I said, not believing quite how calm I sounded.

"You'd better be, because he's coming over," said Will, looking worried. I squeezed his hand and smiled at him, then grabbed another drink off a passing waiter and downed half of it in one go.

"Bella!" I looked up and there he was, the big beautiful bastard... I tried not to remember the first time we met, when we'd ended up having a drunken shag in his trashy hotel room the night he'd beaten me to a Smoking Gun crime writer's award. And then I burped, because I'd drunk my glass of bubbly too fast.

He leaned in to kiss me on the cheek. "You look great, the extra weight suits you." And just like that I was cured. He was still an absolute wanker. I looked around; our messy and acrimonious divorce was common knowledge, of course, and had filled a few column inches at the time as news of his numerous infidelities and my subsequent withdrawal from writing (and life) had spread. Sure enough, the passengers around us were looking over, watching to see how we would react to each other. *Let's give them something to watch,* I thought.

"Oh my god!" I cried. "I'm surprised to see you looking so well. They treated the syphilis, then? Did they manage to save your penis?" Will guffawed loudly before clapping a hand over his mouth, while Joel's wide smile faltered for a moment and he looked around to see who had heard before he could stop himself. I looked penitent. "Sorry, I shouldn't have said anything." I turned to the watching crowd. "It's a sore point," I explained to them.

He was silent for a second, then forced a loud, hearty and unconvincing laugh. "Still the same old Bella," he said, with a smile that didn't reach his eyes. His gaze flickered over to Will, who was still standing patiently next to me, grinning. Will wiped the smile off his face abruptly and put his hand out to shake.

"I'm Will. You must be Joel?" he said, in a friendly, man-to-man tone. "Bella's told me so much about you."

Joel's lip curled slightly as he looked back at me. "I bet she has…"

"Yes," said Will. "I thought she was joking, though." He looked Joel up and down, then held his arm out to me. "I believe they're about to announce dinner. Shall we?"

"I'd be delighted," I said, smiling at him. God, he was just The Best. Forget The Look, what every woman *really* needs is a man who sticks up for her, makes her laugh and buys her sanitary products without complaining. I took his arm and we headed for the door.

"You are *so* getting lucky tonight," I murmured to him.

"Was there ever any doubt of that?" he asked, smiling, and I had to admit there wasn't.

CHAPTER 3

There were several different restaurants on board, but the murder mystery was taking place in a smaller, more intimate venue just off the extremely grand, two deck high Excelsior dining room. We walked through the Excelsior, which had dialled up the red and gold velvet theme to 11, and up the sweeping staircase. A smiling hostess in a gorgeous red Chinese silk dress, richly embroidered, greeted us with a smile and showed us through an imposing double door, mirrored and decorated with gilded ornamental wrought ironwork. We had entered the Pearl of the Orient…

Inside, the interior designer had been given the brief 'deluxe opium den', and had run with it. The room was lined with hand-painted Chinoiserie wallpaper in peacock shades of deep blue and green, with colourful exotic birds lurking amongst the emerald fronds of trees and ferns, and the occasional beautiful pinky white rose. At one end of the room was a bar, decorated with more mirrors and again overlaid with gilded ironwork, portraying golden koi carp darting in and out of contorted seaweed. Overhead, an array of pendant lights hung over the dining tables, simple bright white globes that lit up the gilded ceiling like clusters of pearls. The name had made it sound like a Chinese takeaway, but it was an Oriental vision of Paradise.

"Go ahead if you need to swear," said Will out of the corner of his mouth, seeing me gawp.

The Captain stood in the middle of the room, resplendent in his white dress uniform, talking animatedly to the Chief Purser, who saw us enter and nodded slightly. The Captain whirled round and smiled as he saw us. He was a well built man, who had clearly fully enjoyed the dining facilities on this vessel, and he had a great big beaming smile.

"Ms Tyson! And Mr Carmichael!" he said, as he strode over to us, hand already outstretched in greeting. He had a loud, hearty voice. I sensed Will's immediate approval of the man for getting our names right. "I'm Captain Butler. So pleased to have you on board." He grabbed my hand and pumped it up and down energetically, then repeated the process on Will's. "So pleased. Sorry I didn't get to have a drink with you earlier, so much to organise on a trip like this."

"Of course," I said, resisting the urge to rub the feeling back into my hand; he had a firm grip. "A ship like this must take some running…"

"She's magnificent, isn't she?" he boomed. "I've had the fortune to be in charge of her for three years, and I still can't quite believe my luck. This is the first murder mystery cruise we've had, though, so I'm relying on your criminal expertise to help us run it smoothly."

"I'll do my best," I said.

"And you're Interpol, I believe?" The Captain turned to Will. "Everyone will want you on their team, won't they?"

"I'm semi-retired," said Will. "And there's only one team I'm on."

"And that's exactly as it should be," said the Captain. "The other teams have got great leaders as well though, so you won't have it all your own way. Maureen - you met the Chief Purser earlier, didn't you? - she's overseeing a team on my behalf. I wanted to be involved but I'm just too busy to do more than dip in and out."

The other diners were starting to enter. I looked around, recognising the members of my team that we'd already met.

"How many guests are taking part?" I asked. The Captain turned to the Chief Purser, who had joined us.

"There are just over two thousand passengers on the ship," she said, "but of course we couldn't have that many people playing, particularly not on our first foray into it. We've limited the murder mystery experience to just twenty, so you'll have five guests on your team." She smiled. "Of course, they're not necessarily all paying guests. We have our murder victims, our murderer and a few suspects in there as well."

I smiled. "Not a bad acting gig, is it? Although I suppose if you get murdered straight away you end up confined to your cabin for the whole cruise."

The Captain laughed. "Yes, we thought we'd give them one night of freedom before we start bumping them off."

"So who's the fourth team leader?" asked Will. "We saw Joel Quigley in the bar."

"And that was a *marvellous* surprise," I muttered under my breath.

Captain Butler and the Purser exchanged uncomfortable looks. "Sorry about that," said the Captain. "I hope it won't cause you any awkwardness or embarrassment."

"Not as long as he's one of the victims," I said. The Captain snorted, amused.

"I don't think that's part of the plan," he said, "although of course I could have a word with the murderer…" He looked over my shoulder and smiled. "Here he is now, with the other team leader." I turned around to see who my other rival was, the smile dying on my lips. "Have you met Louise before?"

"Mother fudger!" I growled. Will looked at me, surprised. "Bloody Louise bloody Meyers."

Bloody Louise bloody Meyers (not the name she was born with, obviously) stood in the doorway, arm draped languidly through Joel's.

She was dressed in a glittery black 1920s style flapper dress, her glossy brown hair cut in a smooth bob and her thin lips smeared in bright red lipstick. She paused by the mirrored doors for a moment, framed by them, and looked around to make sure everyone was watching her make an entrance. They weren't. She threw back her head to laugh loudly - causing Joel, who hadn't said anything to provoke such a violent reaction, to jump out of his skin - and all eyes turned towards her. She revelled in it, tossing her hair again and bestowing a 'yes-adoring-fans-it-really-is-me' look at the assembled passengers.

Fudging heck. Now I knew why Susie had been so stressed out earlier, and it had nothing to do with us running late. She'd found out who the other team leaders were and knew exactly how I'd react to them…

Joel whispered something in her ear and Louise laughed again, her eyes - which weren't amused - darting around the room until they settled on me. She smiled broadly, showing off her crooked front teeth, and tossed her hair *again*. What was she, a bloody show pony?

"Is she in a shampoo advert or something?" asked Will. I laughed weakly but he could tell my heart was sinking at the thought of being stuck on a boat with the two people I despised most in the entire world (those not involved in politics, anyway). He squeezed my hand gently. "Fork them both."

"I may not be able to keep up the non-swearing thing," I murmured, then took a deep breath as they approached.

"Bella Tyson!" Bloody Louise. You had to hand it to her, she might have the most strident Northern accent since Ena Sharples had graced the cobblestones of Coronation Street, but she did 'sincere' almost convincingly. She must've been practising. "Well aren't you a sight for sore eyes."

"Not as big a sight as you," I simpered, knowing that in about three hours' time I'd sit bolt upright in bed and come out with a really biting, witty, and perfect retort, and the only audience would be Will, snoring next to me. "Such a lovely surprise to see you here."

She smiled. "Yeah, cruises are not usually my kind of thing, they're so - " she licked her lips, as if trying to get rid of a nasty taste in her mouth - *"middle aged and middle class."* She looked at Will.

"Yeah, the middle classes have got all the best holiday destinations," I said. Her eyes narrowed slightly as she tried to work out if I was being sarcastic or not, but she didn't say anything. "Still, it's a nice change from Skegness, innit?"

"Most things are," said Joel, disloyally. Typical Joel. Her lips tightened for a second.

"Nowt wrong with staying in touch with your roots," she said. "Speaking of which, Bell, I think yours need doing. Or are you embracing the grey?"

"Mother Nature's highlights," I said. "I'm happy with who I am, I don't feel the need to put on a show." *Just a big pair of pants to hide the middle aged spread.*

"The wisdom of age." Louise smiled at me, like an orca smiling at a baby seal on a wildlife programme; you knew something nasty was about to happen. She opened her mouth to follow up with the killer remark but Joel stepped in and inadvertently saved me.

"We should probably go and say hello to Captain Birdseye over there," he said. Louise looked put out for a second, then she smiled seductively at him.

"I wonder if he's got a spare captain's hat?" she said. "I'd *love* to see you in one of those…" She stroked his arm, gazing up at him, and sang in a low, breathy voice. "You can leave your hat on…"

Joel laughed, but even he looked a bit surprised, and I got the impression that however close Louise was trying to make them look, the relationship was so new it was practically box fresh and probably still had the sticky price label on it somewhere. I wouldn't have put it past Joel to try and make me jealous, but I was surprised that Louise - actually, no I wasn't surprised, I wouldn't have put anything past her as she so clearly hated my guts.

"That woman so clearly hates my guts," I said, as they left us.

"I get the feeling it's mutual," said Will. I nodded vehemently. "So what started it off?"

I'd met bloody Louise bloody Meyers on a writers' panel at the Harrogate Crime Writing Festival. In her 30 years on this planet she'd managed to write two half-arsed crime novels and one 'real life' memoir about her terrible childhood, charting her rags to riches rise to, well, mediocrity. I had 18 years and 15 books on her, and an army of loyal readers, and she really should not have bothered me as much as she did - but she did. She'd written about her life of poverty and crime in t'back streets of Manchester, emphasising how humble and grateful she was for the life she had now whilst also banging on and on and on about how much she'd suffered. Every time you thought she'd hit peak suffering, no, something *else* would come up on social media about how she'd been bullied or abused or gaslit or rejected by her parents or something, until she'd built an entire career on her own victimhood. Self pity appeared to sell a lot of books, too.

So we'd both been guests on a panel entitled 'Using Genre to Subvert Societal Norms' (yes, I know exactly how that sounds, but there were actually some good points to be made). It was all going swimmingly until bloody Louise piped up.

"Of course," she said, "all of this means bugger all if you're writing from the working class stand point. Agents and publishers say they want diverse voices but they don't take you seriously if you went to an ordinary working class comprehensive."

Seriously? I looked at her. "I went to a state school and it hasn't stopped me."

"Yeah, but then you were in London - "

"London's not just Harrods and the Houses of Parliament, is it? I went to the same sort of school as you did. Most of the people in this room did. I didn't spend my adolescence conjugating Latin verbs and playing lacrosse, I bunked off and went shoplifting in the Whitgift Centre." The audience laughed and Louise shot a deadly look at me, but I was in full swing now.
"I wasn't part of some mythical Bloomsbury-esque Croydon Set, there wasn't any South London Writers' Salon. Class has got nothing to do with anything."

"You can't say there's no snobbery," Louise protested. "When I wrote my first two novels, no one would even look at them because I didn't 'fit'." I groaned, but she carried on. "I pitched them both to agents and they just weren't interested once they 'eard my accent and realised I 'adn't gone t'right university," she said, dropping Hs left, right and centre as her accent got stronger, whether on purpose to make a point or because she'd been suppressing it. I'd noticed in the past that she seemed to be simultaneously proud of her background whilst also having a massive chip on her shoulder about it, but it was quite amusing to see it in action.

"Do you know how many people in the industry have asked me if I have a degree?" I said. "None. Literally no one cares."

"Well I suppose back in your day there wasn't so much pressure on women to make something of themselves academically," she sneered. *Back in my day?!* I was momentarily speechless. Believe me when I say that doesn't happen very often (yeah, I know, you believe

25

me). "It's different now, women are expected to contribute. I've 'ad to work twice as 'ard as them with degrees."

The panel Chair, a well-known TV presenter who was currently looking like they wished they were anywhere but here, gazed at me pleadingly. *Please calm it down.*

I took a deep breath and prepared to be magnanimous, for the sake of the Chair, but then she delivered the killer blow.

"In your day women were expected to just stay at home and look after the children." She looked me up and down. "If you could keep 'old of your man long enough to 'ave them, of course."

I was so hurt and angry that for a moment I seriously considered leaping up and bitchslapping her in the kidneys (why I thought of her kidneys I don't really know, but I was so angry I wasn't worried about making sense.) But instead I took another deep breath and smiled thinly at her.

"You're right, Louise, you have worked hard. Well done," I said shortly. She looked at me, suddenly suspicious. "Everyone, a round of applause for Louise, for rising above all her obvious social disadvantages." I clapped sarcastically. And, after a few seconds, so did everyone else, albeit less sarcastically and more hesitantly.

It wasn't at all awkward.

Will looked at me, a shocked but sympathetic expression on his face.

"Ooh…" he said.

"I know, I should have risen above it," I said.

"No, you should have bitchslapped her in the kidneys," he said. "God I love it when you're violent."

"Pervert. Anyway she spent the rest of the panel making snide remarks about my age and toy boys." Will glanced involuntarily over towards Joel, then dragged his eyes back to me. I sighed. "I'd just found out that he was cheating on me with someone twenty years younger. It was kind of an open secret, the sort everybody else knows before you do. She found my weak spot and tortured me with it."

"It looks like she's still trying to torture you with it," said Will, watching me as I watched Louise pout and flutter and paw at Joel and do everything except drop to her knees and get to work on his little fella right there and then in front of the Chief Purser. Will put his hand on my arm and I turned to him, uncomfortably aware of how closely I'd been scrutinising them. He stared into my eyes, suddenly intense. "But it won't work now, will it? Because you don't care about him any more."

OH MY GOD I was *such* a bit - female dog. I took Will's face in my hands and kissed him hard on the lips.

"You know what? It actually *isn't* working, because I don't give a sh - " I hesitated. He grinned.

"You can say it for emphasis if you want to."

"Good. I really don't give a shit about Joel any more. I look at him, and I look at you, and you're the one who makes my heart beat faster."

Will smiled. "I am glad about that. Because if you still loved him, I'd have to push him overboard."

I laughed. Sort of. I wasn't sure if he was joking or not.

CHAPTER 4

The Captain tapped his wine glass - which only contained water, by the looks of it - and said a few words to welcome everybody to the murder mystery cruise. Then we all sat down to an amazing dinner.

As I tucked into a plate of tiger prawns braised in a black truffle broth with hand made squid ink noodles (I suffer so hard for my art!), I looked around the room at my group of amateur detectives.

There were four tables arranged around the intimate dining room, each one seating between four and six diners including the team leaders, myself, Joel, Maureen the Chief Purser and bloody Louise. At my table were Will and the honeymooning couple we had met earlier, Harvey and Michael, the two man-hating/hunting besties, Sylvia and Heather, and Zoé, a single lady in her mid-30s who excitedly introduced herself as my biggest fan, 'but not in a creepy way'. Yeah, right… I made a mental note to make sure we locked the cabin door that night.

Zoé was enthusiastic and excited, but she was sweet and harmless. She also didn't seem like the typical cruise goer, and as she talked about her job in a book shop I wondered how she'd managed to afford this trip; the cruise on its own was expensive enough, and the murder mystery game had been a hot ticket that hadn't come cheap… I didn't have to wonder for long though.

"I couldn't believe it when they told me I'd won!" trilled Zoé.

"Won?"

"This trip. The book shop I work at - they put the names of all their top salespeople into a raffle and this trip was the prize." She tried to look modest but failed miserably; she was obviously quite proud of herself. "I was the top salesperson out of all their branches in the South West."

"Wow!" I said. "That's brilliant. What a generous prize, too."

"Yes," she said, her smile fading slightly. "It was meant to be for two, but my husband - " She stopped abruptly, looking down at the plate in front of her. The rest of us exchanged uncomfortable looks. Sylvia, who was sitting next to her, patted her on the hand.

"Never mind, love, we'll make sure you have a lovely time anyway," she said, and we all murmured in agreement. I picked up the bottle of wine in front of me and reached across to refill her glass.

"Here's to my team of amateur detectives," I said. I stood up and raised my glass. "Leave no stone unturned, no suspect unquestioned, and most of all, no glass of wine undrunk!"

The diners laughed and raised their glasses too. I sipped carefully at my drink - I'd already had too much champagne, and as I rarely drink there was a real danger that if I had much more, I would suddenly find myself dancing on the table singing 'Joleene' with my massive pants on my head. Or, equally (maybe more) likely, someone else's pants on my head. And I was saving that particular treat for the last night of the cruise…

Out of the corner of my eye I saw Zoé knock back her whole glass of wine in one, and I thought to myself, *there's one unhappy lady, right there.*

The rest of the evening passed without much incident. I went around the other tables during the next couple of courses, talking to the rest of the amateur detectives. There was a lovely Indian couple, celebrating their 40th wedding anniversary, who clearly adored each other; a Jamaican lady, who was loud and funny and gorgeous, while her husband was tall, skinny and possibly The Whitest Man In The World™;

and an elderly lady who made out she was deaf (shouting WHAAAAT?? every time her harrassed daughter spoke to her) but who could hear perfectly well whenever alcohol was mentioned. The nondescript couple we'd met in the bar earlier were on the Chief Purser's team, being (if it were possible) even more bland and forgettable, and I instantly marked them down as suspicious; they were being *too* normal, and when I mentioned it to Will, he thought so too.

"They're trying too hard to blend into the background," he said. "They're clearly homicidal maniacs. He's going to kill her for her life insurance."

I shook my head. "Nah, my money is on her bumping him off for shagging his secretary." Will looked thoughtful for a moment, watching them discreetly as they ate.

"He's definitely guilty of something," I said. "Look how attentive he is - he's pouring her more wine without her even asking - maybe you're right, he's going to get her pissed and push her off the top deck."

"But I'm attentive to you, my love," protested Will. "He might just adore her, the way I adore you." We watched them again for a moment, then shared a look. "Nah!" We both laughed.

"God, we're nasty, suspicious people aren't we?" I said.

"I really hope they are actors and not just on holiday," said Will.

I managed to ignore both Joel and bloody Louise, even though her voice was loud and shrill and really carried across the entire room. Several times I saw Harvey and Michael exchange looks at the sound of her cackling.

"I hate to be a bitch, but *oh my god!*" muttered Harvey. "I've not heard so much fake laughter since your brother's best man speech at the wedding."

Michael shuddered. "I still have nightmares about that speech. That laugh just brings it all back." He saw me looking at them and gave a rueful smile. "Sorry, I shouldn't speak ill of one of your fellow writers - "

"Don't hold back on my account," I said. Zoé laughed.

"You don't follow Bella on Twitter, then," she said. "She *hates* her."

I cringed. "No, no, we just have a - complicated relationship."

"*Hates* her," said Zoé again, grinning. I laughed.

"Stop it, you'll get me into trouble! I'm a professional, you know…"

Heather - who up to now had been concentrating on clearing her plates of food and finding the bottom of her wine glass, over and over again - looked over at bloody Louise and *harrumphed* disdainfully.

"By 'eck as like, I'm not as good looking as I think I am, am I?" she said, in a perfect rendering of Louise's nasal Northern drawl. We all laughed. "She reminds me of my husband's - sorry, *ex*-husband's - secretary. She wanted a raise and he gave her one, alright. He gave her several." She drained her wine glass again and stared at it morosely. "He's probably giving her one as we speak."

"Okay!" said Sylvia brightly. "I think we might head back to our cabin now…"

Dinner and hosting duties done for the night, Will and I decided to take a walk around the deck. The Captain had already told us there would be no murders until the next night, so we determined to make the most of this little bit of free time.

Land was already far behind us, with the only lights visible out to sea from the container ships that plied the same route as us between the US and Europe. But the darkness meant that the stars overhead were bright and felt closer, somehow, than they did on land. Hand in hand we strolled along the deck towards the bow, or the pointy bit at the front, as us naval types call it.

"What's the betting there's a queue of passengers right at the front, re-enacting that bit out of *Titanic*?" I said, and Will laughed.

"I thought you'd want to do that," he said.

"God no," I said. "But you can paint me like one of your French girls if you like."

"Can't we just have sex?"

"Oh alright then…"

We stopped at the sight of a queue of couples at the bow and laughed, then walked on until we found a quiet spot. This ship was so huge that even with so many passengers (most of whom, admittedly, were inside as it was a chilly evening) - even with 2000 other people on board, not to mention the staff, we could still find a private corner to ourselves. I nestled into Will, marvelling as ever at how well we fitted together physically; I had always gone for taller men (like Joel, who was 6'2"), but Will was actually the perfect size. When we hugged, my head fitted snugly into the curve between his head and his shoulder, and we could snog standing up for *hours* without me getting a crick in my neck. Which is more important than you might think.

He took my hands, threading his fingers through mine, and pulled me closer. His lips searched for mine and we kissed, gently, tenderly. I breathed in the scent of him - a combination of aftershave, soap, and an indefinable fragrance that was just Essence of Will. His cheek felt smooth and warm against mine. I felt almost dizzy with the unaccustomed champagne, the cold night air and the rush of happiness that went through me as I stood there with him. *I am so lucky*, I thought. *Nothing can ruin this cruise, not even Joel and Louise.*

But I was about to be proved spectacularly wrong.

CHAPTER 5

I woke up the next morning after the best night's sleep I'd had in ages. The gentle rocking motion of the ship, combined with the alcohol and the sea air, had left me dead to the world the moment my head hit the pillow.

I looked up at the ceiling, enjoying the feel of the soft, crisp bed linen on my skin (my duvet cover never feels like that) and the pale golden sunlight filtering through the curtains. At this time of year sunshine was never guaranteed, but the last two days had been beautiful in that slightly melancholic way that only late summer/early autumn can be, even out here at sea. I turned to look at Will, but he was still out for the count; after taking a sabbatical from Interpol after the events in Venice, he was losing the habit of getting up for work in the mornings and learning to sleep in.

Wake up and kiss me, I thought, staring hard at his peacefully sleeping face; but he didn't. I tried again, glaring harder - still nothing. I toyed with the idea of waking him up, but it was early and we didn't need to be awake at this time, so I let him sleep.

I reached out to the bedside table for my phone. I may be approaching the menopause but I am a complete bloody millennial when it comes to my phone. I read on it, I Google stuff constantly, I'm all over social media like an ill-fitting suit, and occasionally I even text people. The one thing I never do is actually ring anybody, apart from Will and, once a year at Christmas, my sister Megan (who is just as bad as me at talking on the phone and prefers to communicate via the medium of selfies on Facebook).

I switched my phone on and immediately 8000 (give or take) notifications pinged, making Will murmur in his sleep but still not wake up. I hurriedly turned the volume down.

Approximately 95% of those 8000 (give or take) notifications were from Twitter. Although, as far as I could remember, I hadn't posted anything on there for the last couple of days. I opened it up and scrolled down to find out what was happening.

I nearly dropped the phone.

Staring up at me from the screen was a photograph of Joel the bastard unfaithful ex-husband and bloody Louise bloody Meyers, hand in hand at the bar last night. He had a big fat smug grin on his irritatingly gorgeous face, while she gazed up at him adoringly. The photo was part of a post shared by one of the less-scrupulous British tabloids (which makes it sound like some of them actually *have* scruples). The headline above it was, 'Jilted Joel finds love again with lovely Louise'. And someone had been 'kind' enough to tag me, so every time someone commented on it, I got another ping on my phone. There were a lot of comments. A LOT.

It was enough to make the bile rise. 'Jilted Joel'? Yes, I'd jilted him alright, after discovering he'd slept with the entire female contingent of our local Weatherspoons. He hardly deserved such a sympathetic headline. And 'lovely Louise'? Just - no.

I clicked on the link and brought up the article. It was just a few lines long, but it still managed to mention me and my age (of course), but the worse thing was the second photograph.

It was a photograph of me, scowling. The website had managed to insinuate that it was taken in the bar as I glared at the happy couple, jealous, when in actual fact I could see it had been taken much earlier in the evening when I was talking to my detective team; and I wasn't scowling, I was telling them a funny story and the photographer had caught me, mid-expression. But when had the truth ever mattered to a tabloid?

Two can play at that game, I thought. I retweeted the article, adding my own comment above it:

Annabelle Tyson　　@AnnabelleTysonYepItsReallyMe

SO happy for @THEJoelQuigley and @RealLouMeyers ! Don't they make a lovely couple? Such a wonderful surprise to share this #MurderMysteryCruise with you, looking forward to testing out our detective skills! Let's hope the 'murderer' doesn't get you... ;-)

And I hit enter before I could change my mind. Although spending a week on the high seas with those two was slightly less appealing to me than getting my legs waxed, a root canal filled and a cervical smear done ALL AT THE SAME TIME BY THE SAME PERSON, I didn't give a damn about them seeing each other. They thoroughly deserved one another.

"You typed that through gritted teeth," said Will, beside me. I laughed and bent over to kiss him.

"Not really. I don't care about them," I said. "And if they're together, hopefully they'll be too busy with each other to annoy us."

Will pulled me down for a cuddle. He was lovely and warm.

"You seem to forget that *we'll* be too busy with each other to even notice them," he said. I liked the sound of that and snuggled closer. He didn't speak but I could feel him thinking.

"What is it?" I asked. He sat up, dislodging me.

"Show me that post," he said. I handed him the phone and he studied it. "Who took these photos?"

"I dunno." I looked at them again, more closely. "There's a ship's photographer on board, isn't there? I don't remember seeing them there last night, though."

"No," said Will. "And these don't look like professional photos. Plus I would assume that any photographer employed by the cruise line would have to sign something to say they can't leak pictures to the press."

"Yeah…" I looked at them carefully again. "And the crew would be subject to the same rules, wouldn't they? So it's probably a passenger."

We looked at each other, slightly alarmed. I'm quite well known, but I'm not the sort of well known that has the press following me around and taking photos. The thought that someone on this ship was potentially going to be watching our every move in case we did something they deemed newsworthy was a bit perturbing. Added to that, the angle the photos had been taken at made it clear they'd been done surreptitiously; rather than asking if they could take a photo or even just openly snapping one, the photographer had secreted themselves somewhere. And to then send them off to the press, hinting that I was jealous… The sneaky way it had been done made me feel very uncomfortable.

Will scrolled down, reading the phone screen. I made a grab for the phone.

"Don't read the comments," I said. "It's Twitter. They're either really lovely or really horrible."

His face clouded over. "Apparently you traded down when you swapped Joel for me," he said. I grabbed the phone.

"You and I both know that's bollocks," I said. "*Everyone* knows that's bollocks. I traded WAY up - "

"You swapped the 'hottest crime writer in the world' for a man who's 'short, balding and middle-aged'."

"Well that's *obviously* completely wrong, because *I'm* the hottest crime writer in the world," I said, trying to make a joke out of it. Will laughed, but not really. I took his face in my hands - his lovely, sweet and slightly sad face - and gazed into his eyes. "You have to ignore it. It's rubbish. I wouldn't swap you for Joel Quigley, Tom Hardy or Chris Hemsworth - "

"I notice you didn't mention Tom Hiddleston," he said.

"I'm not making promises I can't keep," I said. He did laugh then. I kissed him on the lips. "You are the only man I want. You've ruined other men for me now. None of them could ever hope to measure up." He opened his mouth to speak but I stopped him with another kiss. "Not even Tom. And definitely not Joel. I love you and no one else."

"Prove it."

"Again? Oh alright…"

So I proved it, and then we got up and went for breakfast. We toyed with the idea of eating in our cabin, but Will said we should make it clear we weren't hiding away. He was right. We had to ignore the rubbish on Twitter (and wherever else it had spread to by now) and carry on as normal.

We opted to eat in the executive breakfast room, which was slightly less 'in-your-face glamour' than the Excelsior and the Pearl and more 'subdued grandeur'. It was fairly quiet, reserved for the occupants of the penthouses and suites, and I hoped that the type of passenger who could afford a suite would not be the sort who'd be interested in social media gossip.

Harvey and Michael were already at a table. They stopped talking and looked up as we sat down, and I knew immediately by the looks on their faces what they'd been talking about.

"Morning!" I said breezily. I wasn't going to mention it if they weren't. They did, though.

"Oh honey," said Harvey sympathetically, reaching out to squeeze my hand.

"You saw it then?" said Will. They nodded.

"What a load of old rubbish!" said Michael hotly. "You reacted perfectly normally if you ask me. And that *terrible* photo of you - "

"Thanks…" I muttered.

"I didn't mean it was *terrible*, I meant - well, you know. They caught you in full flow." Michael was clearly quite offended on my behalf.

"Who took the photos, that's what I want to know," said Harvey. Will and I exchanged looks.

"Yes, we'd quite like to know that too," said Will.

"What I'd really like though," I said, picking up my tea cup, "is to forget all about it and enjoy the cruise."

Harvey and Michael nodded in agreement. I launched myself head first into a Full English and tried not to imagine someone sharing a photo of me tucking into a sausage on social media.

CHAPTER 6

After breakfast we took a stroll around the ship. It was enormous and we'd seen hardly any of it. Apparently there were shops, a 'fitness zone' (gym to you and me), three swimming pools, two hot tubs, a theatre, a cinema, a nightclub and more places to eat than you could shake a stick at.

We reached the beauty salon, and stopped to gaze in at the row of women - and a few men - being scrubbed by a whole battalion of hairdressers, manicurists and beauticians. I jumped as a well groomed, heavily (but tastefully) made up woman appeared in front of me.

"Ms Tyson," she purred. "Lovely to see you. Would you like to make an appointment?"

"Oh, I…" Truth be told, I do sometimes wish I was more polished - it's all I can do some days to wash my hair and shave my armpits - but I feel completely out of my depth in beauty salons. Will noticed my discomfort and came to my rescue.

"Could you book us both in?" he said, running his fingers through his hair. "I need a trim. My wife is already the most beautiful woman on the ship, but she deserves a bit of pampering."

Behind us there was a collective *aahhh* as every woman in the salon melted. Even the salon manager, who was far too professional to actually melt, clutched her heart as she made our appointment. Will smiled at me and took my arm as we walked away, and I thought, *that'll show anyone who believes what they read on Twitter…*

We were just passing the pursers' desk (kind of like the concierge desk at a hotel) when the duty purser hailed us.

"Message for you!" he said, handing me a piece of paper. It was an invitation, beautifully handwritten on the ship's own luxury stationery.

"You are cordially invited to the library. Tell no one."

The library was wonderful, if completely out of place on a boat. It should by rights have been in a large country house or stately home. It was lined with floor to ceiling bookshelves and mahogany panelling, with most of the books being leather-bound and gold-tooled. They were clearly more for show than reading, although there were a few lower shelves full of popular novels (lots by me, a few by Joel, none by Louise, as far as I could see). There was even a library ladder, the sort on a rail that went around the room so you could reach books on the higher shelves. I immediately had library envy.

"I have *always* wanted a library with a sliding ladder," I said to Will.

"I can just see you up there, whizzing around the shelves," he said. "Not looking for a book, just whizzing around."

I looked around, furtively. "Let's come back at night and have a go on it!" He laughed.

"It's a date."

In the corner of the library was a coffee bar, with a shiny brass coffee machine that looked like something out of a steampunk novel - all valves and knobs and steam escaping. Leather Chesterfield sofas and comfortable wing-backed chairs were dotted around the room, with coffee tables displaying an array of magazines and newspapers. I fully expected to look out of the window and see a croquet lawn, a summer house and a herd of deer beyond the ha-ha. I had no idea what a bloody ha-ha looked like or how to recognise one, but it was the sort of thing every self-respecting country estate had. Ha ha ha.

One thing that most self-respecting country estates do NOT have, however, is a dead body sprawled on the Axminster.

It took me a while to notice their chest moving up and down, ever so gently. *Thank god for that*, I thought. I may be well known for writing about murder, but what's less well known is that sometimes my job seems to encroach upon real life. This was not the first dead body I'd come across, but luckily it was the first corpse who was still breathing.

They were sprawled (relatively comfortably, I thought - the murderer had been quite considerate) on the floor, eyes wide open and staring up at the ceiling. I watched them for a while, waiting for them to blink, but they were world class starers. My eyes started to water in sympathy.

"Well well well," said Will. "I didn't expect that."

We'd confidently expected the victim (and murderer) to be Mr and Mrs Too Innocent, but instead the lovely Indian man I'd spoken to last night was lying in front of us, a bloody dagger not really sticking out of his chest. In a nearby chair, weeping, was his lovely Indian not-really-wife. Her clothes were covered in blood. I had to hand it to the cruise line, it had done well.

The murder mystery players gathered around the corpse. Sylvia and Heather were there in suspiciously new and un-sweaty fitness gear; apparently they had just been about to start a 'Fit and Fab and 50 Plus' class at the gym when they'd received their invitation. Harvey and Michael were carrying Gucci shopping bags, so they'd been adding to their already extensive designer wardrobe. The other players turned up in dribs and drabs, and I felt for the corpse; he was having to stay still for an inordinately long time, and his wife's sobs were beginning to run dry.

The Chief Purser nodded to me as she entered, and gestured for Will and I to step back and let the paying guests take charge of the investigation. They gathered around the body and prodded him, turned him over, studied the wound and looked around for the murder weapon.

"By 'eck it's right posh in 'ere, innit?" Bloody Louise could not enter a room quietly. It just wasn't in her DNA. "Ooh, 'as someone died? What happened, did they read Bella's last book and die of boredom?"

"No," I said. "They choked on your 'real life' memoir, because it's so hard to swallow." I smiled sweetly at her and turned away, catching a glimpse of Joel's mocking face as I did so. I turned back to glare at him, and to my surprise he wasn't mocking me, he actually looked uncomfortable. It wasn't an expression I was used to seeing on his face.

I rather liked it.

After half an hour everyone had got fed up of poking the poor corpse (who had started wriggling slightly and probably needed a toilet break), so we adjourned to a nearby coffee shop for tea and a cake buffet (I know, right? how bloody marvellous is that idea?! I decided I was going to live on this ship for ever). The grieving widow dried her eyes and allowed herself to be questioned over a Victoria sponge and a cup of Earl Grey.

Louise and Joel wandered up to the counter to order coffee. The barista offered them both cake plates, but Louise waved hers away.

"Not for me, thanks," she said loudly. "Some of us are watching our figures, int that right Bell? Of course, some of our figures are easier to spot than others."

Joel muttered under his breath. "That's enough." She laughed and, unabashed, sat down across the room with her coffee.

Zoé, who had missed all the fun in the library, bounced into the seat next to me, watching as I finished my carrot cake slightly less enthusiastically than I'd started it.

"I can't believe I missed a dead body!" she cried. The people at the table next to us (who weren't part of the game) looked at us, alarmed. She ignored them and leaned in close to me.

"You poor thing!" she said. "I saw that awful Tweet this morning! How did they get those photos? It was so mean of them to tell everyone you were jealous."

I could feel my cheeks getting hot. She was right next to me, why did she have to talk so loudly? "I'm not jealous," I said. She looked surprised.

"No, of course you're not…" She turned her gaze on Will, who had gone to get a glass of water, for a second then back to me. "Of course you're not." She leaned back and *really obviously* watched Louise and Joel across the room. "How are you holding up, though? Really? With those two rubbing it in your face…"

As she spoke, 'those two' looked over at us. Louise smiled; Joel just stared at me for a moment, then looked away. I waited for the ground to open up and swallow me but it stayed resolutely solid beneath my feet.

"I am not jealous," I growled at Zoé under my breath. Couldn't she take a hint and shut the fudge up?

"I just hope the mysterious photographer doesn't pop up and get another incriminating photo of you," she said, shaking her head.

"I AM NOT - " Heads were turning and I forced myself to lower my voice. "I am not jealous, Zoé, honestly. Will and I are very happy and absolutely fine and we're just ignoring it, okay? Please do the same." She looked for a moment like she might cry, and I immediately

43

felt terrible. "I'm really touched by your concern, honestly, I am. Thank you. But let's not talk about it, okay?"

"Okay." She looked at me sympathetically. "I did feel for you when it all came out about Joel, though." *Christ almighty, if you don't stop talking I swear to God I will throw something at you.* She looked down at her plate of untouched Battenburg and her bottom lip trembled. "I know what it's like to put your heart into something and have someone you thought the world of let you down." She looked over at Louise, but the faraway expression in her eyes told me she wasn't seeing the loudmouthed Northern bint in her mind. "I know what it's like when someone steals it away from you."

Holy crap, this was all getting a bit too emotional for me. Will sat down next to me, immediately sensing there was something going on and deciding to ignore it.

"Oh hi Zoé!" he said brightly. "You missed the floor show. But at least you got here before the cake ran out." He smiled at her, then turned to me. "Everything okay?" he asked, making it clear he knew it wasn't.

"It's fine," I said, leaning over to kiss him. I just hoped it was.

CHAPTER 7

We spent the afternoon killing time before our pampering session at the salon. Mine took longer than Will's, because quite frankly there's a lot of me to pamper and now I'd bitten the bullet and let a beauty therapist get at me, I wasn't leaving until I'd been pumiced and polished and tweaked and painted and smoothed and curled to within an inch of my life.

Will looked up from the magazine he was reading as I stood in front of him, feeling slightly self conscious but marvellous. His jaw dropped. Literally. I have never had a man drop his jaw for me before in my entire life.

"That bad?" I asked, but I knew it wasn't.

"Oh my god, you look amazing," he said, his eyes wide. I felt my heart flip, and vowed to actually make an effort more often. He stood up and took my hand, looking me up and down. "You always look amazing, but this is next level…"

We made it back to the cabin without stopping for a bunk up on route (although it was touch and go). Will said he wanted to fully appreciate the fruits of the beauty therapist's labour but I didn't want him messing my hair up, so I told him he'd have to wait until later. And then we got into our dinner outfits.

Tonight's entertainment was a fancy dress party. Will had groaned when he'd read that, but I was quite excited; this would be the first time I could go in a couple's costume. In the past I'd always gone as something really obscure that no one had got, or something cool, clever and impossible to go for a pee in.

I wore a tight-fitting pencil skirt with a slit up the side and stiletto heels; not my usual kind of thing, but when I looked in the mirror I was amazed how good it looked. A thin sweater, with a scarf around my neck and a beret at a jaunty angle, completed the outfit. Next to me, Will wore a sharp double-breasted suit with wide leg trousers and a trilby.

"Nice…" he said, nodding approvingly as I posed, flashing a bit of leg. "But don't forget this."

He handed me a gun. I knew it was only a toy but it still felt cold, heavy and realistic. I pointed it at my reflection and he laughed.

"That is the first thing *everyone* does when they get given a gun," he said. "Everyone does the stance. Even in the Army. Although it's a bit different with an assault weapon…" He held up his own hand gun and we stood side by side, admiring ourselves.

"Bonnie and Clyde…" I said. "It kind of suits us, doesn't it?" Our eyes met in the mirror for a moment, then we both lowered our guns, letting our arms hang by our sides.

"Shall we go?" said Will.

We made our way to the Pearl - all the murder mystery dinners were being held there, which was slightly disappointing as there were several other restaurants on board that I liked the look of. But then I wasn't paying for it, so I wasn't going to complain. The room was pretty full and Harvey and Michael were already there at the restaurant bar, dressed as Batman and Robin. Sylvia and Heather were with them, dressed up as Agnetha and Anni-Frid from ABBA, in courageously short glam rock tunics and knee high boots. Heather looked like she'd already been at the bar for some time and was quite happy in her outfit, but every now and then Sylvia tugged at the hem of her dress, trying to pull it down.

"Wow, ladies, you are rocking those outfits!" I said, making a point of looking Sylvia up and down admiringly. "You've got the legs for it." She smiled at me gratefully.

"Ahem!" Michael cleared his throat and gestured to himself and the other half of the Dynamic Duo.

"You've got nice legs too," I said, placatingly. "But those outfits are so tight I can see what you had for lunch."

"I *told* you," said Harvey. Will laughed and clapped him on the back as I reached for one of the glasses of champagne lined up on the bar. Michael sidled up to me and murmured quietly.

"We ran into that bitch Louise earlier, when we were picking up the costumes," he said. "She said Harvey should be dressing up as Fatman, not Batman. He was really upset."

"Oh no!" I said, mortified that I might have inadvertently added to Harvey's misery.

"There was no need for it, the cow," said Michael. "We weren't even talking to her and she just took it upon herself to insult him."

Will, bless him, had heard our conversation. He offered Harvey a glass of champagne and said, "Of course, you can pull off a costume like that. I couldn't, I'm much too flabby." Which was completely untrue but a really nice thing to say. Harvey smiled broadly and Michael looked relieved.

"Oh he's a keeper," he whispered to me, and I nodded proudly. My husband is such a sweetheart.

Zoé scooted across the room to join us, draped in a nun's habit and severe-looking wimple. I was surprised that she'd chosen such a loose-fitting and unflattering outfit, but then if she was recovering from a broken heart (which seemed likely, from what she'd said earlier) perhaps she wasn't ready to start putting herself out there yet.

"Ooh, Bonnie and Clyde! That's perfect!" she squealed. "You both look really untrustworthy."

I laughed. "Thank you, Sister Zoé. I think."

I looked around at the other diners. Mr and Mrs Too Innocent were there, him dressed in lederhosen and her looking like a menopausal Heidi. Among the other guests we had the Queen (complete with toy Corgi), a bloke in a white tux who kept going round saying 'the name's Bond, Jame-sh Bond' in a terrible Sean Connery voice, Freddie Krueger (I didn't fancy his chances using the cutlery at dinner, but then again maybe he wouldn't need it), and a Jamaican Marilyn Monroe who looked completely wrong but absolutely gorgeous at the same time. As I watched, an elderly, hearing impaired fairy godmother shuffled in on the arm of a downtrodden and rather dowdy Cinderella, who looked like she would kill for a glass slipper and a pumpkin coach if it meant she could get some time on her own. I felt a brief pang of sympathy and thanked my lucky stars that my mum was an incredibly spritely 80 year old with a massive circle of friends and a better social life than mine, who'd told me several times that if she ever became a burden I was to pack her off to a nursing home stat (to which I always replied that she needn't worry, I bloody would).

Zoé looked around and then spoke to me in that annoyingly loud confidential whisper of hers. "No sign of Joel and Louise," she said, raising her eyebrows meaningfully.

Heather *harrummph*ed at the mention of Louise; it seemed to be a Pavlovian response.

"With any luck the murderer's struck again and we won't have to put up with her slobbering all over him," she said, and we all laughed.

The Chief Purser, who was dressed as a rhinestone-spangled cowgirl with a massive blonde Dolly Parton wig, entered looking harassed. I guessed the Captain had probably had a few choice words with her about the leaked photos, and felt a pang of sympathy for her. She looked longingly at the champagne on the bar, then asked for a tonic water. She took a long pull at her drink, but it clearly wasn't having the desired effect.

"Is everyone here?" she said, looking around.

"Not yet," said Zoé, looking at me meaningfully. I ignored her. We all knew what was going to happen; Joel and Louise were obviously holding on so they would be the last ones in and could make a grand entrance.

The door of the Pearl opened, letting in noise from the dining room of the Excelsior beyond it, and we all turned to look; only to see a surprised looking Karl, who was no doubt wondering why we were all staring at him. He smiled awkwardly and scuttled over to the Chief Purser.

"We're not late, are we?" Everybody's eyes swivelled back to the doorway, where Louise was posing. Joel stood next to her, with an arrogant smile on his face; as well he might, because (of course) he looked gorgeous. Not that he had any effect on me any more, other than causing me to feel mildly irritated.

I'd expected them to come dressed in a couple's costume - maybe as the world's greatest lovers, like Maid Marian and Robin Hood, or Lancelot and Guinevere, or Donald Trump and his comb-over - but they weren't, which led me to the conclusion again that this was a very new relationship. Joel was dressed in dark red trousers and a white military style tunic with gold piping and a gold sash; a regular Prince Charmless. Louise was draped in a long white sleeveless dress, with a gold belt and a large round metallic collar, both studded with gemstones in lapis blue. She wore a crown, a simple band around her head studded with more fake lapis lazuli. A long cape of the same deep turquoise blue hung down behind her, the ends attached to thick gold bangles at her wrists, so that it fanned out like wings as she stretched out her arms. Her eyes were outlined with thick black kohl.

"There's never an asp when you need one, is there?" I muttered.

Louise went straight to her table and sat down, leaving Joel to get her a drink. He approached the bar, making for the exact spot I was standing in.

"Evening," he said. "What have you come as?"

"Your mum," I said. How could I always write great dialogue in my books yet be so rubbish at comebacks in real life? "What are you meant to be, the bell boy?"

"Prince Charming, actually." He drew himself up, as if steeling himself against my reply. That surprised me. Surely he couldn't really care what I said to him? Maybe he could. I cursed my complete inability to come up with a sarcastic comment to capitalise on this new knowledge, but there was nothing I could do.

"Don't tell me - Liberace!" said Will, moving closer to grab another drink. I smirked. I could always rely on him.

Joel smiled thinly. "Yeah, something like that." He picked up two glasses of champagne and turned away.

"Don't hang around the lobby!" I called after him. "People will keep giving you luggage."

"Ha ha," he said, not turning around. Harvey held up a hand to me and we high-fived.

Dinner began. The food was amazing, as it had been the night before, and I started to feel less miffed about not being able to try the other restaurants on board. Halfway through our main course we were interrupted by a burst of terrible music; some kind of awful gangster rap (the only music in the world I loathe), with an angry bloke shouting over the top:

Snitches, end up in ditches,

While the bitches, get all the riches...

"WHAT?!" cried the deaf fairy across the room, bewildered. Will and I smothered our giggles and the entire assembly of diners, staff and murder mystery players looked around as Zoé, blushing furiously, reached under her nun's habit and pulled out her mobile phone.

"My ring tone," she mumbled, looking incredibly embarrassed. I felt bad for her.

"That music is - interesting," I said, trying to play it down and make a joke of it.

"My friend at work is always changing my ring tone for a laugh," she said. "I don't really like that sort of music…"

She fiddled with the phone and then tucked it back under her habit. The poor woman looked mortified. I patted her hand.

Between courses we wandered between tables, talking about the corpse in the library, and that led on to that old question: how do you get away with murder?

"Planning," said Harvey firmly. "Lots of planning." There was murmured agreement around the room.

"Oh, I don't know…" I said. Louise scoffed.

"Don't be ridiculous," she said. "Of course you have to plan! You can't just walk up to someone and bump 'em off. You need an alibi." Heather nodded reluctantly.

"Yes," she said. "You need to get a murder weapon, then you need to know how to dispose of it, how to get in and out of his office without anyone seeing you, how to wipe the CCTV tapes, how to get rid of his body…" We all looked at her. She shrugged. "I can dream, can't I?"

I laughed. "True. But I still think a crime of passion, an opportunist murder, can be easier to get away with. As long as you're not a complete idiot." I noticed Joel watching me closely and smiled evilly. "Obviously I've thought about how to kill someone... I'm talking from a writing perspective, of course. Will? What do you think?"

Will had just returned from the bar, bearing drinks for the two of us and Zoé.

"The problem with planning everything is, yes, you might be able to get rid of the body (for example), but if the police have even the slightest suspicion about you they will look at your bank statements, at CCTV footage around your home, they will track where your car and your mobile phone have been, and they will be able to prove that two days before the murder you went out and bought a machete and bleach and a very large suitcase, maybe some latex gloves... They will look at your search history and see that you Googled 'remote woodland' and looked up the place where the body was found. All of your planning is what will give you away."

"Really?" Zoé looked fascinated. "But surely you're more likely to get caught in the act, with an opportunist murder?" She was so caught up in the conversation that she absentmindedly picked up my drink, raised it to her mouth and then, realising it was my white wine, handed it to me with an *"Oops! Sorry!"* before reaching for her own orange juice. I smiled and discreetly put it back on the table, wishing I'd gone for a soft drink myself; I'd had too much wine already, and I didn't think it would be a good look for one of the hosts to start throwing her arms around people and telling them she fancied a kebab.

Will thought about it (getting away with murder, not getting a kebab). "Not necessarily. The main thing is to not be seen, or if you are, to look like you should be there so no one really notices you. There have been several high profile crimes - burglary rather than murder - where the thieves walked straight in off the street in high vis jackets or uniforms, not making any attempt to sneak about, and everyone ignored them because they fitted in."

Zoé looked thoughtful, and I wondered for a moment if she was planning to bump off her husband like Heather was. *Nah*, I thought. She was still at the broken hearted stage; she hadn't got to red hot hatred and the desire for revenge yet.

"The other thing about planning," said Will, "is that all the other people you've factored in won't necessarily act the way you expect them to." He smiled meaningfully at Heather. "So the guard at the reception desk might normally slope off for a coffee at 10.30 every morning, leaving the desk unmanned long enough for you to sneak in, but what happens if he gets stuck in traffic that day and is late, so he doesn't go for his coffee? What happens if he's done someone a favour and they get him one, so he doesn't have to leave the desk? Then how do you get in?"

"You need to be able to think on your feet," I said, and Will nodded.

We had dessert (Death by Chocolate, of course), then the Chief Purser announced a game; the one where you have a name on a Post It note stuck to your forehead, and you have to walk around asking everyone questions until you work out who you are. I walked around asking the usual questions - *am I male or female? What colour is my hair? If I was a biscuit, would I be a Jammie Dodger or a Hobnob?* - and it was all going well (I was convinced I was either Oprah Winfrey or the Pope at one point, but then I was quite drunk, despite leaving my wine untouched and starting on sparkling water), until I ran almost literally into Louise.

She did not look well. She was even paler than usual (native Mancunians aren't naturally tanned) and staggering around. I took her arm to stop her falling over and guided her into a chair.

"I'm fine, I'm fine…" she said, but she clearly wasn't. I looked around for Joel but he was talking to Harvey and Michael.

"You are not fine," I said. "You need to call it a night. Where's your cabin?"

"It's just along the corridor," she slurred, and I remembered that some of the suites were on the same level as this private dining room. She struggled to her feet, but she was swaying so badly that there was no way she would make it back on her own. I looked around for Karl, who had been helping out behind the bar, but he was nowhere to be seen. Sylvia was chatting with the Chief Purser, while Will was with the suspiciously innocent couple; he'd told me he was keeping an eye on them, because he was convinced they were the murderers. I sighed; it looked like I was escorting Louise back to her cabin.

I draped her arm around my shoulder and hauled her up.

"What are you doing?" Zoé was by my side in an instant, making me jump. I told her what I intended to do. "You can't go, you're one of the guests of honour," she said. She gestured to another steward I didn't know, who was lurking nearby. "We'll do it. You stay here."

The steward - a good looking blonde guy of about 30 - came over and helped pick up Louise without a word. I looked at them and grabbed Zoé's arm before they left.

"Be discreet," I said. She raised an eyebrow. "I don't want this ending up on Twitter. No matter how much I dislike her." Zoé looked at me, then smiled.

"Okay." She turned and began to drag Louise out. I just hoped our mystery photographer wasn't lurking under a nearby table.

CHAPTER 8

It took Joel about ten minutes to realise his lover had unceremoniously disappeared. He asked around, but Zoé had in fact been discreet enough to ensure that no one else knew where she'd gone. Eventually he approached me, sheepishly.

"Have you seen Louise?" he asked. I pondered for a moment.

"Tall skinny irritating woman, with a voice like Geoffrey Boycott on helium and an ego the size of Old Trafford? Yeah, I seen her…" He looked at me, exasperated, and I relented. "She's not well, Zoé took her back to her cabin. Maybe you should go and check on her. I'm sure you know where it is."

He smiled. "Yeah, I know where it is. It's not as big as mine."

"That figures," I said, dismissively. We stood awkwardly for a moment. Then -

"Louise bloody Meyers though - " "I'm sorry about Twitter - "

I smiled thinly. "It was you who leaked the photos, then?"

"No! I don't know who it was…" He didn't look convincing, and to his credit he realised it. "I don't know, but it might have been Louise. If I'd known she was going to do it I'd have stopped her."

"You think she'd have listened to you?" I asked sceptically. He grinned.

"Not a bloody chance. But I should go and check on her."

Five minutes later Joel and Zoé returned, chatting amicably. I looked over and she gave me a thumbs up, which I took to mean Louise had been safely delivered to her room and was sleeping it off.

I turned back to the game where Will had just worked out that he was Barak Obama, as the lights went out. I grabbed his arm and he whispered in my ear.

"Here we go…"

There was a commotion in the darkness - it was pitch black - and a sudden brief flash of light - no more than a sliver - appeared somewhere to the side of the room. Was it the door opening, somebody slipping outside? But that was on the other side of the room, wasn't it? There were the sounds of a scuffle and chairs being knocked over, and a surprisingly authentic cry of fear, then a few muffled laughs. It was difficult to take it seriously, but the Chief Purser rallied magnificently.

"It's okay, everybody!" she called, "Just stay where you are, and the lights will be back on in a minute."

From nearby came a familiar noise -

Snitches, end up in ditches,

While the bitches, get all the riches.

- followed by a loud -

"WHAT?!"

Everyone laughed, the mood completely ruined. I could almost see Zoé's red cheeks glowing in the darkness. The phone shut off abruptly but she didn't speak and I felt bad for her; she must be so embarrassed.

It stayed dark. More laughter.

"Do you need 50p for the meter?" some wag called out - I suspected it was the poor man's James Bond. There's always one, isn't there…

And *still* the lights didn't come on. I heard the Chief Purser sigh angrily.

56

"Where's Karl?" she hissed. The steward behind the bar answered quietly, obviously in the negative, and she hissed again. "Then *you* turn the bloody lights on!"

There was the sound of someone fumbling around and an 'ow!' as they walked into something and finally, *finally*, after what felt like hours but was probably only about 5 minutes, the lights came back on and we were all left blinking at the sudden brightness.

There was a body slouched across one of the tables. *How unhygienic,* I thought. *I'm glad we already had pudding.*

A dark red stain was slowly spreading across the tablecloth... It looked very realistic, until the corpse farted softly (I mean, I know gas builds up in dead bodies and it has to escape somehow, but this one wasn't even cold yet) and those of us close enough to hear giggled.

This time, the corpse was dressed in a crew member's uniform. I recognised the young man who had given me the invitation to the murder in the library.

The other guests stood frozen in surprise for a few seconds, then swarmed around the corpse, gingerly at first - the blood was thick and glutinous, and did look quite real - then exclaiming as they realised who it was. I noticed a few of them looking around to try and work out who had been standing nearby; next to me, Will nodded approvingly. I could see Harvey and Michael prodding the not-really-deceased, and I knew they were just trying to make him laugh. Naughty boys.

The poor grieving widow from earlier (who had, rather unrealistically in my view, joined us for dinner) gave it a minute, then screamed and swooned into a handily placed chair, after looking round and making sure it was there. Zoé appeared from behind me, holding a glass of brandy she had managed to procure from the bar. She gave it to the woman, who knocked it back delicately but quickly and pointedly looked at the empty glass. The Chief Purser took it from her with a warning look, and the widow subsided back into gentle sobs.

Sylvia rolled her eyes at Zoé. "You do know she's just acting, right? She knew this was going to happen. The rest of us didn't."

"No," said Harvey. "It was all a bit of a shock. I could do with a brandy myself."

"Sorry," said Zoé. "I just got caught up in the moment." She bent down and picked up her phone, which had ended up on the floor in the melée, and scuttled away again.

Will, the Chief Purser and I faded into the background, letting the amateurs do the detecting. Joel said loudly, "I wonder what happened to the murder weapon?" before joining us. They immediately all began scuttling around looking for a knife.

Joel sighed. "Why do they automatically assume it was a knife? There are so many other things he could have been stabbed with."

"And that's why you're a crime writer," I said. "You don't immediately think of the obvious thing."

Will looked at me in surprise, and to be honest I was surprised myself that I'd actually said something that could be construed as 'nice' to Joel. I smiled.

"But of course in real life it normally *is* the obvious thing, isn't it?" I said, turning to Will. He nodded.

"In my experience, yes. Which is why I'm a policeman of sorts and not a writer…"

I turned as a purser - a real one, rather than a fake dead one - *ahem*ed behind me. He smiled apologetically and held out a piece of paper.

"Message for you," he said. I took it; another handwritten note on the ship's stationery.

Come to my cabin. P9-4. We need to talk, LM

"When did you get this?" I asked, frowning.

"A couple of minutes ago," he said. "Ms Meyers rang the pursers station. I brought it straight here."

I thanked him and he left.

"What's the matter?" asked Will. I could feel Joel watching me carefully. I showed Will the message and he looked surprised. "Well that's a turn up for the books. Do you want me to come with you?"

"Is there something wrong with Louise?" asked Joel. I shrugged and showed him the message. "Ah... I think she might want to call a truce."

"Really?" I was incredulous, but he nodded.

"I told her she was out of line. She's really not that bad, you know. You bring out the worst in her."

I opened my mouth to protest. So it was my fault, was it? The way she swanned around and constantly made snide remarks about me? But Will touched my arm.

"Maybe just go and talk to her," he said gently. "You act like it doesn't bother you, but I know you. You want everyone to like you."

Damn him, he was right. I hate conflict. I hated being at war with her, even when she bloody deserved it. I sighed.

"Alright, I'm going," I said. "If she starts mouthing off again and it ends up in fisticuffs, I'm blaming you."

CHAPTER 9

I headed out of the Pearl, through the Excelsior upper level dining area and out into a corridor. The more expensive penthouses - like mine - were on the next level up, but this one still had a mixture of exclusive suites and bigger cabins, handily located for the private dining rooms.

P9-4 was close by, luckily for Louise; she wouldn't have made it back if it had been too far, even with Zoé and the steward helping her. I took a deep breath as I stood outside the door. From the next cabin I could hear the sound of a woman laughing, a deep, throaty laugh followed by a moan of pleasure. No prizes for guessing what was going on there, then. I wished I was back in my own cabin, making the same sort of noises with Will. But needs must. If Louise was holding out an olive branch it would be childish not to take it.

I knocked. And waited. No answer. I knocked again. If she was playing silly buggers with me… Fork her, I wasn't hanging about. I banged on the door again in frustration and then stopped as it moved under my hand. It was unlocked.

Ooh that wasn't good. Spidey senses tingling, I opened it and called out.

"Louise? Are you alright?"

I went inside, leaving the door open behind me.

There was no sign of her in the main room. I looked around, convinced now that she was playing some sort of stupid joke on me, and then stopped as I saw a foot, stretched out on the floor behind the bed. *Oh bloody hell…* Not wanting to but having to, I forced myself to edge around the bed and then froze in horror.

Louise lay on the floor, eyes wide in unseeing terror, hands clutching weakly at her throat. Blood oozed sluggishly but relentlessly through her fingers as they scrabbled at something sticking out, dark and sticky against her white skin. Blood puddled around her head, staining the soft cream carpet crimson. *It'll be a right bugger getting that deep pile clean* flashed inappropriately across my mind. I dropped to my knees, narrowly missing a small pool of vomit next to her, and saw the corkscrew rammed into her artery, its evil twisted hook tearing through the flesh. Paralysed with shock, I thought I saw a flicker of recognition as she stared into my eyes, all the while trying in feeble panic to pull the corkscrew out. I had this sudden, horrific vision of her succeeding, of her neck popping like a champagne cork and blood spurting everywhere. I grabbed her hand and held it still.

"Leave it!" I said urgently. I put a hand on her cheek. It was cold. "Leave it, it'll make it worse if you pull it out. We have to stem the blood flow…" I looked around, then tugged at the scarf around my neck and pressed it onto her wound. "It's okay Louise, I've got you, we'll get help…" I looked around helplessly, but her phone was on the other side of the room and I'd left mine back in my own cabin. I didn't want to move and lessen the pressure on her wound, even though a voice in the back of my head whispered that it was too late, she was already gone and I was - for want of a better phrase - flogging a dead horse. *What the hell do you want me to do?* I hissed at that voice. *Abandon her? Let her bleed to death without even trying?*

I looked down at her face, hoping against hope to hear that bloody awful voice of hers sneering that she'd fooled me, that it was all a game and I was a bloody idiot for falling for it. I'd even have settled for a snarky comment about my age or weight or grey hair. But I knew the likelihood of my ever hearing that voice again was getting less and less. All of a sudden I remembered the couple next door.

"Help!" I yelled at the top of my lungs. "Please, someone help me!"

Karl and Heather were the first ones to show up. They found me bent over Louise, covered in her blood, crying as I realised the life had already left her eyes. I wouldn't let go of her hand or take the pressure off her wound until Will arrived and ever so gently prised my fingers away from hers. I looked up into his face and saw my own shock and horror mirrored there.

The captain came, and the ship's doctor arrived at a run with a full medical kit, but he didn't even bother to open his bag; there was no point. It was too late.

The ship's head of security took charge of the situation, although it was clear that the stunned man had never had to deal with anything quite like this before. Will offered his assistance, but it was firmly (although politely) declined. Two security guards escorted us back to our cabin, where the doctor examined me and placed my blood-stained clothing into plastic bags. He then swabbed under my fingernails, much to Will's consternation; but I barely noticed anything he did. All I could see was Louise's eyes, staring into mine, pleading with me to please, *please* not let her die. And I'd failed.

I ran to the bathroom and threw up, then stayed on the floor by the toilet, shaking, just in case I needed to do it again. I heard Will talking to the doctor, sounding slightly pissed off, and then the sound of the door shutting as he left.

Will came and sat on the floor next to me. He cleaned my face with a flannel and draped a bath towel around my shoulders like a blanket, then put his arm around me and stayed there on the tiles with me.

Eventually I felt well enough to stand up. Will helped me out of the bathrobe I'd changed into and turned on the shower, then sat on the toilet while I stood under the hot jets, soaping and scrubbing all traces of Louise out of my hair and skin pores. The thought of that made me retch again and I had to steady myself against the shower screen. Will was on his feet in a second, ready to grab me, but I recovered. I was so glad that he was there.

I put on my pyjamas and sat on the bed as Will made some tea.

"What time is it?" I asked him. I felt exhausted but strangely wide awake at the same time.

"Nearly 2am," he said. He looked wiped out as well. He handed me a mug, watching as my hand trembled, then sat down next to me. I leaned against him and closed my eyes.

There was a knock on the cabin door. I jumped, but Will put his hand on my leg.

"It's okay," he said. "I've got a good idea who that will be."

There were two vaguely familiar men outside in uniform. Will stood aside to let them in, making it clear he wasn't very happy about it, then sat down next to me again. One of the men stood near the door while the other pulled up a chair and sat in front of me.

"Bella, this is Harry Carter," Will said. "Harry is the head of security, here on the boat."

"I know you," I said. "I saw you at Louise's cabin…" My voice trailed off as saw the scene again.

"Mrs Tyson - " he began.

"Mrs Carmichael," corrected Will.

"Bella," I said. Harry smiled, without warmth.

"Bella. I need to ask you some questions about what happened."

63

That was the last thing I wanted to think about, but I knew I would think about it anyway, so I may as well tell him what he wanted to know.

"Okay, well, I knocked on the door but there was no answer. I thought she was playing a trick on me, so I was going to leave, but then I realised the door was open so I went in and there she was…" I wiped my eyes, not even really aware I was crying again.

"Why did you go to Ms Meyers' cabin?" asked Harry. Will shifted in annoyance.

"We told you that earlier - "

"Yes, but I want to hear it from Bella."

"Why do you need me to go over this again?" I just wanted to lie down and shut my eyes. "I already told you all this."

"It's just routine."

"If it's routine, can't we do it in the morning? I feel awful, I just want to lie down."

Harry didn't answer but looked at me steadily.

"What?" I asked, confused. "Why do we have to do this right now?"

"Because you're a suspect," said Will, angrily. "Bella, he thinks you did it."

CHAPTER 10

'Time stood still'. Writers use that phrase all the time - I've even used it myself, when I wanted to slow a story down and take stock, but I've never actually experienced it in real life.

Except at that moment. Everything froze. I couldn't breathe. Harry looked at me, and Will glared at Harry, and I shut my eyes so I wouldn't have to look at either of them. Only then I saw Louise lying on the carpet bleeding to death in front of me, so I opened them again. Harry was still staring at me.

"He thinks - " Will started, but I stopped him.

"He thinks I killed her," I said. The words sounded faintly ridiculous. Me, kill someone? I was the least aggressive, biggest coward out of anyone I knew. Why would I kill Louise?

"Why on earth would I kill her?" I asked. Will gripped my hand tightly, and for a moment I thought he was warning me to keep quiet, in case I might say something to incriminate myself. Angrily, I turned to look at him. "Don't tell me *you* think I did it too?"

Will looked shocked. "Of course not! You're not a killer. I know you wouldn't hurt anyone." He looked at Harry. "You don't know my wife - "

"I know that she had a well-publicised feud with the deceased," said Harry. "A feud that's blown up over the last few days on Twitter. I know that she was found next to the deceased, restraining her with a scarf and holding the murder weapon in place - "

"I was trying to stop her bleeding to death!" I protested. The whole thing was ludicrous.

"I know that the deceased was having a relationship with her ex-husband, which by all accounts your wife wasn't happy about."

"What accounts?" I exclaimed, exasperated. "Who said I wasn't happy about it? I wasn't bloody jealous! I - "

"There was a threat made on Twitter," said Harry, "Something about hoping the murderer didn't get Ms Meyers 'by mistake'. And then you asked one of the passengers to make the deceased disappear 'discreetly' so no one would realise she had left the dining room…"

I scoffed, incredulous. "Oh for god's sake! I told her I didn't want it to end up on Twitter that Louise had got legless and had to be helped back to her cabin. I was trying to be nice!"

"There's also the matter of the murder weapon," said Harry. He spoke with the air of Hercule Poirot, delivering his deductions and about to deliver the killer blow. "The deceased was killed by a blow to the carotid artery with a corkscrew. Does that sound familiar?"

"No…" But it did. I started to get a nasty feeling.

"Really? You've never written a murder where the murderer kills the victim with a corkscrew to the neck?"

Will looked at me, his mouth falling open slightly. He's my biggest fan, and he's read all my books, and it rang a bell with him too.

I shrugged. "One of my DCI Fletcher books had a similar murder - "

"The exact same murder," insisted Harry.

"Okay, it was the exact same method," I said. "I wasn't hiding it from you, I didn't remember it. I've written a lot of books and killed a lot of people."

Harry raised his eyebrows. I shook my head in irritation.

"You know what I mean. So the murderer copied my book. So what?" But I was started to feel sweaty and panicky.

"So this is your case against my wife, is it?" Will sounded calm, but I knew he was barely keeping it together. He got to his feet and pointed a finger right in Harry's face. "You come to our cabin when my wife has just been through the most distressing experience of her life, when she's still in shock, and you accuse her of murder based on - well, it's not even evidence, is it? You accuse her based on wild conjecture, gossip and speculation?" He took a step forward, his fists now clenched in barely contained anger.

The other security guard, who I'd almost forgotten about, stepped in front of him, but Harry gestured him away and faced Will steadily.

"Mr Carmichael," he said. "I'm just doing my job. A murder has taken place on this ship, and a murderer is on the loose. The safety of every single passenger and member of the crew is my responsibility, and I will not be prevented from fulfilling that responsibility. If you persist in obstructing my investigation I will place you both under house arrest and you will be confined to your cabin until we reach New York, when you will be handed over to the authorities."

I looked at Will. I could not believe this was happening, and clearly neither could he. I knew I was innocent, but no one else did, and at that moment I felt completely and utterly alone. Even Will - did he really believe me? Or was he just sticking up for me because I was his wife, and because, after I'd covered for him in Venice, he owed me?

Will reached out and pulled me towards him, and I burst into tears. I felt his reassuring warmth as I sobbed into his shoulder and knew that whatever he thought had happened in that cabin, he would defend me to the death anyway.

Harry sighed heavily. I hoped he didn't expect me to feel sympathy for him, shouldering this huge burden of responsibility, because if he did he was shit out of luck.

"Mrs Ty - Bella," he corrected himself. "I'll level with you. There is no one else on this ship who has any motive for killing Ms Meyers."

"As far as you know," I interrupted him.

"As far as I know, yes," allowed Harry. "As far as we are aware, only you and Mr Quigley had even met her before this cruise, and most of her interactions had been with the two of you and a few other passengers. You were in her cabin - " he held up a hand as I opened my mouth to interrupt him again - "yes, I know, she invited you. There are witnesses who corroborate you getting the message from her. But none of them can shed any light on why she might do that or what her intentions were. The murder method - "

"That is just ridiculous," Will interjected sharply.

"The murder method is tenuous," said Harry. "I'll admit that. But everything else points to you."

I hugged Will tighter. This was turning into a nightmare.

"You are confined to your cabin while we investigate," said Harry. "There will be security guards posted outside your door, so please don't try to leave. We do have a secure holding facility - "

"A prison cell," I corrected him, wiping my nose.

"Yes," he said. "A prison cell. I think you will be more comfortable here, so please don't force me to use it."

"What about me?" demanded Will. "Can I leave, or am I under arrest as well?" I clutched at him; I didn't want him to leave me. He smiled gently. "I need to leave the cabin if I'm going to clear your name," he said.

"You are free to come and go as you please," said Harry. "But I will not have you interfering with or obstructing my investigation."

"As an officer of Interpol I have the authority to investigate a murder, particularly when it occurs in international territories," said Will, drawing himself up to his full height (which wasn't that high, but it was high enough for me). "Legally, this ship doesn't come under the jurisdiction of either the UK or the US - "

"The Captain has authority over this ship when it's in international waters," said Harry, drawing *himself* up too. They looked like two middle aged, rutting stags, fighting over a female in heat. Watching someone bleed to death, being accused of murder, having two men fighting over me - it was turning into an evening of firsts...

"The Captain is a sensible man," said Will. "A sensible man doesn't turn down any offers of experienced help. How many homicide investigations have you led?"

Harry stared at him for a moment, then sighed.

"Fine. But I will be watching you. Yours is hardly an objective view point, and I won't have you leading or influencing witnesses." He turned to the security guard behind him and nodded, and they both turned to leave. He stopped at the door and looked back. "Get some sleep, Bella. I will need to talk to you again."

I flopped back onto the bed, exhausted, as I heard the door shut. I stared up at the ceiling and felt the mattress move as Will lay down next to me, but I didn't look at him.

"Go on then," I said. I felt him roll over to gaze at me.

"Go on then what?"

"Ask me if I did it." I swallowed hard, fighting back the tears again, but I was determined not to cry any more.

"No," said Will. I turned to see him watching me closely.

"You mean you don't want to know?" I said, in a small voice. He smiled and shook his head.

"No, you looney, I mean I don't need to ask. I know you didn't do it." He reached out and stroked a lock of my formerly glamorous hairdo out of my eyes, and I felt a pang for the hard work of the beauty therapist and hairdresser, completely ruined by the night's events. *We should have had that bunk up earlier.* "You are the softest, warmest, most compassionate person I've ever met." He laughed gently. "I mean yes, you have got a bit of a gob on you and you're good at sarcastic comebacks - "

"Usually two hours too late," I said.

"Not always. Words are your weapons, not sharp pointy things." He pulled me to him and kissed me on the forehead, then we slowly undressed each other and fell asleep wrapped in each other's arms.

CHAPTER 11

We slept late the next morning. I woke with an aching head and sore, puffy eyes. Will made tea as I swallowed an aspirin and stood under the shower again; I hoped it would clear my head, but part of me also wanted to scrub myself all over again, just in case any traces of Louise lingered.

We sat and drank our tea and looked at the room service menu, but neither of us felt like eating. I was strangely calm and no longer perpetually on the verge of bursting into tears, in fact I felt absolutely fine - if you ignored the massive panicky knot of anxiety lurking in the pit of my stomach that left no room for breakfast.

I picked up my phone, more out of habit than a desire to look at anything, but Will put his hand on mine with a warning glance.

"Are you sure you want to look at that?" he asked. I thought about it. He was probably right to be wary, but at the same time I wanted to know if I was already facing trial by social media.

"Sticks and stones," I said lightly. "I'm going in…"

As I'd expected, #RIPLouiseMeyers was trending on Twitter. The same tabloid newspaper as before had posted a story about her murder, but they had stopped short of accusing me of committing it, just saying that I had been among the last to see her and was unavailable to comment. The same though could not be said of the Twitterati, who all had their own theories as to what had happened, most of which hinged on my supposed bitter jealousy over her bonking my ex.

"Is it bad?" asked Will tentatively. I laughed, but not really.

"I've been found guilty and completely exonerated," I said lightly. "I'm a jealous bitch who's so much happier with my lovely new husband than I ever was with Joel, who I apparently am desperate to get back together with. So you know, it could be worse…"

My voice trailed off. I'd been tagged in a post by someone I didn't know (not unusual in itself - although it was usually someone slagging off one of my books and kindly letting me know I was a crap writer). But there was no text, just a hashtag - #Guilty - and a picture. A picture of me, being led away from Louise's cabin covered in her blood. I went cold.

"What is it?" Will saw the blood drain from my face, and was on his feet and next to me in a second. He saw the photo and plopped down onto the chair next to me.

"Who the hell is taking these pictures?" I cried.

"And leaking them online," said Will grimly. "Although I notice they've posted it directly this time, not sent it to the newspapers."

"The newspapers aren't daft," I said. "They know I'd sue their arses if they shared this." I glared at my phone, then jumped out of my skin as it rang. Susie.

"Oh my GOD Bella, what's going on?" she shrieked. I held the phone away from my ear. "I just heard about Louise. I should've told you as soon as I found out she was going to be on the ship, but I honestly didn't find out until the last minute. I'm so sorry, it's all my fault this has happened - "

"Of course it isn't your fault," I said, trying to calm her down, although to be fair I was the one facing a murder charge, not her, and I did feel a moment's irritation that we seemed to be doing things the wrong way round. She should have been reassuring me, by rights.

"I just feel so bad…" she said. *How do you think I bloody feel?!!!*

"Have you seen Twitter yet?" I asked, and she went quiet. I could hear her tapping away at her laptop. Then -

"What in the name of Mark Zuckerberg?!" Susie sounded like she was having a coronary on the other end of the phone. I held it further away from my ear.

"Er, I think that's Facebook - " I said. She ignored me.

"I can't BELIEVE Twitter have let that go - you do mean the picture, right? Oh my god, you have seen that picture, haven't you? I haven't just made things worse - "

"Yes I've seen the picture," I said. "I want you to get onto Twitter and threaten to sue the bejesus out of them unless they take it down now. And I want to know who posted it."

"The username is Fletcher92DM," Susie said. I went cold. In my horror at the sight of that photo, I hadn't even noticed the username. The main character in the series of books I was famous for - including the one with the corkscrew murder - was DCI Daisy Fletcher, badge number 92DM... I could hear more typing. "They're new. This is the only thing they've posted. We could trace their IP address..."

"No point," I said. "I know exactly where they are, they're on this bloody ship, hiding in pot plants and behind doorways, waiting to jump out and take a photo of me."

Susie swore - although she never really swore because she was far too posh, she just exclaimed slightly bizarre things in lieu of a good cussing - Susie had a bit of a random outburst and then calmed down long enough to listen to my requests: to get that photo off Twitter, get that user banned, and threaten the tabloid with legal action if they posted any more photographs of me. I didn't hold out too much hope for the last one, although there was a chance that the fact there was now an ongoing criminal investigation might persuade the editor that it wasn't worth the risk.

"Oh, and have a word with Louise's agent," I said. "Give her my condolences."

I got her off the phone, and looked over at Will. He was smiling.

"What?" I asked.

"You're ready to fight now, aren't you?" he said, and I realised with surprise that I was. I no longer felt like crying, or hiding away in my cabin (notwithstanding the fact I'd been told not to leave). I was desperate to get out there and find out who had murdered Louise - because it sure as hell hadn't been me.

The first thing we had to work out was when exactly Louise had been attacked. That was easy; she had called the pursers' desk to invite me to her cabin, and it had only taken the duty purser a few minutes to come to the Pearl and find me. I'd been a little reluctant to go and hadn't exactly hurried there, but that still only gave the murderer a window of about six or seven minutes at the most to enter the cabin, attack Louise and leave. It had been cutting it very fine, and it was surprising that I hadn't passed them in the corridor.

"They could have gone into a neighbouring cabin," I said. "Louise wasn't pouring with blood, but there must have been - " I swallowed hard, feeling a bit sick - "there must've been a bit of a spurt when they stabbed her. They must have got blood on them, so they could have cleaned themselves up and stayed there until all the fuss died down."

Will thought about it. "But there would have been security guards and members of the crew in the corridor for hours afterwards. There are probably still some out there now. The murderer wouldn't be able to slip out unseen."

"Unless they *were* seen," I said. Will looked puzzled. "Remember what we were talking about, over dinner? That if you look

74

like you belong, no one will notice you. Who would have access to Louise's cabin, and the neighbouring ones, and would be able to slip out unnoticed?"

"A member of the crew," said Will.

We looked at each other. There were so many crew members on the ship that it was impossible to recognise who should be on that deck and who shouldn't. And once they were in uniform it was difficult to tell some of them apart, certainly at a brief glance, anyway.

"Of course, it could still be a passenger," said Will. "If it was someone staying on the same deck, they could have attacked Louise then just holed up in their cabin until today. It was quite late in the evening, so they wouldn't have been missed if they'd just stayed there and gone for breakfast this morning."

I nodded. "We need to know who's staying in those cabins."

There was a loud, urgent banging on the cabin door, and we both jumped out of our skins.

"If that's Harry..." I started, but Will stopped me with a kiss.

"It will be fine," he said. "You're innocent."

But when he opened the door, it wasn't Harry. It was Zoé. She pushed past Will and wrapped me in a great big hug, then stood back looking slightly embarrassed.

"Sorry," she said, "but I just wanted to make sure you were okay! What people are saying about you is horrible!"

"What are people saying about me?" I asked. She opened her mouth to speak, but I laughed softly and stopped her. "I'm joking. I can guess."

"It's not true, though," she said, and I wasn't sure if that was a statement or a question. "I mean, I wouldn't blame you if - "

"No of course it's not true," I said, trying not to snap at her. She was sweet, and she was concerned about me, yet there was something about her that really irritated me. I fought it down. "It was really nice of you to come and see me."

She smiled and was about to speak again, when her phone rang. The familiar, charming refrain - *snitches, end up in ditches* - rang through the cabin as she quickly grabbed it and turned it off, blushing.

"You really need to change that ring tone," I said lightly, and she nodded.

"I know," she said. "I was so embarrassed when it went off last night! Right in the middle of the murder! You don't think everyone heard it, do you?" she asked, with a hopeful expression on her face. I hated to dash it.

"I think they probably all did, I'm afraid," I said gently, remembering the laughter in the dark room. "Don't worry about it, it lightened the mood, didn't it?"

She laughed. "Yes, it probably did."

Will cleared his throat. "Are you okay if I leave you for a bit? I want to go and talk to the Chief Purser, about - what we were just talking about."

I nodded, and Zoé looked between the two of us, open mouthed.

"Ooh, that all sounds very mysterious!" she squealed. "Is it to do with the murder?"

I looked at Will, and he shrugged. What harm could it do?

"We're going to clear my name," I said. She squealed again.

"It's a real life murder mystery!" she said. She just stopped herself clapping her hands together in excitement. "I mean…do you need a hand?"

Will and I exchanged looks. "I don't know…" Will sounded dubious, but she ignored him.

"The murder mystery's been cancelled," she said, "and you've got a whole team of amateur detectives sitting around with nothing to do. Let us help you!"

I suddenly felt on the verge of tears again. "You believe me, then? You don't think I did it?"

Zoé smiled. "I know you didn't do it," she said, grasping my hand and squeezing it. I stood up, wiped my eyes, blew my nose and smiled at her.

"Then the game is afoot."

CHAPTER 12

Will went to talk to the Chief Purser and ask her about the passengers in the cabins near Louise, and Zoé left soon after to 'rally the troops', as she put it. I didn't think my amateur detectives would be that likely to help, but just knowing that not everyone thought I was guilty was reassuring.

      I made some tea and sat down with a pen and paper, hoping that if I could just relax, some flash of insight or inspiration would flash through my mind and I would instantly know who the murderer was, or at least how to clear my own name. But inspiration remained conspicuous by its absence. My stomach rumbled; I must be feeling better. Food would help (food always helps, particularly chocolate and bacon, though probably not both at once). I ordered breakfast - or lunch, looking at the time - from room service and went to stand out on the balcony, watching the late summer sunshine highlighting the ripples of the waves. It was quite fresh out here in the middle of the Atlantic, but there was very little wind and the sea was calm. I pulled my long cardigan around me and breathed in deeply. In my mind I looked proper dramatic, like the cover of a romantic novel; you know the type, where the back view (never the front) of a woman gazes wistfully out to sea, or at the Eiffel Tower or some mountains or something (I don't know how she manages to look wistful when all you can see is her back, but she does). She's probably wearing a floaty dress and clasping a summer hat to her head, too - the women on these book covers are never wearing trainers or clutching a Tesco's Bag for Life like normal women.

And the book's always called *The Little (Something) in the (Somewhere),* or *The (Something or Other's) Daughter.*

But knowing my luck the only book cover I would ever personally grace would be called *The Middle-aged Writer Who Got Seagull Shit on Her Cardy.* Either that or 'The Countess of Monte Cristo'.

There was a loud knock on the door of the cabin; brunch! I opened the door to the steward, who placed the plate of Eggs Benedict with extra bacon (for brain power) on the table. I tipped the steward and sat down, ready to tuck in, as he turned to leave.

"I see guilt hasn't affected your appetite," said Joel, making me jump. I leapt up and glared at the steward, who stood apologetically in the doorway.

"I'm sorry, madam," he said. "Mr Quigley just - "

"It's okay," I said. "Mr Quigley has a habit of turning up where he's not expected. This ship, my cabin, other women's knickers…"

"I'm not here for an argument," said Joel.

"No? What *are* you here for?" I noticed the steward hopping about in the doorway, looking embarrassed. "It's fine, you can go." He escaped gratefully as Joel sat down, eyeing my bacon. *You can keep your thieving mitts off that*, I thought. "Oh please, do make yourself at home," I said sarcastically.

"I will." He reached out to snaffle a rasher and I slapped his hand.

"I see grief hasn't affected *your* appetite," I said. He looked affronted.

"I am upset!" he said. I looked at him, and he bristled. "Don't look at me like that! I am. I'm shocked. I was fond of her."

"'Fond'? You romantic fool."

He looked at me for a moment, then gave a small laugh. "Yeah, that sounds bad doesn't it? I didn't even really know her that well. But she was alright, you know?"

"I'll take your word for that." I picked up my knife and fork and looked at him. "Are we done?"

He sighed. "You still hate me, then?"

"Why on earth would I hate you?" I said, and for a moment I thought he was actually going to answer that. But he obviously thought better of it.

"Fair enough. Look, I just wanted to come and make sure you were okay - " he eyed my massive plate of food - "I can see you are. I wanted to say, I know you didn't kill her." I was surprised to hear a slight hoarseness in his voice, like he was suppressing some emotion. I looked at him and was even more surprised to see a look of genuine worry on his face. "I want you to know, I'm on your side. I know you, Bell. You're not a killer."

I felt tears pricking my eyes again. *Damn you, Quigley!* I swallowed hard, trying not to show that I was actually quite touched by his concern.

"I don't suppose you know why your girlfriend invited me to her cabin just as she was about to get done in, do you?" I asked. He shook his head.

"I don't know. Like I said before, maybe she was going to call a truce. She didn't tell me she was going to talk to you, but then we weren't joined at the hip." He looked embarrassed - another first. "I mean, we were joined at the hip in that we, you know, physically - "

"Yeah, yeah, believe it or not I had guessed you were doing the horizontal macarena," I said, rolling my eyes. He snorted.

"Horizontal macarena… You always did have a way with words."

"Maybe I should think about becoming a writer, what do you reckon?"

"Nah, you're not *that* good," he said, grinning. I flapped a hand at him.

"If you're not going to help me, bugger off so I can eat my breakfast," I said. He stood up as I pointedly picked up my knife and fork.

"You do realise she was mad jealous of you, don't you?" he said, and my hand stopped halfway to my mouth with a forkful of poached egg on it.

"She was jealous of me?" I was astounded.

"Why is that such a surprise?" Joel seemed equally astounded that *I* was astounded. "I mean, look at you…"

Exactly, I thought, though I wasn't about to say it out loud. *Overweight and approaching 50.*

Joel though, the bastard, seemed to know what I was thinking. "Look at your career," he said, clarifying it. "You're an amazing writer, you've had bestsellers all over the place. Louise liked to say her background and her lack of education had held her back, but she knew it was just an excuse. You had the same kind of childhood and it didn't stop you. She was in awe of you."

"In awe of me?" I still didn't quite believe it.

"And then, of course…" Joel's voice trailed away as he stared at me.

"What?" I said, but his gaze was starting to make me feel hot.

"She knew that I still - you know what I'm trying to say, don't make me say it." I just stared at him, thinking, *you have got to be feckin' kidding me.* "She knew I regretted what happened - that I still had feelings - "

The egg on my fork slipped off and smooshed into a puddle of hollandaise with a loud and farty-sounding splat. Joel stopped and looked at it, then at me, sitting there with my mouth open. I hastily shut it.

"Your bacon's getting cold," he said, and turned and left.

My bacon *was* getting cold. I ate it thoughtfully. There was a lot to unpack from that conversation. Joel still - I swerved around that thought. Louise had been jealous of me? It seemed unlikely. But then, I did have a string of bestsellers and awards and lots of readers, and what did she have over me? Her relative youth, and lots of media attention, which she had always courted. She had written a wildly successful memoir, which had sold loads but had also caused a fair bit of controversy, as there were whispers that *maybe* not *all* of it was strictly true. I'd thought that was a very diplomatic way of putting it, because I'd read it and the whole thing sounded like bollocks to me. But who knew? There were certain things in my own childhood (and more recent past) that I'd kept to myself, and if I suddenly came out with them now doubtless not everyone would believe me. And it hardly mattered now anyway, because she was dead.

Maybe one of the figures from her murky past was on this ship, and had seized the opportunity to wreak revenge upon her for outing them in her book? But that seemed unlikely; they were low level criminals on the streets of Manchester, and if anything the notoriety that had accompanied Louise's book had probably given them huge props amongst their fellow felons. No, whoever had killed Louise had had a grudge against her *now*, not from her past.

Listen to me! Hercule Poirot without the moustache. Although as a woman of a certain age I did have a small one that kept appearing (along with a few random hairs on my chinny chin chin), and the 'little

82

grey cells' were becoming outnumbered by long grey hairs, but you know what I mean. I shook my head and mopped up runny egg yolk and hollandaise sauce with a hunk of toasted English muffin.

The thought of hunks and English muffins immediately led me back to Joel. He still - there was no avoiding it forever - he still had feelings for me! I had some choice feelings for him, too, but I assumed his were of the more romantic persuasion, rather than the sort that led to you Googling 'how to make a voodoo doll' and ordering pins.

When I had met Joel at the Smoking Gun awards, many years ago now, he'd been the new e*nfant terrible* of British crime writing while I was, I suppose, part of the establishment. Why he'd fancied me in the first place I could never quite work out, but he had. He'd celebrated his win over me in the Best Crime Novel award by plying me with drinks and badgering me for a bunk up. I'm not a complete pushover but it's safe to say I wasn't much of a challenge after the second bottle. It had however grown into something much more than that, and by the time the awards came around again we were married. We laughed, we talked about books and movies, we had fun. But it wasn't enough for him - *no,* I reminded myself sharply, *I* wasn't enough for him - and he'd cheated on me with a string of casual lovers, most of them one or two night stands, 'nothing serious', as he'd put it. It might not have been serious to him, but it was to me. I've never exactly been a nun (what can I say? I'm a part time hedonist. I love pleasures of all kinds, including but not limited to sex) but I have always been a monogamist, a one-man (at a time) woman. Well, there was that once in South America, when I was travelling - but it was all consensual and I never did it again, forget I even mentioned it.

Anyway... I finished eating and sat back in my chair, stuffed full of food and wild thoughts.

Will returned soon after that, bearing a passenger list and a map of the ship. The Chief Purser, it seemed, was convinced of neither my guilt or my innocence, she just wanted the murder solved as quickly and quietly as possible, with the minimum of fuss or publicity. If that meant helping Will in his unofficial investigation, so be it. The Captain too was happy for - or maybe resigned to - Will poking around, as long as he did it discreetly. How Harry, the head of security, felt about it we knew only too well, but it looked like there was nothing he could do about it.

Will kissed me and smiled when he saw that I'd eaten.

"You're feeling better, then," he said. I nodded. I decided not to mention Joel's visit until I'd had time to process it.

"What have you got there?" I asked, as he spread out the map, trying not to get hollandaise sauce on it.

"It's a floor plan of Louise's deck," he said. "We can mark out who was where when she died."

There was a polite knock on the door and I groaned.

"Who is that now?" I said. "This bloody cabin has been like Clapham Junction this morning." Will raised an eye brow; as far as he was aware Zoé had been my only visitor. *Dammit.* "Joel popped by," I said lightly, and his other eye brow joined the first.

"What did he want?" he asked, but there was another knock before I could reply.

"Housekeeping!" came the muffled voice from behind the door. I opened it as Will gathered the map and passenger list up again.

"I'm terribly sorry," I said, trying to sound lighthearted, "but I can't leave."

"I know, madam," said the room cleaner, a young Asian woman. "I can work around you."

Will opened the glass doors onto the balcony and gestured me outside. I smiled at the cleaner and followed him, shutting the door behind me.

We sat on the sun loungers and watched the seagulls swooping low over the waves. Will cleared his throat and spoke without looking at me.

"So, what did Joel want?"

To declare his undiminished, undying love for me, I thought. Not helping, Bella…

"He wanted to see if I was okay," I said.

"Hmm."

I turned to him, reaching out a hand to grab his. "Don't 'hmm' like that!" I said, earnestly. "Honestly, you don't need to worry about Joel. He just wanted to let me know he doesn't think I'm guilty, and after seeing that bloody picture on Twitter I need to hear that from as many people as possible."

Will smiled at me. "Sorry," he said. "I'm being an idiot."

"Yes you are. But you're *my* idiot…"

He laughed and kissed my hand, and we stayed like that until the cleaner knocked on the window to signal that she was done.

CHAPTER 13

Will spread out the map again on the now-empty table, and laid a note pad next to it. The cabins were clearly marked out, either side of the wide corridor, with the Pearl and its kitchens at one end of the ship, and a bar and viewing lounge at the other.

"There are so many cabins!" I cried in dismay. I knew the corridor was long, but there were far more than I'd realised. Will nodded.

"There are 110 cabins on that deck," he said. "But just here - " he tapped the middle of the map - "there's a wall of lifts and a staircase down to the Excelsior's lower level, on the deck below. The only way of accessing the other end of the corridor is to go down those stairs and up the other side, so I think we can discount all the cabins beyond that point - I don't think the murderer would want to risk being seen by anyone in the Excelsior, as they wouldn't have had time to clean themselves up before leaving the murder scene. Louise rang the pursers' desk at 9:33 exactly - I checked, they have a daily log where they enter all phone calls and so on. The duty purser came straight up to the Pearl, which I reckon would take four, maybe five minutes, so say 9:37, 9:38. You moaned a bit - don't look like that, you did - but you'd still left the Pearl by 9:40. It can't have taken you long to reach the cabin?"

"Only about two minutes," I said. I traced my route on the map. "I came out of the Pearl and walked through the Excelsior upstairs bar, then out past the kitchen, to her cabin there…"

"So at the very most, the murderer had ten minutes between her calling the pursers' desk and you arriving at the cabin, to get into her room, attack her and leave without being seen."

"Hmm…" Something was bothering me, niggling at my brain, but I couldn't put my finger on it. Will looked at me.

"What is it?"

"Why was the murderer in such a hurry? I mean, I know you wouldn't want to hang around after you'd just topped someone, but they literally got in - she let them in or they broke in, we don't know, but the lock wasn't broken - they got in, stabby stabby - " I absentmindedly mimed a Norman Bates-style stabbing - "…then straight back out again."

"Why were they in such a hurry, unless they knew you were coming?"

"Exactly." I shut my eyes, saw Louise bleeding out in front of me, and opened them again quickly. "How long does it take for someone to bleed to death?" I asked. Will looked thoughtful.

"Depends on the wound," he said. "If her throat had been slit all the way across - " he swallowed hard, and I knew he was remembering a crime scene in Venice - "it would have been quick. She'd have been unconscious in 60 seconds, maybe less, and dead pretty soon after. But it was a small puncture wound, and with the corkscrew left in and her holding her neck trying to stop the bleeding - and then you, trying to stem it with your scarf - who knows? It could have taken a lot longer. You could never have saved her, even if the blood only looked like a trickle. Even in a hospital it would have been touch and go. They'd have to take the corkscrew out at some point, and then she would have been gushing." I grimaced and he stopped abruptly. "Sorry. Not a nice thought."

"So who had the cabins nearby?" I asked. Will took up a pen and consulted his list, adding names to the cabins as he spoke.

"Well, out of the people who we know had contact with Louise - basically the other murder mystery players - the Bauers were opposite -"

"Who?" I didn't recognise the name.

"Mr and Mrs Too Innocent. It looks like they're genuine holidaymakers and not actors after all," said Will. I laughed.

"Well, we're both rubbish detectives, then," I said. But then something occurred to me. "Unless…"

"Unless what?"

'Bauer, Meyers - they're both German surnames. We know that Louise was full of Scheiße when it came to her childhood, so could there be some kind of Teutonic connection there?" It seemed unlikely, but stranger things happen at sea.

Will shook his head doubtfully. "I don't think so. That's pretty tenuous, even for a mystery writer…" He dodged the slap I aimed at him.

"I'm just spitballing here," I said, thinking aloud. "Maybe there's some kind of family connection from the past, and they were here to confront her or bump her off. That would account for their suspicious actions…"

Will laughed. "What suspicious actions? I think we were looking a bit too hard for dodgy characters."

"Yeah…" I said, slightly reluctantly. "I guess they probably are completely legit, even if he should be locked up for wearing those lederhosen. Okay, who else have we got?"

"Next to the Bauers are Lauren Donaldson and Peter Maguire."

"The gorgeous Jamaican Marilyn Monroe and the skinny bloke who's so white he's almost reflective?"

Will laughed. "Yes, that's them. He *is* terribly white, isn't he? Nice couple though."

"What have we got on them?"

"Absolutely bugger all at the moment, I need to do some digging. They were on Louise's team, though."

"Okay. What about the cabin next to Louise? There were definitely people in there," I said, remembering the moans and groans I'd heard as I knocked on the cabin door.

Will looked at his list. "That's Sylvia and Heather."

I was surprised. "Sylvia and Heather? But I heard…" It suddenly clicked, how Heather and Karl had both turned up so quickly, and at the same time. "Karl, the randy little - I bet he's got a woman in every port." Will looked at me, puzzled. "Karl and Heather were the first people to get to me." Will still looked puzzled. "Together. Looking red in the face and slightly dishevelled."

Understanding dawned. "Ahhh…" Will laughed, amazed. "Karl and Heather? She's old enough to be his mother."

"And rich enough for it not to matter," I said. "She told me her ex owned and ran one of the biggest manufacturing companies in the UK and I get the impression she's done rather well out of the divorce settlement. I might be cynical, but I hope she just sees it as a bit of holiday fun. Something to get back at her ex-husband."

"The one who's sleeping with his secretary. Who looks like Louise…" Will looked at me meaningfully.

"I know," I said. "And I know she disliked Louise because of that. But it's hardly a strong enough motive for murder, is it? And I'm certain she was with Karl. She was definitely in her cabin with someone, anyway. It sounded like they were very busy, and were on the verge of finishing being busy at any minute, if you know what I mean."

We both sat for a moment, involuntarily imagining Heather and Karl getting jiggy with it. I shuddered and turned back to the map.

"So this room here - " I tapped the blueprint. "This is the Pearl, yeah? Who's in the cabin between that and Louise?"

Will consulted his list again. "Ah yes. They used to let that out with Louise's cabin as a connecting room, usually for passengers with children. But the Chief Purser said they used to get complaints about the noise so they stopped renting it out - it's right next to the Pearl's kitchen. The chef uses it as a store room."

"So could the murderer have holed up in there and got clean?" I wondered. Will looked thoughtful.

"I don't think so," he said. "I think the connecting door is blocked up, or locked at the very least, so they couldn't have used that. There is a door out into the corridor… I think that's normally locked too, but the chef might leave it open during service in case they need anything." He made a note on his writing pad. "I need to go and do some digging."

I sighed. "I just wish I could come with you." I looked around the cabin. As prisons went it was pretty plush, and most jails don't come with room service, but even so I was already starting to go stir crazy.

"I'm going to have a word with the Captain," said Will. "This is not on, confining you to your cabin! They're treating you as if you're guilty with absolutely no proof of anything."

There was a knock on the door. I rolled my eyes.

"I might be stuck in here but it feels like the whole bloody world wants to visit," I said. Will opened the door, and I knew from the set of his shoulders that he wasn't pleased to see whoever was on our doorstep.

"Oh," he said, then turned to me. "It's the judge, jury and executioner."

90

Behind him, Harry sighed heavily. "There's no need for that, Mr Carmichael," he said. Will opened his mouth to say something but I stopped him.

"Come in, then," I said. "What can I do for you?"

Harry entered, followed by one of the security guards who had been posted outside. The guard nodded at me, looking slightly embarrassed, I thought; they probably hadn't expected anything like this when they had taken the job. The guard headed towards the kitchenette area and stopped, looking askance at Harry, who nodded. Harry spoke as his colleague began searching the cupboards.

"As you know, the murder weapon was a corkscrew. Every single cabin on this ship has one." Harry looked at the guard, who shook his head. "The ordinary cabins - the Silver class passengers - have plain silver coloured corkscrews, but the penthouses like this and Louise's - what we call the Diamond class cabins - have corkscrews with diamond-cut crystal handles. There are only 20 Diamond class cabins, with 20 corkscrews on board." Will and I looked at each other, perplexed; what did this have to do with anything?

"Okay," said Will. "But you've already got the murder weapon - "

"It was still stuck in the victim's neck, or did you miss that?" I asked, sarcastically. Harry just smiled thinly.

"Where is your corkscrew, Mrs Tyson?" Harry knew he was using the wrong surname, I could tell, and he was trying to wind Will up. I put my hand on Will's arm.

"It's Mrs Carmichael, as you well know, and the last time I saw the corkscrew it was on the side there, next to the ice bucket. Why?" But I was starting to get a nasty feeling. The guard shook his head, and Harry spoke again, this time with an irritatingly calm satisfaction.

"We assumed at first that Ms Meyers had been stabbed with the corkscrew from her own room," he said. "But in the course of removing the victim's body, we discovered that corkscrew on the table. So the murder weapon came from another cabin."

"It didn't come from here," I said. "I saw it this morning. I moved it off the table with the ice bucket when the steward brought brunch."

"Well it doesn't appear to be here now," said Harry. I shook my head.

"Of course it's bloody here! Look properly. The cleaner came in and tidied up, they've probably put it in the wrong drawer."

The guard shook his head again, but wouldn't meet my eyes. Harry smiled grimly.

"Added to the fact that I'm pretty confident the police will find your fingerprints all over the murder weapon - "

"Of course they will, you moron!" This guy was a regular Inspector Morse. Not. "I had my hands all over it, trying to stop Louise pulling it out and bleeding to death faster!"

"Mrs Tyson - "

"It's Carmichael." I hissed. I was so furious I could have punched the smug smile off his face, but I resorted to sarcasm instead of violence. "So what you're saying is, I planned Louise's murder, just like I planned all those murders in my books, you know, the ones that none of my readers ever solve before the end. The ones that I'm famous for. I deliberately chose the corkscrew to be the murder weapon - the very *distinctive* corkscrew, which would immediately narrow down the field of suspects to the occupants of those 20 cabins, rather than something that could have been used by all 3000-odd people on this boat. I picked it up before we went to dinner, because I knew I wouldn't have an opportunity to come back to my cabin, and took it with me, ready to stab her." I looked at him, unable to keep the contempt off my face. "Where did I put this corkscrew? It's got a large, cold handle, and I didn't have a handbag, so what did I do with it? Hide it in my cleavage? Stick it up my - "

"Bella's right, this is preposterous!" Will's voice was relatively calm, but his hands were balled into fists and I could tell he was on the verge of slamming Harry into a wall. Or possibly through one. I could see the security guard getting ready to leap into action if necessary, and Harry himself looked like he was limbering up for a fight, and suddenly I'd had more than enough of all this testosterone. I hate confrontation at the best of times, and this one was getting out of hand, everything was starting to spin out of control, and I needed to do something before there was a punch up in my cabin and things got even worse. So I did the only thing I could think of to do.

I fainted.

I *say* I fainted. I did a massive swoon and dropped to the floor, making sure not to hit my head on the way down. There was stunned silence for a moment, then Will was kneeling next to me, looking anxiously into my face. He stroked some hair off my cheek and gazed into my eyes.

"What happened?" I asked, groggily.

"Bella! It's alright, darling, you fainted, don't try to get up." I winked at him and he coughed suddenly, violently, trying to hide a laugh. Will got himself under control and glared up at Harry. "You see what all your ridiculous accusations have done?" he said angrily. "My poor wife…" His poor wife shifted; I'd landed as carefully as I could, but I'd trapped my leg underneath myself and (sadly) I weigh far too much to stay like that for long.

"I need to get up…" I said in a timid voice, nothing like my own.

"What in God's name is going on?" Captain Butler's anything but timid voice boomed across the cabin, sounding shocked at the ridiculous tableau that confronted him. I struggled to my feet (I am a consummate actress, even under pressure) and staggered to the bed, hand clasped to my head.

Harry looked alarmed and I realised that whatever he was up to, he hadn't passed it by the Captain.

"Captain Butler," he started, but the Captain held his hand up to stop him and turned to me. Will sat down on the bed next to me and held my hand.

"The Chief Purser tells me Mr Carter has confined you to your cabin," he said. "Is that right?"

"Yes," I said, trying to sound calm. I got the feeling that getting angry with the head of security was one thing, but it was probably not a good idea to get pissed off at the Captain of the ship when we had another 4 days at sea.

"Have you confessed to the murder of Ms Meyers?" he asked. Will and I exchanged shocked looks.

"What? No, of course I haven't!" I protested. I was about to say more but the Captain nodded.

"I thought as much. Under what grounds are you holding Ms Tyson here?" Captain Butler turned back to Harry, who looked flustered.

"The evidence - " he began. Will snorted.

"What evidence?" he asked, scornfully. "Captain, if I ran an investigation this badly - "

The Captain held his hand up again, this time to stop both men talking. No resorting to undignified fake fainting for him. He was a big, heavy-set man, and I got the impression that once he was on the floor he'd have a struggle to get up again, so it was probably just as well.

"Mr Carter, I think you and I need to discuss this in my cabin," said the Captain, then he addressed me. "Ms Tyson, my apologies. I believe the phrase is 'innocent until proven guilty', isn't it? You are of course free to rejoin the rest of the passengers. The police in New York have been informed and they will doubtless want to question you when we dock, but for now please try to enjoy the rest of the cruise."

"Thank you…" I said.

The Captain stood back and gestured for Harry to leave. The head of security glared at me, probably expecting me to look smug; but I wasn't feeling smug, I was feeling - relieved? Not quite the right word - it wasn't as if this was over yet, not by a long shot - but at least I could get out of this cabin and help Will clear my name. Harry glared at me and left, followed by the Captain, who walked with the air of someone who couldn't *wait* to get back to the privacy of his own cabin and completely explode.

We were left alone in the cabin. Alone, that is, apart from the security guard, who stood there looking slightly gormless and embarrassed. Will looked him, eyebrows raised.

"Oh - yes - sorry," said the security guard, and he headed for the door. But he stopped again and looked at me. "I am sorry about that, Ms Tyson," he said, "but I honestly couldn't find your corkscrew. You might want to have a better look for it."

CHAPTER 14

Of course, now that I was allowed to leave the cabin I wasn't sure if I wanted to. Joel and Zoé believed I was innocent, but Zoé had also said that people were talking about me and saying nasty things. Well, that was no surprise; once you hit a certain level of success or fame there's always someone, somewhere, saying nasty things about you. But they weren't normally accusing me of murder.

Social media seemed split pretty much 50-50 on whether or not I was guilty, and I guessed that the passengers on this ship might well fall into the same divisions. I hoped that those who knew me from the murder mystery game would think better of me, but you can never tell. From what Zoé had said about my team of amateur detectives, I thought that maybe Harvey and Michael at least believed in my innocence; but who knew about anyone else?

There was only one way I was going to find out. Suddenly staying in the cabin and living off room service until we reached New York seemed more attractive than ever…

But Will was having none of it, and he was right (he has a bloody annoying habit of often being right).

"Get your glad rags on, do your hair and make up and come for a walk," he said. I lay back on the bed.

"Do we have to? Can't we stay here and make our own entertainment…?" That usually worked, but he laughed and shook his head.

"Oh no, I'm not falling for that one - well, not right now, anyway - you're trying to appeal to my base sexual urges just so that you can hide away in here."

I sat up. "'Base sexual urges'? Ooh, that is *so* hot, I'm genuinely turned on now…"

But he grabbed my hand and pulled me to my feet.

"Behave, woman! Tidy yourself up. I've sworn to clear your name, and I will, but I could do with a bit of help."

I sighed and went into the bathroom, flinching at my reflection in the mirror. I even looked guilty to my own eyes, and I knew I hadn't done it.

I cleaned my teeth and applied a good couple of inches of foundation to cover the dark circles under my eyes - any more, and my reading glasses wouldn't fit round my head - then tossed my hair about to make it look like I was young and carefree (it didn't work on either score and just looked like I'd been dragged through the hairspray aisle at Boots). I plastered on a fake smile and presented myself to Will, who managed to repress a shudder but not before I'd seen it.

"That bad?" I asked.

"No, no, no… Just relax, will you? You didn't do it." He smoothed my mad hair down and tucked a few rogue strands behind one ear, then kissed my cheek. "Stop trying to look like nothing's happened. You've been through a terrible ordeal. It's okay to let people know you're having a hard time."

I hugged him tightly and wished we were back on land, back home in Wimbledon without ever having set foot on this bloody cruise ship. Will kissed me again and smiled.

"There's only 4 more days until we reach New York," he said. "The police there won't be anything like Harry Carter. He's out of his depth and clutching at straws, and he's desperate to prove his worth by solving this murder. Unfortunately by the time we dock the trail will have started to go cold…"

"So if we want the murderer brought to justice, we'll have to find them," I finished. He nodded. "We'd better get on with it, then. This murder ain't going to solve itself, is it?"

Brave words are one thing. Actions are another. We walked down the corridor, and I smiled confidently at the few people we came across. *I can do this*, I thought. And then we went downstairs and into the main entertainment deck.

You know in old Westerns, when the hero walks into a cowboy bar full of gamblers and desperados, smoking, drinking and gambling while some old timer plays the piano, and suddenly everything goes quiet as they turn to look at him? It was almost (but not quite) totally unlike that. It didn't go quiet, if anything the noise level picked up as people turned to each other and gossiped as I passed. Most of them tried to be discreet but some of them made no attempt to hide it, *ooh*ing and *aah*ing as I went past and loudly sounding off about my guilt or otherwise.

I ignored them all. I could feel my cheeks burning, but I firmly bit my tongue and resisted the urge to confront the onlookers with an aggressive "WHAT?" or suggest that they maybe take a picture, it'd last longer. That had been the standard comeback in my youth, but of course these days everyone has a bloody camera in their pocket, and I'd learnt the hard way that if you say, "Why don't you take a picture, it'll last longer?" the buggers actually will.

Will clutched my hand tightly and led me through them all, past the shops and the beauty salon, past the entrances into bars and restaurants and the cinema, and outside to the swimming pool area, which was rather less crowded being the end of summer and not as warm as it could be. A few die hard octogenarians were sitting in deck chairs, soaking up the late September rays, and a couple of kids splashed in the pool. Will turned towards the pool side bar and sat on a bar stool, with an attempt at nonchalance that was slightly spoilt by the fact that he's only about 5'6" and the stools were high. I struggled onto one next to him, my feet dangling in the air.

"Let's have a drink," he suggested.

"No alcohol for me," I said. Honestly, I barely drink normally, and I'd had more wine in the last two days than I'd had in the two years preceding that. Damn you, all inclusive holidays. My liver would need three weeks at a monastic retreat in the mountains if I carried on drinking at that rate. "I need to keep sharp."

Will nodded and handed me the cocktail menu. "Have a Virgin Mojito or something," he said. "Something with an umbrella and fruit that tells everyone you're on holiday."

We both ordered mocktails - Will doesn't normally drink much either, and we have this running competition when we go out to see who can order the campest drink (it's normally not me). And then we decided to go over what we knew.

"Okay, so - the murderer had a window of around seven to ten minutes in which to get into Louise's cabin, stab her - " Will stopped as the bartender, with raised eyebrows, set two glasses full of pink liquid, fruit and sparkly stuff in front of us. If these drinks didn't say BACK OFF MAN I'M AN INNOCENT TOURIST then nothing would. I smiled at the bartender.

"Thank you!" The bartender nodded and moved away, although I had the distinct impression they were eavesdropping. I sucked up the incongruously sweet and girly drink as Will carried on outlining the grisly murder.

"They must've arrived at her cabin after 9.33, quickly done the deed, and then scarpered," he said. I nodded.

"Okay, first of all - how did they get into the cabin?" I asked, watching Will stir the fruit around his drink with a swizzle stick decorated with thin strands of silver tinsel.

"If Louise let them in, it was someone she knew," said Will.

"Or someone like a steward, someone you'd let in without suspecting them of foul play." I picked a grape out of my drink and ate it. "But when Louise left the Pearl she was completely legless. I can't imagine her being able to get up and let someone in."

"When did she leave?" asked Will. "Did she have to time to get back to her cabin and throw up? Sometimes being sick can sober you up pretty quickly."

"She left before the murder - the pretend murder," I clarified. "Probably ten, fifteen minutes before the lights went out. Then the murder took - I dunno, another five minutes? The lights were out for ages."

"The Chief Purser said they were only meant to be out for a minute, and then Karl was supposed to turn them back on but he didn't," said Will.

"Because he was getting jiggy in the next cabin along with Heather," I said, adding mentally, *Respect, sister*. Because she was at least 25 years older than him and deserved a good time.

Will sucked at his straw, making a slurping noise as he reached the bottom of the glass. It was a good job these were non-alcoholic, as we'd both knocked them back in seconds, self consciously toying with the straws as we felt (or imagined) other passengers watching us.

"Anyway...," I said. " Louise had been gone about 25 minutes when she called the pursers' desk. I'm actually amazed she managed to even do that, but then I suppose the phone's next to the bed so she didn't have to stand up or anything."

I reached the end of my own drink and stared across the deck at the kids in the swimming pool. It seemed like the last place on earth a murderer would be hiding, but someone had killed Louise and whoever they were, they were out there, probably watching me and thanking their lucky stars that I'd blundered onto the murder scene and taken the heat off them.

"So," I said, pushing my glass away and signalling to the bartender for two more drinks, "we're still none the wiser as to whether she knew her killer or not. I still think she'd have been unlikely to have let them in herself, because she was so wasted, which makes me think it was someone with a key."

"A crew member?" asked Will. "That ties in with them being able to hide in a cabin and clean themselves up before leaving that deck…"

"Yep." Something else had occurred to me. "A crew member also might be able to insinuate themselves into the investigation, so they'd know what was going on. When they realised that I was looking good for it, they could have decided to help things along by stealing our corkscrew and planting it in Louise's cabin, making it look like ours was the murder weapon."

"Maybe…" Will looked at me. "You said you'd had a lot of visitors this morning. Who exactly came to see you?"

I smiled guiltily. "To be honest it might not have been this morning. I told Harry Carter that I saw the corkscrew when I ordered my lunch, but between you and me - I don't actually remember the last time I saw it. We definitely had it when we were getting ready for the fancy dress, because you opened that bottle of wine, remember? And we had a lot of visitors after I found her." I shook my head to clear it. It seemed unbelievable that all this had only happened the night before. "Last night. The Captain popped by. The doctor was in our cabin for ages. Harry came in, and there were a couple of security guards. Then this morning there was the steward who brought my lunch, and the cleaner, and then Harry and the security guard again…"

"And Zoé, and Joel," Will pointed out.

"Yes, but they were in the Pearl when Louise was murdered, weren't they? They were there when the duty purser came up with the message."

"True." Will agreed reluctantly.

"Joel can be called many things, most of them not particularly complimentary, but not a murderer," I said gently. He smiled.

"Sorry. I am inclined to think ill of him for the way he treated you," he said. "But I should really be thanking him. If he'd treated you the way he should have done, we would never have met."

I squeezed his hand. "He did us both a favour."

"There you are!" Zoé stood in front of us, breathless. "I've been looking for you everywhere. You're needed in the library."

I grimaced. "Not another amateurish murder, I hope?"

"No," she said, tugging me off the stool. "Your team of eager detectives awaits!"

CHAPTER 15

My would-be saviours were waiting in the library, with coffee and cake. My waistline gave up, waved a little white flag and accepted a slice of lemon drizzle cake. I thanked whoever had invented elasticated waistbands as I studied my team.

I was touched to see Michael and Harvey, taking time out of their busy designer shopping schedule just to clear my name. Sylvia and Heather were there too, Heather in particular looking militant on my behalf. I wondered if Sylvia knew what her cabin mate had been up to…

Michael and Harvey both leapt up and enveloped me a big double hug. It was sweet, even if it meant I could hardly breathe.

"Thank you…" I gasped. They got the hint and released me.

"Poor Bella," said Michael. "The whole thing is just *horrible.* And so ridiculous! As if you would ever hurt anyone!"

Zoé sat down next to Heather, with a troubled look on her face.

"It *is* ridiculous," she said, "but I can kind of see why they think it's you." There were a few exclamations and protestations around the table. Zoé shook her head. "No. no, don't get me wrong, I don't think Bella did it either, but…"

But?!! Thanks, Zoé… I bit my lip but Heather glared at her.

"I was there, Zoé," she said, angrily. "I saw poor Bella trying to save that woman's life. There's no way she did it."

I sat quietly, bemused as they all discussed me like I wasn't there.

"I'm not saying she did!" protested Zoé. "I know she didn't do it! But they'll say she's the only one on this ship who had a grudge against Louise - "

"I didn't have a grudge against Louise," I said mildly. "I mean, I didn't like her, I don't deny that. But I didn't have a grudge…"

"They'll say, look at the photographs on Twitter," Zoé went on, ignoring me. "They'll say, what about the long-standing feud between the two of them? What about the jealousy over her relationship with Joel - "

"I wasn't jealous," I said, looking at Will. "Honestly, I couldn't give a toss."

"And then what about the murder itself? That was in one of your books." Zoé sat back with an almost satisfied look on her face.

"Who the bloody hell are you, the case for the prosecution?" snapped Harvey. "We're supposed to be proving her innocence, not fitting her up!"

"I'm just saying what the police will say," said Zoé, defensively.

"To be fair," I said, "I've lost count of the number of murders I've committed in my books, but at some point I must've used every conceivable murder method and weapon known to Man."

"Yeah…" said Sylvia, but I could see she was a little less convinced of my innocence than her roomie. "The security people searched our cabin today, did they search yours?"

Harvey and Michael nodded, Zoé shook her head.

"No, why did they do that?" she asked. "What were they looking for?"

"Corkscrews," I said. She looked puzzled.

"But they've already got the murder weapon."

"They told me that all the penthouse cabins have very distinctive corkscrews, and they found Louise's one still in her cabin after they moved her body," said Sylvia. "So that means…"

"That means the murder weapon came from another penthouse cabin." Zoé worked it out aloud. "So the murderer - the murderer must be a passenger in one of the penthouses!" She turned to me excitedly. "But that's brilliant! All we have to do is find out which cabin is missing their corkscrew - "

I sighed heavily. "It's mine."

"What?" Zoé looked puzzled. "But you - you didn't - "

"Of course she bloody didn't!" snapped Will. "Someone took it from our cabin and planted it in Louise's room."

"Who would do that?" Sylvia now looked quite sceptical. "And why?"

"To throw suspicion onto me and off them," I said.

"But why you?" asked Michael. Harvey nudged him in the ribs. "What? It's a reasonable question."

"We think someone saw that the finger of suspicion was being pointed at Bella and they decided to keep it that way." Will looked around the table. "I know Bella, and I know she didn't kill anyone. If you believe differently, then perhaps you should be off enjoying yourself at the spa or getting your nails done rather than being here."

For a moment I thought Sylvia was going to leave. But she exchanged glances with Heather, who glared at her meaningfully, and bit into her cake instead.

"So who had access to your cabin?" asked Zoé. I laughed.

"You mean apart from you?" She looked shocked and I quickly reassured her. "It's alright, I'm joking. There were quite a few crew members popping in and out - "

"And Joel," said Will. All eyes widened and looked at me. *Thanks babe*, I thought.

"Yes, and Joel, briefly." I sipped at my café latte, willing my cheeks not to get hot. "But of course we know neither Joel or Zoé murdered Louise - " Zoé was mid-sip and almost choked. " - because they were both in the Pearl at the time."

Michael patted Zoé on the back. "We all know where you were, sweetheart." he said, then he started to sing. "*Snitches, end up in ditches, and this music, gives me the itches…*"

Everyone laughed, except for Zoé who blushed. "Oh don't!" she said. "I was so embarrassed."

"So anyway…" I said. "There were crew members popping in and out all the time." I stopped as something occurred to me. "Zoé, do you know who that steward was, the one who helped you get Louise back to her cabin?"

Zoé shook her head. "No, sorry. I hadn't seen him before, I don't know where he normally works. Why?"

"Well, not to put too fine a point on it, Louise was as smashed as a plate at a Greek wedding. She could barely stand up when she left the Pearl."

Zoé nodded. "Yes, we had to almost carry her."

"She wasn't in a fit state to let the killer into her cabin," I said. "So how did they get in?"

"When the cabin door shuts behind you, it automatically locks," said Will. "Maybe you put it on the latch as you left, so you could check on her later?"

Zoé shook her head. "No, we didn't even think of that. We were just going to let her sleep it off."

"You and the steward?"

"Me and Joel." Zoé looked meaningfully at me. *Don't look at me like that every time his name comes up!* "I'd propped the door open to carry her inside, then the steward left - I was trying to be discreet, like you said, so I sent him away - and then Joel stuck his head around the door to make sure she was alright. But we made sure the door shut behind us when we left."

"So the murderer must have had a key card…" said Heather thoughtfully. "There are spare keys at the pursers' desk. Mine wouldn't work properly yesterday, so I took it down there and they programmed a new one for me."

"Exactly," said Will. "A crew member - not necessarily someone on the pursers' desk - might be able to get hold of a duplicate or a master key." He looked carefully at Zoé. "Or maybe they took Louise's own key after you carried her inside."

"You think the guy who helped me carry her back to the cabin might be the killer?" Zoé looked alarmed, and even shuddered a little bit. "That's pretty scary, to think I was on my own with him…"

"I'm sure you were never in any danger, honey," said Harvey, patting her hand, but she still looked worried.

"Would you recognise him if you saw him again?" asked Will. Zoé thought for a minute, then shook her head.

"I don't know… You don't think he'd - you don't think he'd target me next, if he thought I could identify him?" The poor girl looked terrified. I fought down a massive irrational and unsympathetic surge of irritation - I was starting to get used to situations like this, but it was probably a bit much for an unassuming bookseller to handle - and smiled at her.

"No, of course not. We don't even know if he's involved. I'd just like to talk to him."

Sylvia hadn't said anything for a while, but now I could see that she was itching to say something. *Spit it out, woman,* I thought.

"Is something on your mind, Sylvia?" said Will calmly, on my wavelength as usual, and I could've kissed him.

"Let's say the murderer got in with a key, or the door was left unlocked by mistake," she said. "So how did *Bella* get into Louise's cabin? I'm no murderer but I'm damn sure I'd make certain I'd locked the door behind me after I left."

"Maybe they were disturbed?" suggested Harvey. "Maybe they heard someone in the corridor and panicked, and ran off without shutting the door properly?"

"Hmm…" I thought about it. It didn't feel right, but I didn't know why.

"That makes sense," said Will vaguely, because actually, it didn't. Like it didn't make sense that the murderer was in such a rush to attack her and then leave. Did they know I was on my way there? Maybe they'd overheard Louise talking to the duty purser on the phone, as they lurked outside her cabin waiting to kill her…

But then why leave the door unlocked, so there was a real danger of me finding the body? I'd have knocked, then got angry at Louise's lack of response and just gone back to the Pearl. The body wouldn't have been discovered until much later, probably not until the next afternoon at the earliest, as we would have assumed she was sleeping off her hangover.

Maybe I was overthinking it. Maybe the killer *had* accidentally knocked the latch up or just not pulled the door all the way shut after them. Killers weren't always the most intelligent people; an intelligent person would know that killing someone on a ship in the middle of the Atlantic was an idiotic move, as there was a finite pool of suspects and no way to escape.

The murderer was trapped on a ship full of people looking for them. But of course that also meant that we were trapped on the ship with a killer…

CHAPTER 16

It was a slightly downcast and less enthusiastic group of detectives who left the library. Will and I went back to our cabin to mull over what had been discussed, and the only conclusion we were able to come to was that we had no conclusions. The team's support, though well meaning, had just underlined what we were up against; circumstantial evidence overseen by the court of public opinion via social media, half of whom had already decided I was guilty because they hated my books (or me personally, usually because I was successful and they didn't deem me worthy of it or were jealous). All of which should have been easy enough to dismiss, only there wasn't any firm evidence that anyone *else* had killed Louise. And in the absence of that, I was looking good for it.

What evidence there was - or 'evidence', as Will insisted on calling it, complete with air quotations, in order to show his contempt for it - was probably unlikely to get me convicted; Will had far more faith in the New York police than that. But *probably unlikely* still meant *possibly likely*. And of course, mud sticks. If we didn't find out who had really killed Louise my name would be forever linked with her death, and I would always be viewed with suspicion.

Will got out his notebook - a policeman to the end. We looked at each other.

"So what do we do now?" I asked.

"We write down what we know." He smiled. "The first thing we know is that you didn't do it. We work backwards from there."

Will drew out a timeline. We didn't know the exact times; hardly anyone wears a watch these days, using their phones instead, and even then how often do you check the time when you're at a party (unless it's crap and you're wondering when you can escape without it looking rude)? But the Chief Purser had told us what time the lights went out, so we were able to guesstimate from that when Louise had gone back to her cabin, what time Joel and Zoé had returned to the Pearl, and what time I had left. We were able to narrow that down to a period of between 7 and 10 minutes when the attack had taken place, between Louise calling the pursers' desk and me finding her.

"So we kind of already knew that…" I said, my mind starting to wander. I was wondering what prison food was like. At least I'd have plenty of time to write. Hell, I might even lose some weight…

"I know we did," said Will patiently. "That's the framework we build on. Now we start to fill in the gaps. First, we mark out where everyone was when the murder took place."

"There are about 3,000 people on this ship," I pointed out.

"I know. But most of them would never even have known Louise was on board - " I raised my eyebrows and he laughed. "Okay, with that awful laugh of hers and her need to be the centre of attention, they might have spotted her. But the only people who really had any interaction with her, and therefore the most opportunity or motive to kill her, are our murder mystery party and the crew who served her deck and in the Pearl."

"There could be someone else on the ship who knew her, and who purposely steered clear of her until they got the chance to strike," I said. Will shook his head.

"Not really. It looks like this was an opportunist murder. The murderer saw that she was pretty much incapacitated and would be an easy target. They may even have had the opportunity to take her key while Zoé and Joel were preoccupied with making sure she was okay."

"That steward," I said, and this time he nodded.

"Yes," he said. "Although of course we have no idea what their motive would be, but they had the greatest opportunity."

"We need to find them."

"We will."

I looked at his timeline. "So who was in the Pearl when the murder happened? That's the easiest place to start."

"Well, you were for some of that period, obviously. We were with Joel, and the Chief Purser…"

I thought back to the other murder - the pretend one - and who had gathered around the body, which must have been happening as Louise made her final phone call.

"Okay, Harvey and Michael were all over the pretend corpse, laughing at the poor man. Sylvia, but not Heather or Karl - we've got a pretty good idea where they were."

Will nodded. "Yes, but we can't discount those two. They were in the cabin next door when you showed up - I know you heard them apparently going at it like a couple of Duracell bunnies, but they could feasibly have bumped off Louise then run next door and made ooh and aah noises when they heard you coming."

"If that's the case then they both deserve a BAFTA for the Most Convincing Sex Noises, because it sounded like I wasn't the only one coming."

Will laughed. "I thought most women could fake a convincing orgasm? Or did When Harry Met Sally lie to me?"

"I can honestly say I've never had to fake it with you, babe," I said loyally, fluttering my eyelashes. He laughed again and leaned across the table to kiss me.

112

"Thank you. I don't even care if you're lying."

I studied the timeline again. "The Bauers were there, and the other two - what were their names again? Laura and…?"

Will consulted his notes. "Lauren Donaldson and Peter Maguire. Yes, all four of them were on Louise's team. The Bauers were poking around looking for the murder weapon - the pretend murder weapon - but I noticed at the time the other two were hanging back a bit." He looked at me, with a small but triumphant smile on his face.

"What?"

"I reckon they're actors, and they were hanging back because one of them was the pretend murderer."

'Well that's brilliant, detective, but let's concentrate on the real murder, shall we?"

Will laughed. "Sorry. Who else was there?"

"The old dear - you know, the deaf one whose hearing dramatically improves every time she's offered a free drink? And the younger one who I assume is her daughter, I don't know their names…"

Will looked at his list. "I think that's Doris and Sarah Pullman. Not much of a holiday for the daughter."

"No, poor woman. Then there was James Bond and Moneypenny - "

We went through the list of names, and sure enough everyone was in the Pearl throughout the whole murder window. Everyone, except me.

"Oh, and Zoé was there of course."

"Where was she?" asked Will, marking her down on the timeline. "I don't remember seeing her when the lights came up."

"No, but her phone went off in the dark, remember? And then she gave the grieving widow a brandy."

113

Will nodded. "Oh yes, the Chief Purser wasn't too happy about that."

"She must've been near the bar, behind us," I said. "Talking of which, who was serving at the bar?"

Before Will could consult his list there was a knock at the door. He stood up but I stopped him.

"I'll get it," I said. "I'm not hiding."

It was Joel. I tried to keep my voice normal as I invited him in, and managed to sound almost as though he hadn't told me he still loved me the last time I saw him. To be fair, he hadn't actually *said* it, but the sight of him was still enough to give me palpitations. Or maybe it was indigestion from the lemon drizzle cake earlier.

"I ran into that stroppy middle aged bird - "

"Heather," said Will and I simultaneously.

"Yeah, her, she said you were trying to clear your name?"

"That's right," said Will stiffly, drawing himself up to his full height which, next to Joel, made him look like an angry hobbit. "My wife's innocent and I intend to prove it."

"Good," said Joel. "I'll help."

I looked at him in surprise. "You will?"

"Of course I will," he said. "I told you, Bell. I know you're not a killer." He looked at Will. "Look, mate, I think we got off on the wrong foot. I want to help."

Will stared at him for a moment, and I thought he was going to tell him to get lost. But then his shoulders sagged and he relaxed.

"Okay," he said. "You'd better sit down."

Joel sat down at the table and looked at the timeline.

"This is when the murder took place, yeah?" he said. "And you're working out who was where at the time." I nodded. He studied the list of names.

"Doris and Sarah - they were on my team. Doris is a right old character, constantly demanding attention. If I was her daughter I'd be putting arsenic in her cocoa... Lauren and Pete - Louise was pretty chummy with those two, she said they weren't quite who they seemed..."

Will grinned at me triumphantly. "Told you!" Joel looked at me, puzzled, but I wasn't going down that rabbit hole.

"Yeah, we need to talk to them... But it would be more useful now if you could help us pin down what happened earlier, when you and Zoé left Louise in her cabin."

"Well, I didn't actually see Louise," he said, "but I did hear her. I stuck my head around the door to check everything was okay and Zoé was just coming out of the bathroom. She said Louise was in there, throwing up. She turned round and told her I was outside and Louise said she'd see me in the morning."

"Letting you off the hook," I said. "I bet you were relieved."

"Just a bit." Joel grinned.

"So," I said. "Louise is in the bathroom, suffering from alcohol poisoning - "

Joel put his hand up. "Woah woah woah! Are you saying Louise was drunk?"

I looked at him in surprise. "I told you she was."

"No, you said she was ill," said Joel. "She can't have been drunk. That woman could drink Oliver Reed under the table."

"I saw her," I said. "She was reeling around all over the place. She certainly *looked* drunk."

"Doubt it." Joel shook his head. "The first time I met her, at the - " He stopped and looked at me, sheepishly. "I met her at the Smoking Gun Awards last year, and we..."

"Skip to the relevant bit," I said quickly.

"We drank all night, and then we went back to my hotel room." Joel looked straight into my eyes. *That's not the bloody relevant bit, you twat*, I thought. "We went to my hotel room, where I passed out on the bed and she gave up and left."

There was silence for a second, and then Will burst out laughing. I cringed, waiting for Joel to punch him or at least say something nasty, but instead he laughed as well. I let out my breath slowly.

"Last of the red hot lovers, I know." Joel smiled ruefully. "That woman had hollow legs. She was a borderline alcoholic. She must've had the best part of two bottles of wine and some spirits, and she was fine - better than me, anyway. She hadn't drunk anywhere near that much the night she was - " He stopped.

Will stopped laughing. "The night she was murdered."

We all sat in silence for a moment. Here we were, joking about Louise, and she was lying in a fridge down in the ship's medical centre.

"She *was* falling over, though," I said. "She wasn't ill, she was - she *seemed* - completely legless."

"Well, she wasn't." Joel was adamant.

"Maybe she was drugged," said Will. I looked at him in shock. "Some kind of date rape drug. That could make her appear drunk and render her completely helpless."

"Drugged? But - when? At dinner? Who would do that?" I tried to imagine one of the murder mystery players slipping something into Louise's drink, but couldn't. It meant that her murder had been very much planned, and not the opportunist crime we'd thought.

"We need a toxicology report on her before we know for certain," said Will, "but I'm not sure the medical facilities on board will be up to it."

"The steward," I said. Joel looked at me. "The one who helped Zoé carry Louise back to her cabin. We'd never seen him before, and we already thought that maybe he'd taken her key and let himself back in after he'd seen how drunk she was, but perhaps he made a point of coming to the Pearl specifically to target her. Perhaps he wasn't even a real crew member - "

Joel stopped me. "Blonde guy, about 5'8", tattoo on his forearm - black ink, Celtic design, yeah?"

"Yeah, that's him. He - "

"He was behind the bar. That other steward - the one who's all tan and white teeth - "

"Karl," Will and I said together.

'Yeah, him. He was flirting with that woman - Heather? Heather - they were flirting in the corner of the bar after dinner, before we started that stupid name game, and I overheard your main suspect tell him to go for it, said he'd cover for him." Joel reached out and tapped the timeline. "He was behind the bar during the murderer's window of opportunity. I think he was the one who took ages turning the lights back on."

Bollocks. There went the theory I had started to work on. "Are you sure?"

"Yeah. I noticed him, because I liked his tattoo and I was thinking about getting one." Joel stared at me defiantly, probably because he knew I was remembering his incredibly low threshold for pain. He could barely handle stubbing his toe, letting alone having someone working on his skin with a needle, but I let it pass.

"Damn. So he couldn't have taken the key without Zoé seeing and then let himself back in…" I was disappointed; I'd thought we could be onto something, and now it seemed we were almost back at square one.

117

Almost. We now knew - or suspected - that Louise had been drugged and deliberately incapacitated.

"Not necessarily," said Will. "He could still have taken the key, and given it to someone else."

"Who?"

"No idea." Will smiled grimly. "I think we need to find this steward…"

CHAPTER 17

That heavy leaden ball of anxiety had settled deep within my guts again, so I decided that the best way to oust it was with a three course dinner with matching wines and a cheese board to finish. We headed to the Pearl, and found the murder mystery players sitting down to eat. They all - well, most of them - welcomed Will and I warmly, although Sylvia seemed out of sorts and wasn't really talking to us or Heather.

We made slightly awkward small talk through the first two courses. Michael asked if we'd found out any more about the steward but Zoé, God bless her, must've seen my discomfort as she deliberately changed the subject and steered the conversation into uncontroversial waters. I smiled at her in gratitude and she beamed back at me. We finished the main course and then, as had become the custom everyone got up and wandered between the tables, talking to the other diners over dessert. I thought it was nice that everyone was still mingling and chatting, even though the murder mystery (the official one, anyway) had been disbanded and there was no need to question each other and look for clues. I say *everyone* was mingling and chatting, but Will and I stayed in our seats; I knew I should get up and put on a brave (and most of all, innocent) face, but I'd spotted too many of the guests at the other tables looking over at me and talking between themselves. Sylvia, in particular, seemed unable to talk to anyone without causing them to peer in my direction in discreet (or not so discreet) scrutiny.

The Chief Purser came over and plonked herself down next to me. She smiled at Harvey as he returned to pick up his glass before wandering off again; but as soon as his back was turned her face dropped. She seemed to have aged over the last couple of days, and let out a heavy sigh before turning to me.

"So how are you holding up?" she asked, in that soft Scottish voice that was so soothing.

"Okay," I said. "How about you? This is not what you wanted on your first murder mystery, is it? A real live corpse turning up."

"A real live corpse," she murmured, amused. "No, we hadn't planned for that. I think we can safely say this is our first and last murder mystery cruise. And possibly my last cruise, full stop."

"The Captain can't hold you responsible!" said Will. "It's hardly your fault, is it?"

She sighed again, toying with a napkin that had been screwed up and discarded on the table in front of her. "I didn't kill anyone, no. But someone leaked those photographs to the paper. It's not a good look, is it? And I knew all about your history with Louise and Joel. When the other writers pulled out and they were the only ones available at short notice to replace them - I should have said something, I should have warned you and made sure you were okay with them - "

"I *was* okay with them," I said, putting my hand on her arm.

"Still," she said, "it was my idea, and the buck stops with me."

We sat in silence for a moment, watching the other diners chatting; several of whom were very studiously (and obviously) trying to avoid looking over at us. No, at me. The Purser turned back to me.

"Joel told me you were trying to find the steward who was helping out behind the bar on the night of the murder," she said. I nodded. "I don't know who it was off the top of my head - we took on a lot of new crew recently and I don't know all of them by name. I do know they weren't supposed to be on duty here, but the crew do sometimes swap shifts with each other, so there's nothing suspicious about that in itself."

"Will you be able to find out who it was?" asked Will, and she nodded.

"Yes, leave it with me." She looked across the room, took a deep breath and got to her feet. "For what it's worth, Bella, I don't think you did it. I believe you were just in the wrong place at the wrong time." She smiled. "Don't lose hope."

Don't lose hope. I sat in the dining room, knowing that I was innocent yet feeling horribly guilty under the weight of the other diners' stares. Even the ones who were on my side - they didn't actually *know* I was innocent; how long would they continue to believe me, if I couldn't find any evidence pointing to someone else?   The more we investigated, the more confusing it got. First it was an opportunistic murder, then it wasn't; by another passenger, except how would they have got in - so by a crew member; but what was their motive? What was *anyone's* motive? Yes, she was an annoying bint and a terrible writer, but if I went around taking out everyone who was guilty of writing unnatural dialogue, convoluted plots with ridiculous twists at the end and clichéd characters, well then there'd be fewer awful books out there and people would be forced to spend their hard earned money on mine instead. Hmm. Yeah, maybe I wouldn't get my defence attorney to use that in their closing arguments…

"Penny for your thoughts?" Will looked at me, a gentle but slightly worried smile on his face.

"A penny? Pah! I don't think for anything less then £2.50." I'm good at bravado, but Will knows me too well to fall for it, and he didn't this time either.

"You're worried." I bit back a sarcastic *no shit, Sherlock*.

"Why on earth should I be worried?" I asked.

"Sorry, it was a stupid thing to say," he said apologetically. "Of course you're worried. But you didn't do it - "

"How do you know that?" I snapped. What the hell was I doing, trying to start a fight with him or something? But he just smiled again.

"Bella, *I know you*. I'm not saying you'd never kill anyone, because as we both know…" He looked serious for a moment. "As we both know, everyone has the potential to be a killer under the right circumstances. But I know you, and I know what motivates you. You didn't like Louise, but you don't like a lot of people - "

"That's not fair!" I cried. "I like everyone!" I thought about it. "Okay, I like most people. Some more than others. I mean, I can't stand *some* people, but most of the time…"

"Like I said, there are a lot of people you don't like, but you don't go around dispatching them. And I have the sneaking suspicion you actually quite enjoyed your feud with Louise." Will was grinning at me now.

"What? You're insane." I dismissed the idea, but there was the distinct possibility that he was right. Some of my finest work had been penned in sarcastic tweets to or about her. I had reached hitherto unknown heights of snark when faced with some of her more outrageous claims on social media, several examples of which had ended up in my books. She annoyed the crap out of me, but she'd also inspired me. I'd been toying with creating a character who was a self obsessed, opportunistic, narcissistic, manic self-publicist writer, who was so far up her own arse she could see her tonsils, but I thought my readers would think her too far-fetched to be real. Someone who was so deluded, arrogant and overly-confident in their own meagre talent that they regularly compared themselves to the great writers who had gone before them, describing themselves as 'Margaret Atwood's heir' or 'the next Maya Angelou'. All of which Louise had done. She'd once updated her Twitter bio, calling herself 'the Queen of True Crime' (seriously, WHO DOES THAT?! You can't proclaim *yourself* the Queen of something) and I had responded by changing my own Twitter bio to 'the 7th Earl of Get the Hell Outta Here With Your Over-Inflated Ego'. Which had gone down well with my fans but not so much with Susie, the ever-diplomatic agent. Funnily enough Louise hadn't reacted to it at all, probably because she was too busy taking herself far too seriously to notice it or to realise it was aimed at her.

Will was still grinning at me.

"Oh alright, I did enjoy it," I admitted. "But I don't think that's necessarily going to convince a jury, do you? *'I couldn't possibly have killed her, your Honour, because I enjoyed taking the piss out of her on social media too much.'* As defences go, it's not very good, is it?"

"Point taken. But it's convinced me. I will always be on your side." Will looked around, then bent close to me. "I'd be on your side even if you *had* topped her."

"Thank you. I'll bear that in mind next time I bump someone off."

"Please do. If you ever need an alibi, I'll cover for you."

"Just say we were having sex. That'd ring true for anyone who knows us."

Will laughed and gave me his version of The Look, which at that moment was a very welcome distraction. It was much less arrogant than Joel's Look, much softer and more considerate; less the kind of the look that said *I want to take you roughly over the kitchen table* and more *I want to take you roughly (with your consent) on the bed, where it's more comfortable and there's much less chance of getting splinters in your crevices, and have wild sex with you whilst making sure you enjoy it as much as I do, possibly more times than I do, and afterwards*

I'll even make you a cup of tea. The kind of look that gets you just as hot as the first one, without the vague feeling of self-loathing that often accompanies it. Or is that just me? Anyway…

He gave me His Look, and I gave him one right back - mine just said *ooh yeah go on then* - and before I quite knew what was happening we'd blown the joint and were making out in the corridor. We stopped at the sound of footsteps coming towards us, no doubt looking highly suspicious to Sarah, downtrodden daughter cum care assistant to the redoubtable Doris, who had obviously managed to escape from her mother's demands for a few minutes and was making her way back to the dining room. We smiled and nodded at her, then pulled ourselves together and made our way to our penthouse, giggling; luckily it was just one deck above, almost exactly above the Pearl. *Right above Louise's cabin*, I thought, then pushed that away; it wasn't conducive to sexy time with Will.

We almost fell through the doorway, snogging furiously and ripping at each other's clothes, rather ineffectually if truth be told; Will was used to whipping my usual t-shirt and jeans off, but this was a fancy cocktail dress, with unaccustomed hooks and buttons. I laughed and pulled away from him, heading further into the room as I struggled to undo myself. But then I stopped, my libido suddenly frozen in its tracks by a metaphorical bucket of cold water.

Someone's been in here.

"Babe - " I started, turning round to face him, then stopped short again. He hadn't hung around; his clothes lay in a heap on the floor. Most of them, anyway.

The sight of Will naked but for a pair of Argyle socks was normally enough to make me all unnecessary, so it was testament to how rattled I was that the only quiver that betrayed me now was one of mild irritation.

"Bloody hell, you move fast," I said. He stepped forward and took me in his arms, reaching around to fiddle with my buttons again.

"And you're being too slow," he murmured, kissing my neck as his fingers got busy in my clothes. "This dress is ridiculous, I may have to rip it…"

I pulled away from him. "Someone's been in here."

"What?" He clearly didn't want to discuss it right now. "Of course they haven't."

"They have!" I said, dancing out of his grip. "Look! My handbag's on the chair."

Will sighed. "So?"

"I put it on the chair, but it slipped off and ended up on the floor as we were leaving. We were almost out of the door so I left it."

"Are you sure?" He looked around. "Is there anything else? Anything missing?"

I looked around the room too, but my eyes kept being drawn back to Will standing naked and now somewhat at half mast next to me. "Put your pants back on babe, your knob's distracting me."

He sighed again and put his boxers on, then ventured further into the room. I followed cautiously, peering around; I couldn't see anything missing, but it just felt *wrong*. Will reached the bathroom and paused, his hand on the door. We looked at each other, both suddenly nervous. He took a deep breath and pushed it open.

I shut my eyes; whatever was lurking in there, I didn't want to see it.

"Oh my god…" said Will, and a chill ran through me.

"What is it?" I said, horrified, following him in.

"There's a bloody massive spider on the ceiling," he said. I punched him. "What? I hate spiders. Pass me a shoe."

I went back into the bedroom and lobbed a shoe at him, then threw myself on the bed as he dealt with the eight-legged intruder.

"Got it!" Will stood in the doorway looking pleased with himself. The whole thing was so ridiculous - him in just his pants and socks, clutching one shoe in triumph - that despite the feeling of mild unease that still lurked at the back of my mind, I giggled. Had someone really been in the cabin? I'd been so certain when we'd entered, but there didn't appear to be anything missing. There were no dead bodies waiting for us, unless - I quickly peered under the bed, but it was a divan and there was only a gap of about an inch between it and the floor - there were no dead bodies, apart from the squashed arachnid in the bathroom. Maybe I'd been mistaken; maybe my bag hadn't moved. Maybe…

"Now, where were we?" Will lay down on the bed next to me, propped up on one elbow, one leg bent upwards at the knee and his tackle thrust out towards me, posing with an eyebrow raised and a 'come hither' look on his face. I rolled my eyes.

"Who are you supposed to be, Mr November?" He grinned and flexed his muscles.

"No, Mr August. Ask me why."

"Why are you Mr August?"

"Because I'm hotter than July."

I burst out laughing, and it was such a genuine release of tension and stress that I threw my arms around him and hugged him tight.

"I love you," I whispered, and he hugged me back even more tightly.

"I love you too," he said, then pulled away to gaze into my eyes. "Does that mean…?"

"Take your pants off," I said. "But leave the socks…"

CHAPTER 18

We had breakfast the next day in yet another dining room, hoping to have a table to ourselves. New York was getting closer and closer, and if we didn't come up with some answers soon I had visions of being carted off by the NYPD's finest.

But wouldn't you know, it seemed that half of the murder mystery players had decided to try the Atlantic Diner for breakfast that morning, too. The Bauers were at a table in the corner and greeted us with a polite nod, while Michael and Harvey shared a table with Lauren Donaldson and Peter Maguire, who we still hadn't had an opportunity to speak to properly. All four of them smiled at us but didn't speak. I began to feel paranoid again. Not long after we sat down Heather and Sylvia entered and took the table next to us. Heather greeted us in a friendly way - she definitely seemed chirpier than at the beginning of the cruise, and I wondered if that was down to the attentions of young Karl - but Sylvia blanked us completely. No need to ask what *she* thought about my innocence or otherwise.

We'd just ordered when Zoé came in. She spotted us and waved, then headed towards us.

"Oh no…" muttered Will, and I had to agree with him.

"I know," I said, 'but be nice. She's an ally. She's quite sweet, really…"

But before she could join us, Karl appeared. He glanced over at Heather, who nodded slightly in my direction, and made his way over to our table. Zoé zig zagged and sat down next to Sylvia instead.

Karl looked nervous, quite unlike the cocky Scouse lothario he normally was.

"Can I have a word?" he said.

"Of course." I gestured to an empty seat. "Please, sit down. What's troubling you?"

He sat down next to Will and lowered his voice.

"I heard you were looking for Rob - the steward who helped take Ms Meyers back to her cabin?" Will and I nodded. "I share a cabin with him."

"We just want to talk to him," said Will. "Please tell him it's nothing to worry about, we're just trying to pin down what happened. If he wants to come to our cabin to talk - "

Karl shook his head. "That's the problem, I haven't seen him since the morning after the murder."

"You mean he's disappeared?" I exchanged glances with Will. Was this Rob lying low - or had something happened to him?

"I don't know," said Karl. "We're not always on the same shifts, so I just assumed he was working - he's normally on the pursers' desk, so he does night shifts sometimes. He must've been back to the cabin because his clean uniform's gone, but it's weird that I haven't seen him at all."

On the next table, Sylvia and Zoé were eavesdropping furiously, leaning as close to us as they could without it being too obvious, while Heather studiously kept her attention on the plate of French toast the waiter had just brought her. I could see Zoé open her mouth to speak, and jumped in quick before she could. *Butt out!*

"It's more than weird though, isn't it?" I said. "Right after a murder. You're worried."

"I am. You see…" Karl glanced over towards Heather again, then back at me. "I don't know him very well. He hasn't been working for the cruise line for very long and this is the first time I've shared with him. He's a bit of a git."

Will and I waited for him to continue. He looked embarrassed.

"The first night of the cruise, he asked me if I was in. I didn't know what he meant, but… He said on his last two cruises he'd made a couple of grand by - " Again, his gaze started towards Heather, but he quickly wrenched it away. "By targeting some of the passengers."

Will raised an eyebrow. I spoke to save Karl - who didn't seem that bad a sort, never mind what was going on with Heather - from further embarrassment.

"I'm assuming you mean some of the more mature, wealthy single ladies on board?"

He nodded. "Yes. I said I wasn't in. I mean, I have been known to - "

"Fraternise?" said Will. He nodded again, the redness in his face matched only by the colour of Heather's cheeks at the next table.

"I like sex, and I like money," he said, avoiding my eyes. "If one of the passengers wants a nice time, and if they feel like treating me for it, then it's a win win as far as I can see. But Rob was talking about stealing from them. He said he'd stolen this woman's diamond necklace on the last passage, and although she must've realised it was him she would never have reported him because she'd be too embarrassed."

"Do you think that's why he disappeared?" I asked, exchanging glances with Will. What if Louise's murder had been a simple robbery gone wrong? What if the dishonest steward had seen the state of her when he'd carried her back to the cabin, and decided to return later to steal from her, only for her to wake up and see him?

But then Joel had seen him behind the bar after the lights had come back up, during the murderer's window of opportunity…

Karl shook his head slowly. "Not exactly. He wasn't supposed to be in the Pearl that night - I was behind the bar, helping out with the murder mystery, doing the lights and making sure the players spotted the murder weapon and everything, but he turned up and offered to take over."

"You didn't call him, so you could go off and - dally?" asked Will. *Dally*. It was such a Will word.

"No, he just turned up. He told me he was on a promise. He said he'd got in with this passenger who was loaded, and a bit of a goer as well by all accounts, and she'd told him to meet her there. He couldn't come along if he was off duty, so he offered to split the shift with me. That's why I didn't worry when he didn't come back to the cabin that night. I thought he must be with her."

"So during the murder - the real one and the pretend one - you were off having a, um, *dally* with - " I *just* stopped myself glancing over at Heather - "one of the passengers? And he stayed at the bar?"

"Yes." Karl looked relieved that I'd said it for him. "I left him the list of instructions the Chief Purser had given me, all the timings and everything - "

I frowned. "You told him when to turn the lights back on? So why didn't he do it until the Purser had a go at him? We were stood in the dark for ages, even after the murder had happened."

Zoé gave a little start, and blushed as we all looked over at her. She got up and moved to the chair next to me.

"I'm so sorry," she said. "I need to tell you something. I haven't slept, thinking about it. I should have told you yesterday, but I just felt a bit embarrassed. And then when you said he might be involved - "

I felt my irritation at her rising, and could see from the set of Will's shoulders that he was getting wound up too. I pushed it down and smiled.

"Don't be embarrassed," I said, although to be honest until I knew what she was going on about I didn't know whether she should be or not. "What's troubling you?" I could see Sylvia edging closer to listen, and even Heather gave up the pretence of eating her untouched breakfast.

"This Robert - I didn't say anything before, because - well, I felt a bit - you see, when the lights went off…"

I felt like screaming at her and giving her a shake. *Just bloody tell me!* But I've learnt from Will that sometimes it's best not to ask, it's better to wait and let people volunteer the information themselves. So I just smiled patiently and waited.

"We were chatting in the bar that night. He said he wasn't really supposed to be working in the Pearl, but he was there meeting someone. He said she had asked him to swap shifts and come to the Pearl so he could help her with something."

"Help her with something?"

She nodded. "He seemed nice, and when you needed some help with Louise, he was standing right near you so I waved him over to give me a hand. We talked when we took her back to her cabin and he…" She flushed. "It's not the sort of thing I normally do, I'm not that kind of girl, but he said he'd like to meet up with me later on. You know about my husband - I just thought, why not? I didn't realise he'd hooked up with this other woman as well. What a rat."

"So when the lights went out…?" Will prompted gently.

"When the lights went out he grabbed me and pulled me behind the bar, and we had a kiss." Zoé looked at us, as if daring us to be disgusted with her. I patted her on the hand.

"That's nothing to be ashamed of," I said. "God, if you knew what I got up to in my youth… So what happened after that?"

"We kissed for ages. We got a bit carried away. Then my phone went off and I was scrabbling around in the dark and dropped it, and he was helping me. And then he finally turned the lights on and the body was there. And I thought, if anyone turns round and sees me here they'll wonder why I'm behind the bar, so I grabbed a drink and gave it to that lady who was acting."

Will and I exchanged looks. So this confirmed what we already knew - that Rob couldn't be the murderer himself - but it was looking more and more likely that he was involved. Who was the mysterious woman he was supposed to be meeting and doing a job for? If it had been the Chief Purser, the steward would have said so - she was one of his superior officers, so there would hardly have been any mystery there. Did that mean it was one of the guests?

Heather and Sylvia had given up any pretence of not-listening and had moved close enough to join in the conversation.

"Do you have any idea who he was supposed to be meeting?" asked Heather. Zoé and Karl both shook their heads, but Sylvia snorted.

"Oh come on! Listen to yourself. A mysterious woman who wanted him to do her a favour? One who was loaded?" She looked straight at me.

"Bearing in mind how much the tickets for the murder mystery cruise were, there was no one in that room who *didn't* have plenty of money," Will pointed out.

"And then when Zoé needed some help, he was right there next to Bella, who, by her own admission just now, was a 'bit of a goer' in her youth - " Sylvia said.

Heather interrupted her. "You don't know what you're talking about. I saw her, trying to save Louise!"

"She didn't save her though, did she?" Sylvia hissed. "You're blinded by her celebrity!"

"I'm not a celebrity…" I said, feebly.

"You even said it yourself, Bella, or DCI Fletcher did anyway in one of your books. The most obvious explanation is usually the truth." Sylvia leapt to her feet and pointed an accusing finger at me. "It seems to me that *you're* the one who was with Louise before she was 'taken ill'. *You're* the one who wanted to - what was the word? - *discreetly* take her back to her cabin." Zoé looked at me, guiltily. "Yes, Zoé told me she stopped you taking her. Where was this steward standing at the time? Right next to you. Waiting to help you carry her back to her cabin and do whatever you intended to do."

"Oh shut up, you daft bat," I said, far more calmly than I felt. The other diners were beginning to look round, listening to Sylvia's accusations.

"Yes, you'd like that wouldn't you?" snarled Sylvia. "This is not one of your books, you know, where no one guesses the twist. This time the twist is Zoé stopped you, so you had to come up with another plan. You got the steward to get hold of Louise's key card or better still, a master key - he worked at the pursers' desk, her could easily get hold of one - so you could let yourself into her cabin later. That bit's always bothered me, but it's obvious really."

"But Louise called her!" said Zoé. "How would Bella have known that she would do that?"

Sylvia shrugged. "She promised one steward money and sexual favours, what's to stop her offering the other purser the same to say he got a message?"

"How bloody ridiculous," I said, laughing humourlessly. I didn't feel like laughing at all, I was beginning to feel very frightened, because as untrue as this whole wild accusation of Sylvia's was, I could see how some people might believe it.

Will stood up and confronted Sylvia, who was the same height as him and almost as well built.

"That's enough, Sylvia," he said, very calmly.

"Oh I've only just got started," she said, furiously. He shook his head.

"I think you should shut up and go back to your cabin," he said. He was so calm and unthreatening, which made him look all the more menacing. I couldn't help feeling that he was actually making things worse. I stood up and took his arm.

"No, I think *we'll* go back to our cabin," I said. He shook my hand off.

"Why should you, Bella? You haven't done anything. I won't stand here and listen to this old crow badmouthing you."

"Well, I'm going back to the cabin, with or without you. I'd prefer with." I pushed my chair out of the way and headed out of the diner. After a few seconds, I could feel Will behind me.

"Oh yes, run away!" called Sylvia after me. "We're on a boat, there's nowhere for you to go…"

CHAPTER 19

Shaken, I headed down the corridor without looking where I was going. I stopped as I reached a dead end and Will caught up with me.

"Bella! Calm down." He took my arm and steered me back through a doorway, out onto a narrow deck at the back of the ship, and then into a deck chair. He dropped into another one next to it.

"Holy crap," I said, fighting back tears. "I'm going to go down for this, aren't I?"

"What, because that miserable old bag suddenly thinks she's Miss Marple?" Will shook his head. "Her theory may sound feasible at first, but it would hardly stand up to scrutiny. She's putting two and two together and coming up with a load of rubbish."

"She's going to turn people against me," I said, remembering the looks on the other diners' faces as I passed them. Even Michael and Harvey had been unable to meet my eyes.

"What people?" said Will. "Only the ones who don't know you." He was right. Why the hell did it bother me that a group of people I'd only just met thought I'd killed someone? Those who really knew me - Will, and Susie, even Joel - knew I was innocent. Plus Heather still believed me, and Zoé as well. And the Chief Purser...

The problem was, I *felt* guilty. I hadn't killed Louise, but Sylvia was right; I hadn't saved her, either. I really had tried. But now she was dead, and suddenly all the little digs I'd had at her over the last couple of years, all the times I'd hated her, the time at Harrogate when I'd wanted to hurt her as badly as she'd hurt me with her jibes and had made her look thoroughly ridiculous in front of the crowd - they all came back to haunt me. I was a bad person. No wonder they thought I'd killed her.

"Unfortunately the police officers who investigate her murder aren't going to know me, are they?" I said. "They'll look at the evidence and they'll get statements from the other passengers and at least half of them are going to say I did it, probably more than half now that Sylvia's gone on the rampage."

"We need to find a way to shut Sylvia up," said Will thoughtfully. I shook my head.

"You can't. The more you try and stop her talking, the guiltier I look. Like I've got something to hide."

We sat and watched the waves for a moment, the turbulent, seething froth and foam that followed in the ship's wake. I knew how it felt.

Will stood up. "Come on," he said, tugging me to my feet.

"Where are we going?" I asked, reluctant to leave our quiet little spot.

"To do some detective work. We need to find this Rob, if we can, and we need to work out who he was going to meet."

"And how do we do that?"

"By talking to all the females on the ship, mysterious or otherwise…"

If Lauren Donaldson was surprised to see us knocking on her cabin door, she didn't show it.

"Oh, hi!" she said pleasantly. She'd changed into tennis gear and was holding a racket. "I was just about to go out."

"Swimming?" I said. She looked puzzled for a moment, then laughed.

"Ha ha ha, good one." She picked up her key card. "Do you mind if we walk and talk? I'm meant to be meeting a friend for a game."

We wandered along the corridor towards the fitness zone.

"I didn't even know they had a tennis court on here," said Will conversationally. Lauren nodded.

"Yes, there's tennis, badminton and squash," she said. "I always make sure I bring my tennis gear with me, otherwise I go a bit stir crazy."

"So you're a regular on this cruise, then?" I said, and she smiled.

"Busted! Yes. I'm not a passenger, as such."

Will did a mini fist pump. "I knew it! You're one of the actors, aren't you?"

She nodded. "I normally perform in the theatre shows - I'm a singer, really. But when they mentioned the murder mystery I jumped at the chance. Of course, now it's been called off I'm at a loose end, so I'm having a holiday at the cruise line's expense." She laughed again, a warm, hearty chuckle that reminded me a bit of the Captain's. "They've forgotten all about us in the chaos, and I'm not going to be the one who reminds them…"

"I don't blame you," said Will. "We won't tell either." He waited for a passing guest to get out of earshot, then stopped. Lauren stopped too.

"Look, you heard all that this morning," he began. She nodded.

"Yes, I did. And I know what you're going to ask - do I know Rob and who he was meeting?" She smiled at me, a look of regret on her face. "I'm sorry but I don't. The entertainment staff don't really work with the stewards, so it takes a while for us to get to know them all. Karl did say he was new and he'd only done a couple of cruises."

"Okay." I thought for a moment. Just because she was an actor employed by the cruise line, it didn't get her off the hook; she could still just as easily be the mysterious female we were looking for. "Tell me, you were on Louise's team, weren't you? Did you talk to her much? Did you tell her who you really were?"

She looked around, suddenly wary, then spoke in a lowered voice. "Between you and me - yes, I did tell her I was one of the actors. I told her who the murderer was so her team would win."

"Why?" I didn't know why but hearing that pissed me off. It was cheating. Never mind that the whole thing had been called off and it hardly mattered now.

"I know I shouldn't have done, but…" She looked around again. "My partner, Pete - they took him on for the murder mystery, but he's actually a filmmaker. He wanted to shoot one of Louise's books - The Cuckoo and the Blackbird, you know that one?"

"Bloody hell, why?" I couldn't stop myself from saying it. That had been Louise's debut novel, and a proper hot mess it had been too. Lauren laughed.

"I know… But the underlying story itself is actually really good, or Pete reckons it could be, anyway. Pete and his producer spoke to her agent, but she was asking a ridiculous sum of money for the movie rights, I mean, it needs to be completely re-written to make sense but she wasn't having it. So…"

"So the two of you accepted this gig in order to get close enough to badger her into giving you the rights," said Will. Lauren looked defensive.

"I think badgering is a bit strong," she protested. "I was making nice to her, getting her to like us…"

"Was it working?" I asked. She laughed.

"Nope. My charm offensive had failed to get anywhere, right up to the point where - " She stopped abruptly, looking at me.

"Right up to the point where I bumped her off, gotcha."

"Sorry, I didn't mean anything by that…" She sighed. "If only the murderer could have held off for a bit longer, I might have made more head way."

"I can see how Louise's death would have been terribly inconvenient," I said, with thinly veiled sarcasm. Lauren looked at me.

"You're the one who hated her," she snapped, and turned and left.

We tracked down the Bauers in the hot tub. They were sharing a cocktail, Mrs Bauer sucking seductively on her straw as Mr Bauer ogled her breasts, or at least the spot in the frothing bubbles where they must've been. We stood and watched them for a moment, amazed.

"What's with them?" I asked Will. Every other time we'd seen them, relations had clearly been quite strained; he'd been attentive, uncomfortably so, like he was on his best behaviour, while she had treated him to icy stares or just plain ignored him.

Mr Bauer looked up and saw us. He gave us a broad smile and waved cheerfully.

"Hello!" he called. "Are you coming in?"

"We don't have our swimming togs," I said, and he laughed.

"Nor do we," he said, winking at me. Will stuttered something and Mrs Bauer laughed.

"Oh *Schnucki*!" cried Mrs Bauer, flapping her hands playfully at him. "Don't tease them." She shifted in the water so we could see the top of her swimsuit. I shrugged and slipped off my shoes, then sat on the edge so I could dip my toes in.

"Ooh that's nice…" I sighed, enjoying the feel of the water jets on the soles of my feet. Will tugged up the legs of his trousers and joined me.

"We have not really spoken properly since that first night, have we?" said Mr Bauer. "I am Klaus, and this is Birgit." He reached up and shook both our hands, which seemed absurdly formal for someone who was almost naked in a hot tub.

"Will and Bella," said Will. They nodded.

We sat in comfortable, companionable silence for a while, then Birgit nudged her husband. He nodded.

"Yes, *Schatzi,* I have been trying to find the words…" We looked at him in surprise, but he just smiled at us, thoughtfully. Finally, he spoke.

"My wife and I came on this cruise with the worst of intentions," he said. I looked at Birgit, and she nodded but didn't speak.

"I have not been a good husband," he began, but Will put his hand out to stop him.

"You don't have to tell us this," he said, and I almost laughed; his upbringing had been terribly middle class and buttoned up, and although he could now open up to me, he still didn't really go for big displays of emotion from others. Whereas I, as a writer, love a bit of gossip and over-sharing; where else am I going to get my characters from?

Luckily for me, Klaus wasn't to be entirely deterred.

"I will not go into details as I do not wish to embarrass my wife," he said. *Dammit, go into details!* "But neither of us intended to be married at the end of this cruise."

I looked at Will. We'd joked about them plotting to kill each other as part of the murder mystery game, when all the time they had been planning something much sadder; a real life divorce. I opened my mouth to speak, but I wasn't entirely sure what to say.

Birgit smiled and put her hand on Klaus's arm, gazing at him adoringly. "I was going to stab him and throw him overboard for cheating on me."

Will and I made choking noises as we tried to hide our surprise. They both laughed; they were winding us up.

"And they say Germans don't have a sense of humour," I said ruefully, and they laughed again.

"No," said Klaus, shaking his head. "My wife wasn't going to murder me. This cruise was a last, probably pointless attempt to save our marriage. We have had some tragedy in our life - the loss of a child - " Will and I both gulped again - "and we had stopped communicating with each other. We had become strangers."

"Oh - oh, I'm so sorry…" I stuttered, completely thrown. And now I kind of wished they weren't telling us this, because anything tragic to do with children and I am in absolute *bits*. I had always thought that when I met the right man I would have kids of my own, but then I met Joel and… I'll spare you the details - maybe another time - but the thought of actually managing to have a child and then losing them… It would surely be too much to bear.

"What changed?" asked Will. The Bauers smiled at each other, then at us.

"You two," said Klaus. "After poor Ms Meyers's murder, watching the way you worked together. The way you never doubted your wife, and the way you relied on him, it reminded us of how we used to be. We used to be a team, like you."

"We sat down and talked," said Birgit. "For the first time in months, we actually sat down and talked about our feelings. About our son, and each other."

I could feel tears welling in my eyes, and when I looked over at Will he was blinking furiously. He's just as big a softy as I am. I cleared my throat noisily and looked at the two smiling Germans.

"So thank you," said Birgit, and on impulse I got into the water and gave them both a big hug. There were a few tears - mostly but not only on mine and Birgit's part - and then I climbed out and Will led me soggily back to the cabin.

CHAPTER 20

"Well that was interesting," I said, as I peeled my wet clothes off. I had almost welcomed the puzzled stares that had accompanied our walk back to the cabin; it made a change from accusatory ones.

Will handed me my dressing gown and I slipped it on.

"But what have we learnt?" I asked him, fumbling for the tie-belt.

"That Germans are a bit weird but basically really nice?" he said. "And that actors are almost as self-obsessed as writers?"

I slapped him, then reached behind me again for my belt.

"No, we learnt bugger all," I said, still fumbling. "We're no closer to finding out who this mysterious woman is."

"Do you need a hand?" asked Will.

"I can't find my belt…" Will spun me round to reach for it.

"It's not there," he said. "It must've come off."

I pulled the robe around me and searched the area round the bed. "At least we can cross the Bauers off the list of suspects. I think they were probably too wrapped up in their own problems to worry about killing Louise. Where the bloody hell is my belt?"

I flopped onto the bed, annoyed. Will had bought me that dressing gown for our first Christmas together. It was a silky Japanese kimono, a beautiful bright turquoise robe patterned with peacocks and colourful birds, with tiny butterflies embroidered on it in gold thread. I always felt slightly decadent and Barbara Cartland-esque in it, like I should be reclining on a chaise reciting my latest novel to a mousey-haired, bespectacled lackey at a typewriter, whilst smoking a cigarette (in a long holder, naturally) and stroking a small dog, possibly with a laudanum habit (me, not the dog).

"I can't believe Lauren gave the game away and told Louise who the murderer was," said Will. "That's just not cricket."

"Well *I* can't believe Peter wanted to film Louise's crappy book," I said. "But it kind of rules Lauren out of the mystery female stakes, doesn't it? She needed Louise alive, at least until she'd sold the movie rights. The rights to all her stuff will got to her estate, whoever inherits that, and there'll be chaos over them. *And* they'll all become bloody bestsellers now…"

Will sat down on the bed next to me.

"What the Bauers said - about their child…" He spoke cautiously. "I know that sort of thing upsets you. Do you want to talk about it?"

"Not really."

He let out a deep breath and relaxed. "Oh thank God."

I reached out and took his hand, and we sat there for a moment in silence. But then he spoke again.

"Obviously we're a bit too old now anyway, but I always just assumed you didn't want children," he said, with a questioning note in his voice.

"I can't have them," I said. "It's fine, I found out a long time ago and I'm used to it now."

"You found out when you were with Joel?"

"Yeah."

"No wonder you hated Louise, after what she said at Harrogate…"

"Yeah." I remembered her comment, in front of everyone. *In your day women were expected to just stay at home and look after the children. If you could keep hold of your man long enough to have them, of course.* "She didn't know," I said. "She can't have done. She was just being nasty about my age and about Joel. But when she said it - in that moment, I really could have killed her."

"Maybe it was another nasty comment that got her murdered," said Will. I shook my head.

"No. I thought that as well at first. But this business with the steward, and her probably being drugged - it was planned, wasn't it? It wasn't someone just hitting out at her because she'd upset or angered them."

I lay back on the bed, staring up at the ceiling as I thought out loud.

"So we've basically discounted Lauren, Birgit Bauer, the Chief Purser - it can't have been her, she could have just ordered the steward to cover the bar at the Pearl without being all cloak and dagger about it - Heather, because she was off banging Karl at the time, and unless she's a master of cunning and deceit and her accusations earlier were all a big show, Sylvia as well. Who does that leave?"

Will lay down next to me. "Doris."

"Yeah, doubt it."

"No, these old biddies can be quite evil and Machiavellian! She could be a criminal mastermind, running a powerful underground organisation that Louise and her family were once part of and are now threatening to destroy by exposing them…"

I looked at him. He was clearly enjoying himself immensely. "Hang on, let me write this down. I may have to use it in my next book."

He laughed. "You're beginning to rub off on me."

I leant forward, my kimono falling open. "Ooh, I hope so…"

So after we finished, um, rubbing off on each other, I put on dry clothes and we went out for lunch. Seriously, this entire cruise had turned into a never-ending buffet of amazing food and sex. The perfect holiday in fact, if I hadn't come across a dying woman…

To be fair, I hadn't actually eaten any of my breakfast - Sylvia had put paid to that - so my stomach rumbled loudly when we entered the Red Lion pub. Yes, they had a 'real' English pub onboard, complete with a mahogany bar, a shiny display of optics behind the counter with every spirit you could think of (plus a few more you couldn't), and a dartboard. I made a mental note to leave immediately if my accuser turned up again while we were eating, as I thought the likelihood of one of us - probably me - being carried off with a dart shoved somewhere painful was quite high.

The waiter placed two plates of crusty bread, cheese, ham and pickles in front of us and my stomach rumbled again. I spread some butter on a hunk of bread and tucked in.

"You can't beat a Ploughman's Lunch," I said, and Will nodded, his cheek bulging with a pickled onion. "There's this proper old country pub I used to go to, near Dorking - it's probably been done up now and turned into a gastropub - but it used to have loads of old ploughs and scythes and stuff like that all over the walls, it was the perfect setting for a rural horror film." I put on a deep, gravelly 'movie trailer' voice. "The Ploughman is back, and he wants his lunch…"

Will laughed. "Well he can't have it. Do you want your pickled onion?"

I've never liked pickled onions. They look too much like eyeballs to me. The fish and chip shop near my dad's flat, where he used to take me and my sister when it was his weekend to have us, had one of those massive jars full of pickled onions on the counter. It used to give me nightmares, every time we had cod and chips.

"Knock yourself out. But you'll have to give your teeth a good clean if you want a repeat of this morning…"

Will grinned, leaned across the table and speared my pickled eyeball with his fork. I shuddered and looked away, in time to see Heather entering the bar.

"Oh bloody hell," I muttered. Will looked over and saw her.

"It's alright, she's on her own," he said.

Heather looked around, then smiled as she spotted us and made her way over. She stood slightly awkwardly in front of us.

"I'm glad I found you," she said. "I just wanted to apologise for Sylvia this morning."

Will and I both made dismissive noises: no need for that, not your fault... But Heather shook her head.

"No, I think it is my fault," she said. "I think Sylvia's feeling a bit left out, because..." She hesitated.

"Because you've made a new friend?" I suggested carefully. She smiled.

"Is it that obvious?" she said.

"Well, you have stopped talking about murdering your ex-husband," said Will. She laughed and pulled up a chair, slipping into it.

"You know about me and...?"

"You and Karl," I said. "Yes. That's how come the two of you arrived on the scene together so quickly, isn't it? You were next door to Louise's cabin." I smiled. "Kudos, by the way. He's a young stud."

She giggled. It was nice to hear; the Heather who'd begun the cruise had not seemed like a giggler. "I know! He's the same age as my eldest. Who'd be horrified."

"They don't have to know, do they?" I said. "Not if it's just a holiday fling..."

She looked at me frankly. "Of course it's just a fling. I'm not an idiot, I know it's not a relationship. I knew he was using me for money, even before his confession this morning, but then I'm using him for sex so it seems fair."

"Sylvia's not happy about it, though?"

"No. This was meant to be a girls' trip. It still is, it's not like I'm spending that much time with him. I think she disapproves of casual sex." Heather giggled again. Blimey, it was starting to become a habit. "Although there is nothing casual about sex the way he does it - let's just say I know what I was missing, all those years with Colin. God, he was boring. Karl makes me feel young and reckless again. Not that I ever was bloody reckless to begin with."

"There's nowt wrong with being old and reckless," I said. "It's never too late to start." Will nodded.

"We're old and reckless all the time," he said. Heather smiled gratefully.

"I knew you two would understand. But Sylvia's been my friend for years. We met at primary school, we got married the same year, had babies the same year, got bloody divorced the same year. I've never not known her! So please don't think badly of her."

"I don't," I said, although I kind of did. The woman had accused me of murder, bribery and being an evil, manipulative old slapper. "I would like her to stop accusing me in front of everyone though…"

Heather nodded. "I know. I told her she was out of order. We had a big argument and she flounced off and I've not seen her since." She stood up. "She'll come round. I'll have another word with her later. I just wanted to apologise."

"No need," I said, smiling warmly at her. "But thank you anyway."

She turned to go, then turned back. "Oh yeah, Zoé wanted to me to tell you there's karaoke on this evening and that you have to go."

Will groaned.

"Don't shoot me, I'm just the messenger," said Heather. "Zoé would have my guts for garters if I didn't pass on the invitation. She seems to think that you're the Karaoke Queen…?"

I grinned at Will and he groaned again. I have mentioned a few times on social media that I like a good singalong. Just putting it out there, in case…

"Oh we'll be there," I said. What better way to prove I wasn't hiding away, wracked with guilt, than by belting out a few bars of 'Copacabana'?

CHAPTER 21

The karaoke was taking place in yet another venue we hadn't come across before - the Gatsby nightclub. The Art Deco theme that ran throughout the ship was given full rein here. Plush, padded, intimate seating booths, perfectly contoured for illicit rendezvous and clandestine champagne drinking, were raised above an eating area full of dining tables and high backed, studded leather chairs, and were separated from the diners by a sleek brass railing. A long, sinuous bar, made from one solid piece of walnut so highly polished that it glowed warmly and reflected the lights of the ornate chandelier above, hugged one side of the dance floor, leaving plenty of room for doing the Charleston or (more likely) un-coordinated jigging about and general Dad dancing. At the other side a sweeping staircase lined with a brass and walnut balustrade mirrored the curve of the bar, circling upwards to a VIP area.

Right at the end of the room was a small stage, with a DJ booth stuck incongruously at one side. And on the other side was the karaoke screen.

I *am* a bit of a karaoke queen, I have to admit. I used to be in a band at university - it was the only reason I lasted there as long as I did, and I spent my grant money (yes, I'm old enough to have had - and wasted - not only free tuition but a full maintenance grant) on a synthesiser rather than text books. I couldn't read music but the band's singer was a genius who could go from playing Chopin to Black Sabbath to Gary Numan without missing a beat, and he would show me how to play stuff. I was quick to pick it up - I think I must actually have had some musical talent lurking there after all - so when we played gigs I would play the guitar on some songs and keyboards on others; and I wrote lyrics to the music he would come up with. But I never sang. I grew up listening to the likes of Toyah and Blondie and Kate Bush; when I was 9 I desperately wanted to be Pauline Black in The Selector. But I was never brave enough to sing.

And then in later years I discovered alcohol, karaoke and that art of not giving a damn that comes with age, and I made up for it. But that was in pubs and wine bars, usually with Susie who would be equally (or more) drunk. This was like singing at Wembley Arena in comparison.

And of course past karaoke audiences hadn't suspected me of being a killer, although I had been known to murder the odd 1980s chart hit.

The bar was busy and most of the tables were full as Will and I entered. Movement caught my eye from one of the booths, where Zoé, Michael and Harvey were comfortably ensconced, and all three waved us over.

"I'm so glad you came!" trilled Zoé, excitedly. "I remember you saying on Facebook once that you like karaoke. I love it! Maybe we could sing something together?"

"That'd be great," I said. I normally don't like to share the limelight - I've sung with some truly terrible singers, and prefer to perform on my own - but I wasn't sure how friendly (or otherwise) this crowd would be, so thought it would be nice to have moral support. Harvey handed me a list of songs.

"Here," he said. "We've already chosen one."

Will glanced at the list briefly, then stood up. "Drinks?"

While he was at the bar, I studied the list.

"Let me guess - Abba?" Joel stood in front of me. I flushed *(why are you going red, stupid cheeks?!)* as he slipped into the booth next to me, taking Will's place.

Zoé looked at Joel with her mouth open, then at me with a gleam in her eye.

"That's a great idea," she said. "We could do 'Dancing Queen'."

I nodded, not really caring. I'd been looking forward to it in our cabin, while we were getting ready, but now we were here I was wondering how many of the people around us had heard Sylvia's accusations, how many had read that piece on Twitter, and how many had already decided I was guilty. Perhaps me singing was a little insensitive? But then I'd no more killed Louise than anyone else on this ship (bar one) - should *they* all stop having fun and hide away in their cabins?

"I'll go and put our name down!" said Zoé excitedly, and she disappeared.

"I think Will needs a hand at the bar," said Michael, and he and Harvey jumped up as well. *Don't everyone bloody leave me with Joel!* I thought, but of course I didn't say anything.

Joel grinned at me. "Was it something I said?"

"No, you smell." *Ooh, great come back, Bella…*

Joel took the list from me and studied it, but I could see that he wasn't really reading it.

"So…" he said eventually. "Have you had a chance to think about what I said the other day?"

For a moment I did not have a clue what he was going on about. And then I realised he meant his confession that he still loved me. The one he'd managed to make without actually saying it. To my surprise I realised that I actually *hadn't* really thought about it after the initial shock.

"Have they got that Taylor Swift one? The one that goes 'we are never getting back together'?" I pretended to study the list again. He laughed gently.

"Okay, I probably deserve that." He looked at me, suddenly serious and intense. God damn it, he did intense really bloody well. And smoulder - boy, could he smoulder. I was almost surprised the seat didn't catch fire beneath his tight, muscular buttocks *stop it Bella!!!*

"I really am sorry," he said. "I treated you very badly."

"You were a total shit."

"Yes, I was. And a bloody idiot. I didn't appreciate what I had. I won't make that mistake again, Bella."

"You won't get the chance to, Joel."

On stage, the MC tapped the mike in the way of MCs, roadies and sound engineers the world over, then welcomed everyone to the Great Gatsby Karaoke night.

"And kicking us off tonight with our very first song, we have Will!"

Not my Will? There must be loads of Wills and Bills and Williams on this ship. But no. I looked over at the stage and there he was, the last person I'd expected to sing tonight. He smiled over at me as the music played and opened his mouth - and then I was lost in his song. *Somewhere beyond the sea...* He never even sang in the shower at home - I sing everywhere - and I was amazed to discover that he had a lovely, mellow singing voice, just right for the old 50s number.

I watched, enchanted, aware that Joel was watching me in return. I heard him sigh.

"He's got a good voice."

"He's got an *amazing* voice," I corrected him. "I had no idea..." I turned to Joel. "*That's* the sort of surprise a woman wants from her husband, not the type that involves finding another woman's pants in his car."

He smiled, and there was definitely a touch of regret in it - not an emotion I'd ever really connected with him.

"He makes you happy, doesn't he?" It was a question, but he could already see the answer on my face.

"Yes. Very. He makes me feel safe." I saw his mouth open, ready to pounce on that, and I stopped him. "I don't mean 'safe' as in boring, I mean he makes me feel secure. I could trust him with my life, not just my heart."

Joel looked at me for a moment, then nodded and got up without saying anything. I turned my attention back to the stage, where Will was coming to the end of the song. He looked to be massively enjoying himself, somewhat to his surprise I thought.

He finished to an enormous round of applause, which also seemed to surprise him, then handed the microphone to the MC and diffidently trotted back to the booth. I jumped up and threw my arms around him as the others returned with the drinks.

"That was a-bloody-mazing!" I cried. He laughed.

"I didn't embarrass you?" he asked. I shook my head.

"Of course not. You know that I'm the embarrassing one in this relationship…"

Up on stage someone began strangling a cat - or possibly singing, I wasn't too sure - to the tune of 'Take On Me', as Heather wandered past the booth. Harvey waved, but she was too busy adjusting the buttons on her blouse to notice him.

"Alright, Heather?" I called. She stopped and looked up guiltily, then automatically glanced over to the other side of the dance floor where Karl was loitering. He winked at her and looked away.

"Yes, I'm fine," she said, a little breathlessly. I inclined my head towards Karl and she laughed as she sat down, Zoé squeezing along the booth to make room. She turned to Will.

"Was that really you singing?" Will nodded, trying not to look too pleased with himself but failing. If I wasn't careful he would be trying to wrestle my karaoke crown from me.

"So are you going to get up there?" he asked.

Heather shook her head. "I'm so tone deaf I couldn't carry a tune in a bucket," she said. "But I did see that Sylvia's put her name down."

Will and I looked at each, surprised.

"Is she here, then?" I asked, looking around. I wasn't sure if singing would be a good idea if she was. Heather shrugged.

"She must be, but I haven't seen her since this morning," she said. "She never could resist karaoke, though. She's put herself down for 'I Will Survive'. She always sings that one."

Several more singers - or 'singers', as some of them could more accurately be called - performed with varying degrees of skill but lots of enthusiasm, and the audience clapped and cheered warmly for all of them. Harvey and Michael got up and sang 'I Got You Babe', scandalising the older and more conservative half of the crowd - *"Margery, there's two men singing a love song to each other up there! It's PC gone mad!"* - and winning over everyone else with their obvious devotion.

I was complimenting the newly weds on their vocal prowess, when a huge cheer went up for the next singer. I looked up, mid-sentence -

" - and when you harmonised that bit at the end - "

- and stopped, mouth hanging open, as I saw the figure on stage. Joel. I wondered for a moment if he was trying to impress or surprise me, the way Will had knocked my socks off with his song; but I dismissed that as being ridiculous. He must know by now I was happy with Will and, looking at him up there, I didn't imagine that he'd have much trouble replacing me. Not that he should even be thinking about that, not when he should really be mourning Louise. Although I got the impression that had been less of a relationship and more of a convenient arrangement.

Joel looked over at me with that arrogant grin of his - I felt a flush starting but shook it off - then the music started, and I knew I was in trouble.

I'd heard Joel singing before - it had been one of our 'things' - singing in the car on long journeys, giving it our all without embarrassment, even with the windows down (although we did normally go a bit quiet at traffic lights). We would take it in turns to choose CDs; sometimes it would be classic rock and pop like ELO (everybody knows and loves at least one ELO tune), sometimes it would be 80s hip hop like the Beastie Boys (I know all the words to 'Licensed to Ill'), and sometimes - when it was Joel's choice - it would be harder rock stuff, like Muse or the Pixies. But tonight he wasn't singing any of our old favourites.

The strains of 'Back For Good' by Take That started up, and most of the women in the room, and no doubt a few of the men, were immediately putty in Joel's hands. I say most, because of course I was completely immune to his charms by now. Honest…

I could feel Will watching me watching my ex-husband, and tore my gaze away from the snake-hipped sex god on stage *oh my GOD Bella, you did not just say that!* to smile at my gorgeous, wonderful, current husband.

"He's not as good as you, is he?" I said. Will shrugged.

"His voice is pretty good."

"I wasn't talking about his singing, I meant generally. He's not as good as you."

Will gave me a big smile which contained a hint of relief, I thought. I leant over and kissed him hard on the lips.

"What was that for?" he asked, a little surprised but pleased.

"Do I need an excuse to kiss you?" The answer was obviously 'no', as he pulled me towards him and leaned in for a proper, full-on, tongues-and-everything pash. We don't normally go in for big PDAs, but sometimes you just gotta show the world you love each other.

On stage, Joel was singing about how he wanted someone back for good - surely not me - and his voice wobbled slightly. I felt a brief (and completely unaccustomed) rush of power. Maybe it *was* me he wanted back. *Tough. You shouldn't have thrown me away,* I thought. And then I felt a bit guilty, because there's never any need to be cruel when it comes to people's feelings. The song finished and Joel disappeared into the crowd at the bar, overwhelmed by a gaggle of over-excited, over-50 divorcées. Never to be seen again…

There was still no sign of Sylvia. I'd looked all over for her, even taking a detour around the entire club when I went to the loo for a pre-performance pee. The MC called her, but she didn't come up to the stage. Heather asked him to put her name further down the list in case she turned up later; Sylvia had never been known to miss a karaoke night at their local British Legion club, not even that time she'd had bronchitis. She'd forced herself out of bed and had drunk half a bottle of Prosecco on top of her antibiotics. Her performance that night had apparently been so memorable it was still talked about in living rooms all across Chesterfield.

I went to the bar for some Dutch courage (although to be fair it was a rather nice New Zealand Sauvignan Blanc I was drinking, so maybe Kiwi courage would be more accurate). But I'd obviously had more than enough liquid bravery, as I didn't spot the outstretched walking stick until I tripped over it. Luckily for me (but not for her) the elderly Doris, reclining on a banquette, was there to break my fall.

I leapt up, mortified; I was already in the frame for one murder, and I didn't want a crushed geriatric on my rap sheet as well. Her daughter, Sarah, leapt up too, reaching out to tug me onto my feet and fuss over me.

"Oh my god, are you okay?" she said, and it occurred to me that it was the first time I'd actually heard her speak; she was always drowned out by her domineering mother.

"I'm fine," I said, "it's your mum I'm worried about."

Sarah lowered her voice and grinned. "She's as tough as old boots."

"WHAT?!" said Doris.

"I'M SO SORRY!" I said loudly. "I HOPE I DIDN'T HURT YOU!"

Doris cackled. "I'm as tough as old boots, me. It's you young ones I worry about." She glanced at Sarah then back at me, with a mischievous glint in her eye. "Take this one here - "

Sarah groaned. "Not now, Mum…"

"Wouldn't say boo to a goose. Too timid - "

"I'm not timid, Mum, I just don't think Miss Tyson wants to hear all about us -"

I could feel the beginnings of an awkward and long-running family dispute rumbling towards me, but for the life of me I couldn't think of a way to get back to my seat without it looking rude (damn you, British manners!!). So I just smiled at Sarah and said, "It's Bella, please."

She smiled back, looking absurdly happy, but Doris carried on.

"She's been trying to find a way to talk to you for the whole cruise," said the elderly matriarch. I could sense Sarah attempting to sink into the ground next to me and felt sorry for her. "The whole point of coming on this cruise was to talk to you."

Sarah blushed furiously. "That's not strictly true - "

"She's a crime writer like you." Doris babbled on, oblivious to or just ignoring the frantic and embarrassed 'zip it' motions of her daughter. "She's a brilliant writer but she just hasn't got anywhere. Too scared to show anyone her writing."

"Well that's not true either!" said Sarah, defensively. "I have sent it out to agents, I'm still waiting to hear back from a few…"

"It can take ages," I said. "Glaciers move quicker than the publishing industry. It took 8 months for my first agent to read my book."

"Maybe Bella could read your book?" Doris suggested, a sly grin on her face. *Awkward.*

A tip for all you writers out there: never ask another writer to read your book, not unless you're friends and you're at basically the same level in your careers. Because if one's more successful than the other, and they say no, then they're stuck up, they've forgotten where they came from, and they don't remember what it's like to struggle… but if they say yes, what then? If the book's terrible, what do you say? And if it's good, what are you supposed to do about it? Yes, I can ask my agent if she'll read it, but she's busy and she hates being asked personal favours for exactly the same reason. I can't get it published for you. And if I do something nice for one writer, I've kind of got to do it for others.

I know all of this. But I still opened my mouth and said, "Send it to my agent, she's always on the lookout for new talent."

Sarah looked even more embarrassed. "I already did."

Oops. Well I wasn't hanging around to find out if Susie had rejected her or just not got back to her yet. I put on my best, most encouraging smile, and said, "Just don't give up. I had a ton of rejections before I got anywhere. Remember, someone out there once rejected the Beatles and Elvis and Harry Potter - not the same person, obviously, that would be weird…" Aware I was babbling, I began backing away and was relieved to see Zoé waving at me from our table. "Oh look, it's my turn to sing now. Nice talking to you!" And with that I made my escape.

"I thought you'd got lost," said Zoé, eyeing Sarah across the room with suspicion as I joined her. I laughed.

"Just don't ask…"

And then it really was time for Zoé and me to sing. I stood on the stage and looked across the club at the crowd; at the people chatting by the bar, and others sitting at their tables, waiting for us to start. *Most of them don't even know who I am*, I thought, *or if they do, they don't care.* That made me feel much better, although I still felt very exposed, up there in the spotlight. Thank God Zoé was with me.

The familiar strains of 'Dancing Queen' came over the loudspeaker. I allowed my foot to tap. Then my hips began to sway…

Zoé had a surprisingly strong voice. She was sometimes so quiet - timid, even - when talking, that I hadn't expected her to be able to belt out a song, but she could. She stayed in tune, knew all the words and even did a bit of a dance. *Dark horse,* I thought approvingly.

I squinted at the screen next to us at the side of the stage, which was showing the words (unlike Zoé I needed a helping hand remembering them). Behind the screen, black curtains closed off the wings, no doubt hiding cabling and stuff like that. I was momentarily distracted as I spotted something sticking out from the bottom of the curtain, but I couldn't make out what it was so I carried on singing. It looked like a shoe.

Next to me, Zoé did a little shimmy. The crowd went wild, and she blushed, and did it again. She gave a little twirl but disaster struck; her feet got tangled in the microphone lead somehow, and she put out her hand to steady herself on the screen.

The screen, which was on a flimsy metal tripod, toppled over and crashed through the black curtain. Everyone laughed, except of course Zoé, who clapped her hand over her mouth.

"It's alright," I said, as the MC rushed over to rescue the screen. "No harm done…" But my words caught in my mouth as the MC pulled back the curtain to untangle the tripod from it, and Zoé let out a scream.

Sylvia had been at the karaoke all along, but she was in no fit state to sing. A plastic bag had been forced over her head, pressed hard against her stricken face, forcing the air out of her lungs. Her eyes bulged unseeingly through the clear plastic, a nasty gash on her forehead smearing gore onto the bag.

That was bad enough. But the thing that made me feel dizzy, that made me stagger backwards and almost fall off the stage, was what was tied around her neck, keeping the bag in place.

It was long, thin strip of silky material, a beautiful turquoise colour patterned with colourful peacocks and embroidered with tiny golden butterflies. The Japanese influence was obvious. It was the missing belt from my kimono.

CHAPTER 21

To say all hell broke loose would be something of an understatement. Zoé lost it completely and ran from the stage, screaming and crying. Heather ran up the stairs and almost threw the MC bodily out of the way in her haste to get to her friend, tearing at the plastic bag in a panic, hoping against hope that if she could just get some air back into her lungs… But it was far too late for that. Heather sank to the floor, with Sylvia's head cradled in her lap, and sobbed heavily; I knew she was thinking about the last time they'd spoken. They'd argued. About me. Something else for me to feel terrible about.

Harry Carter shouldered his way through the crowd that had swarmed towards the stage, all wanting to know what was going on, followed by a couple of security guards.

"Clear the dance floor, please!" he shouted. "Stand back, let the doctor in, nothing to see here!"

"Has someone been taken ill?" an elderly man asked no one in particular.

"You could say that," I said. Will joined me and took my hand, then looked at me in shock as he spotted the belt. We shared an unspoken *oh shit*.

Harry looked at me, thin lipped. "Ms Tyson, here you are, right on the spot again. What a surprise," he said sardonically. I opened my mouth to protest, but what could I say? I had been present at the discovery of two dead (or dying) bodies.

I cleared my throat. "I know, what are the odds?" Will jerked his head around sharply and looked at me, an expression on his face that I could only describe as 'light bulb moment'. But I never got a chance to question him, as Michael, at the foot of the stage, turned to Harvey and spoke loudly.

"I *told you* it was weird, the way she disappeared like that," he said. Others in the crowd, which was showing no signs of dissipating despite Harry's command, were beginning to look over at the newly weds.

"Stop it," said Harvey.

"No!" Michael shook his head and looked straight at me. "The last time anyone saw Sylvia alive, she was accusing *her* of murder. Look at the two of them! They were furious with her, Will even threatened her - "

"No he didn't," I said, trying to sound calm. I didn't want to sound panicky, or as if I was protesting our innocence too much, even if that was how I felt.

"You both told her to shut up and go back to her cabin," said Michael. "And then no one saw her after that! Is that what happened? She went back to her cabin and you followed and shut her up before she turned everyone against you?"

"Of course it bloody isn't!" I said.

"This is not the place to be discussing this," said Will. Harry raised an eyebrow and Will huffed in annoyance. "Do your bloody job, man! Get this crowd out of here and preserve the crime scene, if you can now that half the bloody ship's trampled all over it."

Will's words stung the man into action, and he and the security guards had soon cleared everyone out of the club apart from the MC, who had waddled off into the wings and thrown up; Zoé, who was sitting on a chair Will had brought her with a dazed expression on her face; and Heather, who was still slumped on the floor of the stage. Will had gently persuaded her to let go of Sylvia so the ship's doctor could take a look at the body, and he had soon turned his attention to Heather herself, who was in deep shock.

Carter took statements from us all. I told him the belt around Sylvia's neck was mine - I didn't want him working it out for himself and jumping to conclusions - but to my surprise he didn't gloat; if anything, he looked a bit put out. Maybe he was still shocked by Sylvia's grisly appearance, which, although far less bloody than Louise's, was rather more disturbing. It was too easy to imagine the poor woman struggling for air, fighting for every last breath until finally slowly, painfully succumbing… The look in her eyes was enough to haunt anyone, and I couldn't understand how anyone could watch that terrified expression cross someone's face and carry on squeezing the life out of them.

Will and I stood to one side. I didn't want it to look like we were colluding or anything, but I was desperate to find out exactly what revelation had occurred to him.

"You've thought of something, haven't you?" I whispered. He nodded and opened his mouth to speak, then stopped as Zoé, who was starting to get some colour back in her cheeks, joined us.

"Mr Carter says we can go," she said. She shuddered. "I can't stop seeing poor Sylvia's eyes, staring at me through the plastic bag…" She swayed and Will gallantly thrust out an arm to catch her.

"Steady there," he said softly. "Maybe you should sit down again. Or better still, go and have a lie down in your cabin." She shook her head.

"I can't! I just know that every time I shut my eyes I'm going to see her face again!"

I desperately wanted her to bugger off so Will and I could talk, but the poor girl had had a terrible shock. I've seen a few dead bodies in my time - mostly for research on a book, but occasionally down to being in the wrong place at the wrong time - and it doesn't really get any easier; although, perhaps surprisingly, the bodies I've seen at wakes and funeral homes have creeped me out more. I think it's because they're laid out in nice clothes, made up with their hair done, like they're sleeping or something, but at the same time they are so obviously and completely devoid of life, of what made them *them* - it just feels so wrong. In a weird way, an untouched corpse is somehow more honest; something horrible happened here, Death happened here, and no matter how you try to dress it up, this person is no more. They're not sleeping; they ain't waking up any time soon.

Honest or not, this was doubtless the first time Zoé had seen a murder victim - maybe even the first time she'd seen a dead person - so it was bound to affect her. I should probably have felt more sympathetic towards her, but I did at least hide my irritation.

"How about some fresh air?" I suggested. She nodded and grabbed my arm, linking hers through it.

"I knew you'd understand!" she said, and she looked so grateful that I couldn't tell her I'd meant for her to go on her own. I looked at Will and he smiled, resigned.

"Let's all go," he said.

We went out onto the deck. The wind was picking up, and the sea, which up to now had been placid and calm, was being whipped into frothy peaks under the moonlight. But the ship maintained a steady course, ploughing through the growing waves and barely rocking.

Zoé stood at the rail, looking out to sea, taking deep breaths. I took Will's hand and led him as far away from her as I could without it looking rude.

"What were you going to say?" I asked, but he shook his head.

"Not here. I don't want to mention this to anyone yet, not even your friend there…"

She's not my friend, I nearly said, but stopped myself. She clearly *wanted* to be my friend. She seemed to be the only one (other than Will) who was utterly convinced of my innocence; Heather had been, but whether she would still feel the same after Sylvia's death was anyone's guess. I wasn't in a hurry to find out.

"Is she all right?" said Will, snapping me out of my thoughts. He nodded towards the rail, where Zoé stood, her shoulders shaking. "I think she's crying."

I walked up behind her and put my arm round her. She jumped.

"Sorry," I said. "I didn't mean to surprise you. Are you okay?" I peered at her face, a sympathetic expression on my own.

"I'm fine," she said, "I just keep thinking about Sylvia. Who would do such a thing? And why? What enemies could a woman like Sylvia have?"

That was something I would have liked to know.

It was chilly up on deck, so after about ten minutes we persuaded Zoé to go back to her cabin. It was getting late by now - it must've been after 10pm - so we walked her back to her cabin on the deck 5, then headed back to our own.

I sat on the bed and took off my shoes.

"So that's me done, isn't it?" I said. Will looked confused.

"What do you mean?"

"Well, everyone's going to be convinced it was me now, aren't they? They were already starting to believe Sylvia, and then lo and behold *she* bloody cops it too, and with my belt round her neck. It's like Michael was saying - it looks like I did it to shut her up."

"Or we did it," Will pointed out. "But that wouldn't be a very clever thing to do, would it? It's such an obvious motive for murder that it makes a less convincing case for it being you."

I looked at him. I was tired and I didn't get it. "What?"

He smiled. "Sylvia was making such a song and dance about it earlier, and, yes, I did make it worse by having a go at her. I couldn't help it. That makes us such obvious suspects that we would have to be complete imbeciles to then go and actually murder her, wouldn't we? And we're not complete imbeciles."

"I dunno, I sometimes feel like I am," I said morosely. He shook his head.

"Self pity doesn't suit you."

"I was going more for self deprecation."

He laughed. "What I mean is, it's a ridiculously clumsy attempt to make you look guilty - *so* ridiculously clumsy that they've shot themselves in the foot. No detective worth their salt would believe you could be so stupid, and using your belt is the icing on the cake. The murderer has already tried to tie you into Louise's murder by using a method from one of your books. But anyone who's read your books will know you're far too devious to be that blatant."

"Hmm…" I wasn't sure whether to be insulted or flattered about being called devious, but I went for flattered.

"This is what occurred to me earlier," said Will. I'd almost forgotten his lightbulb moment. "When that - that - "

"Muppet?" I supplied.

"Oh yes, good one. When that muppet Carter pointed out that you'd been at the discovery of both victims, you said 'what are the odds?'" He looked at me triumphantly.

"Um…yeah?"

"Well exactly! What *are* the odds of you stumbling across two dead bodies on a ship with 3000 passengers and crew aboard? It can't be a coincidence, can it?"

"That muppet clearly agrees with you. That's why he thinks I did it."

"But we know you didn't," said Will patiently. "So what is the only other explanation?"

I looked at him, not sure what he was getting at. And then suddenly it hit me.

"The bodies were left for me to find…"

"Yes! So instead of looking for someone who had a grudge against Louise, maybe we should be looking for someone who's got one against you."

CHAPTER 23

Will's words left me reeling. It seemed unlikely, but equally there didn't seem to be any other explanation. Out of a boat-load of people, I had been the one to discover (or jointly discover) two murder victims. Sylvia had said it had always bothered her, how I was able to gain access to Louise's cabin, and it was that that had finally convinced her I was the murderer. Will and I had missed the significance of that unlocked door. We'd accepted it, even if it didn't quite feel right. I'd told myself (as unlikely as it might be) that the murderer had been disturbed or in too much of a hurry to shut the door behind them properly; but any homicidal cruise passenger with an ounce of common sense would have taken an extra 10 seconds to make sure the door was secure, so that they had plenty of time to put some distance between themselves and the scene before the body was discovered.

If the murderer had *wanted* me to find Louise, though… It suddenly made perfect sense.

"But who could have a grudge against me?" I said. "I mean, that's a pretty bloody big grudge, if it's led to someone killing two people. You'd think I'd know if I'd pissed someone off *that* much…"

Will shrugged. "Who knows? The sort of person who could kill two people just to get back at a third is quite possibly a little - "

"Over-sensitive? Bonkers?"

"Both. What they see as a slight - real or imagined - a non-bonkers person would probably not even notice."

"Which is interesting but no help to man nor beast."

"Nope."

Will got up and paced up and down the cabin.

"You definitely don't recognise anyone else on this ship?"

"No," I said, firmly. "The only people I'd seen before this cruise were Joel and Louise."

He looked at me. "Could Joel be trying to get back at you for kicking him out?" I shook my head.

"No. As much as I have spent the last few years hating him, I couldn't say that he's capable of murder. And he - " *wants me back.* I choked off the rest of the sentence.

"What?"

I sighed. "You heard the song. He doesn't want me locked up."

Will didn't speak. He turned and opened the mini bar, which was well stocked with alcohol.

"No point looking in there, we don't have a corkscrew, remember?"

He held up a miniature bottle of vodka in triumph. "Screw top." He unscrewed it and took a swig, then grimaced.

"We have got to get off this ship before we become alcoholics," I said lightly, and he laughed softly.

"I have drunk more this week than I have in the last year," he admitted. He sat next to me and I took the bottle from his hands. I sniffed it, screwed up my nose and drank, finishing with a splutter. He laughed again. "Shall I make some tea?"

"I'll do it," I said.

We sat and drank tea in companionable silence. I could've killed for a Hobnob - we'd planned on having a late dinner after the karaoke, which of course had been completely forgotten about - but I thought that, with the amount I'd eaten on this cruise, I was hardly likely to fade away.

"Okay," I said, "say someone does have a grudge against me. That gives them a motive, a pretty crap one, but a motive nonetheless. I have absolutely no idea who it could be, so we still need to look at who, physically, could have killed Sylvia. And who could have stolen my belt in order to frame me." I shuddered at the idea of the murderer being in our cabin, poking around in our things, carefully choosing their next murder weapon. "So let's look at that first. Who could have got in here? And when?"

"You were certain someone had been in here when we got back from dinner last night," said Will. "If you remember, I was all ready to - "

"Babe, you're always ready for that. So we've both got keys. I had mine on me. Where was yours?"

"I've never used it," said Will. "Whenever I've left the cabin you've either been with me, or stuck in here. You always make a point of patting your pocket or checking your bag for your key, so I haven't bothered with mine."

I looked at him in alarm. "Then whoever took the corkscrew could've taken your key and used it to get in here!"

Will looked around in mild panic, then relaxed. "No, look, it's on the side where I left it, by the kettle. But I will take it with me in future. Just in case…"

"So we're back to the same conclusion we had with Louise's murder. That the murderer had a master key or something."

Will nodded. "It looks like it… But if that's case, how come Harry Carter hasn't discovered that one's missing? Hotels don't give out master keys to everyone. Staff normally have to sign them out so they can keep tabs on them."

"Maybe the murderer takes the key out and puts it back before anyone notices it's gone." I looked at Will. "If they have access to the keys, they must be a crew member."

"Rob, the missing purser," said Will. I nodded.

"Maybe. It depends on whether he's missing because he's lying low, or because he's…" I drew my finger sharply across my throat. "No one seems to have seen him for days, but Karl said he's been back at some point to change his uniform."

Will smiled grimly. "*Someone* came back to change his uniform," he said. "That doesn't mean it was Rob. They could have done away with him, taken his cabin key and stolen his clean uniform."

"Which means the murderer could be running around dressed as a crew member, able to get hold of a master key and, by extension, able to access every single cabin on this ship." We looked at each other, my words sinking in. "That's a comforting thought, isn't it?"

"Yes…" Will looked thoughtful. "Maybe we should go and talk to the duty purser, and find out how easy it would be for someone to access the keys without being challenged."

"Come on then." I stood but he smiled and grabbed my hand.

"It's nearly midnight," he said. "It can wait until the morning. There'll probably only be a skeleton staff on at this time of night, and it might be better when there's a few of them on duty so we can ask them if they've seen anyone looking suspicious. Or seen Rob, for that matter." I sat down, reluctantly admitting he had a point.

"Okay," I said. "But tomorrow, first thing, we go and talk to them. We've only got two more days at sea, and time's running out…"

We went to bed, and after much tossing and turning Will finally fell asleep. I lay next to him, listening to the sound of his breathing and watching the moonlight filter through the curtains. The pattern of the waves rose and fell across the ceiling as the boat ploughed onwards through the swelling sea, reminding me of the nights we'd spent together in Venice; listening to the much gentler tide lapping against the buildings and the early morning boat traffic along the canal. I thought of our first night together, and everything we'd been through since, and thought, *everything will work itself out, it always does*, then fell asleep, hoping I was right.

I dreamt I was running through the dark, winding passages of Venice again, pursued by a skeleton in an immaculate white crew uniform. The skeleton was laughing and, bizarrely enough, humming 'Dancing Queen' in an evil, menacing tone that made me shudder; it sounded like the buzzing of thousands of flies, grating at my nerves, making my flesh crawl as I imagined them feeding on the rotting corpses of Louise and Sylvia.

    I turned left, then left again, passing the restaurant where Will and I had first had dinner together; then another left, through an archway into a narrow, unlit corridor that led into a square full of people dancing. *I'll be safe here*, I thought in my dream; but the dancers all turned away from me. I recognised Zoé and Heather, Michael, Harvey and, um, Benny and Bjorn from Abba. I gave up; none of them were going to help me, least of all the Scandinavian pop stars. *Ungrateful bastards,* I thought, *I bought your Greatest Hits CD!* I turned and fled down another passage way, by now hopelessly lost; but this one ended in a deep, dark canal, its black waters gleaming like ink. I turned, feeling the skeleton behind me, its ivory bones gleaming in a sudden shaft of moonlight. The skeleton reached out to me and I braced myself, waiting for it to push me into the canal. But it just held out a pen and said, 'Will you sign my book?'

CHAPTER 24

I woke the next day feeling surprisingly rested for someone who'd had a night full of mad dreams involving boney book fans and Swedish musicians. Will was already up, shaving in front of the bathroom mirror clad in just a towel, wrapped around his waist. Although he was 50 years old and entering the realms of middle age, he still had a good body. His time in the Army and then the Intelligence services had kept him lean and surprisingly muscular; surprising, because he'd been with me nearly 2 years now, and I like my food - in case you hadn't noticed - and am not keen on any exercise other than the horizontal kind. Although he has occasionally persuaded me to stand up or bend over, and there was that one time when we were both lucky to escape without a hernia…But anyway. I digress.

I lay in bed and watched him pulling faces at himself in the mirror as he shaved. He filled out one cheek with his tongue and caught sight of me from the corner of his eye.

"Morning," he said, running the razor under the tap. "Everything okay?"

"Just admiring the view," I said, giving him a salacious glance and licking my lips suggestively. He threw a hand towel at me.

"Behave yourself! You treat me like a piece of meat."

"No I don't! Although you could have thrown the towel you're wearing at me…" He laughed.

"I was trying not to encourage you. But I'm not sure why…" He dried his face and joined me on the bed. "I just got clean, but I could get dirty again."

I sat up, kissed him hard and threw back the covers. "Nope! No time! This is the day we solve the case!"

"Is it?"

"It has to be. We reach New York tomorrow."

As luck would have it, the same purser who had brought me Louise's message on the night of her death was on duty behind the desk. He nodded at us in a friendly but professional manner as he finished a telephone conversation.

"How can I help you?" he asked, although he obviously had some idea of what we wanted. He lowered his voice as a group of passengers walked by. "The Chief Purser has told me to answer any questions you might have about - that night."

"Thank you," I said, smiling at him and peering at his name badge. David. "We can see you're busy so we won't take up too much of your time. I don't suppose you know Rob? The steward we've been looking for?"

He shook his head. "I don't, sorry. He never worked the desk on the same shift as me, and I don't think he'd done many trips."

"How long have you worked for the cruise line?" asked Will.

"I'm one of the longest serving pursers," said David. "I've worked here for about five years."

"That's a lot of trips," said Will, encouragingly. "You must know this ship like the back of your hand."

David smiled. "I do. Better than the Captain! She's a beauty, isn't she?"

"She is," said Will. "So you know all the nooks and crannies? Maybe there are a few places the crew like to go when they're off duty, to get away from the passengers?"

He smiled. "One or two. Most of us have to share cabins, so it's nice to find a spot to yourself occasionally. Even better when the boss don't know about them either."

"Could Rob be camping out somewhere in one of these secret hidey holes, if he's trying to keep a low profile? Mr Carter is supposed to be looking for him, but I bet he doesn't know the ship as well as you and your mates do."

David thought about it, then slowly shook his head. "There are places where you could tuck yourself away," he said, "but you'd have to come out at some point, to eat and go to the loo."

Will nodded in understanding. "I see, of course… But how about if Rob didn't need to do either of those things? Could he stay hidden, without being discovered?"

"But surely he'd have to eat?" David looked puzzled.

"Not if something had happened to him," said Will, gently. A look of comprehension, followed by shock, crossed the purser's face.

"You mean - if he was dead?" Will nodded and he gulped. "I'll have a think and see if I can come up with any ideas…"

"The other thing we need to ask you about is keys," I said. "Who has access to the spare keys you have here?"

"There aren't any spare keys, as such," David explained. "They're blanks. If a passenger loses their key we take a blank and program it to unlock their cabin."

"And who has access to these blanks?" I asked.

"All the duty pursers. When we use a blank, we enter the card's code number on the computer and then assign the cabin number to it."

"So if someone had taken a blank and assigned it to, say, our cabin, it would show up on the computer?" He nodded. "Could you look up our cabin and see if that happened? And maybe Ms Meyers' cabin?"

The purser quickly typed in a few numbers, then turned the screen around to face us.

"There are currently two key cards assigned to your cabin," he said. "These are the cards' unique code numbers." He pointed to a string of digits on the screen. I took out my key card and compared it, as Will did the same. Both cards matched.

The purser then entered Louise's cabin number. "There was just the one card assigned to Ms Meyers' cabin, when we sailed."

"So if anyone got into either of those cabins, they used one of those cards?" I asked. He nodded. "What about the cleaners? How do they get in to change the bedding when the cabins are empty?"

"There are master keys for each deck," he said. "Those are kept locked up in the Housekeeping department. I helped out in Housekeeping once when we had a really rough crossing and half the cleaners got sick. I've got a strong stomach."

"And there's no way anyone could get hold of one?"

"I think it would be unlikely. Like I said, they're kept under lock and key. Every morning the Head Housekeeper assigns each deck and the corresponding keys to the cleaners working that shift - they work in pairs, so there's two master keys for each deck. But they're signed out at the start of the shift and signed back in as each pair finishes. If any were missing it would soon be noticed, and they could see who had them last."

The desk phone rang and the purser looked at us apologetically. I smiled and nodded, and he picked it up.

I turned to Will. "So there goes that theory," I said. "Rob must have taken Louise's key when him and Zoé took her back to the cabin, and he must've passed it on to the killer."

"The mysterious woman," said Will. "Yes. But then how did she - or Rob, if he's still around - how did they get into our cabin?"

"God knows," I said. I glanced at the purser, who was still talking to a passenger on the phone.

"Of course, madam," said David. "And what cabin number is that? Thank you."

Something clicked in my head. A light bulb went on - a very dim light bulb, maybe one of those old energy-saving ones that take a while to warm up, but a light bulb nonetheless. I looked at Will, but he hadn't noticed a thing.

I turned to the purser, who had finished the call and was entering something into the computer.

"That phone call you just had - what was that?"

He looked surprised. "Just a passenger booking a call for this afternoon." He grinned. "Apparently they had an afternoon nap yesterday and missed the theatre matinée, and they want to make sure they don't miss it again today."

"You asked for the cabin number. Doesn't it come up on the phone, like Caller ID or something?" I could feel Will looking at me, wondering what I was getting at.

David shook his head. "No, it just rings…"

"So when Louise - Ms Meyers - when she rang and gave you the message, how did you know it was her?"

"She said it was her, and gave me her cabin number…" The purser was now looking quite worried.

"Did you recognise her voice?" asked Will. David nodded, but hesitantly.

"I hadn't spoken to her, but I knew she was a Northerner… You don't think…?"

"That it was someone pretending to be her. It could have been. They could have been calling from anywhere." I turned to Will. "Maybe Louise didn't make that call after all…"

178

CHAPTER 25

We left the stunned purser and headed for one of the few cafés we hadn't tried yet. I ordered a pot of tea for two and we sat down, heads spinning somewhat at what could potentially be the most significant discovery of our investigation.

"Or it might be nothing," I said. "It might still have been Louise who called…"

We sat and pondered in silence, as the waiter bought over a tray with a pretty flower patterned tea pot and milk jug, and two bone china cups.

"Shall I be Mother?" asked Will, picking up the pot. I nodded and watched as he poured. Then we sat in silence again, minds working furiously - well, I know mine was, anyway - as we sipped at our tea.

I finished my drink and carefully placed the cup in the saucer.

"You know what this means, of course," said Will.

"That the murderer could have made the call."

"Yes. And you know what *that* means."

I thought hard, but I was still too stunned by the whole idea that it *hadn't* been Louise that I came up blank. "No, what?"

"That our murder window of opportunity is all wrong."

"It is?"

"Of course. We were basing it on Louise being alive when the pursers' desk received that phone call. But if it wasn't her, then the attack could've happened much earlier. The last time she was definitely seen alive - "

"She was alive when I found her. Just."

"The last time she was seen unharmed, then - was when Joel and Zoé left her in the cabin. And that was, what - 5 minutes earlier than we thought?"

I thought about Louise, lying on the carpet, and that slight flicker of recognition in her eyes as she saw me. I hoped I hadn't imagined it, and that she'd known that she wasn't alone as the life left her. "She couldn't have been killed that much earlier, could she? She'd have been dead when I found her, surely?"

Will nodded thoughtfully. "Maybe…but you said it yourself, although she was bleeding steadily it was a small puncture wound, so it could have taken a while." He fiddled with a tea spoon. "And if she was drugged and it had made her drowsy, which seems more than likely, it could have slowed her heart rate, and that could possibly slow down the rate of blood loss. Not much, admittedly, but maybe by a few minutes. I don't know."

I counted backwards in my head, working out the new time line in my head.

"So the murderer made the phone call at 9.33… That's 3 minutes after the lights went out in the Pearl, and about 2 minutes before they came back on. I'm assuming the murder took place just before the phone call - that would make sense, do you think?"

Will shrugged. "Probably. If they left the door unlocked for you to get in, they wouldn't want to leave Louise for long and risk someone else finding her. And like you said, even accounting for a slow rate of blood loss, she would probably have been dead when you found her if it had been much earlier."

"They could have made the call *before* the murder, but if I was bumping someone off I'd want to get it done and get myself away before I set up the body for discovery."

"So the real murder could've taken place at the same time as the pretend one," said Will.

I groaned in frustration. "So we're none the wiser, are we? We already went through who was in the Pearl during the murder mystery, and it was basically everyone."

"Everyone except Heather and Karl," Will pointed out.

"Yeah…but I still think they were genuinely, you know, going for it in the next cabin. It certainly *sounded* genuine from where I was standing."

"Do you remember that first night, when Heather did her impression of Louise? That sounded genuine too."

I shook my head. Heather's impression *had* been uncanny, but too many other things pointed to it being someone else. "I know it did, but think about it. If Heather was the mysterious woman, and she was off with Karl, what was Rob doing in the Pearl without her? Both Karl and Zoé said Rob was supposed to be meeting someone." I shook my head. "And why would she kill Sylvia? She was her best friend. You saw how distraught she was."

Will looked thoughtful. "So who does that leave? We looked at who was in the Pearl when the lights came up. It doesn't mean they were there when the lights were out, though, does it?"

"But how do we find *that* out? It was pitch black, remember. I couldn't make out anyone, could you? And then of course we have no idea when or where Sylvia was murdered, so it's not like we can look at who had the opportunity to kill her - "

"Sorry, am I interrupting something?" Joel stood awkwardly (but undeniably handsomely) by the table.

"Just us banging our heads against a brick wall. What's the matter?" Because now I looked at him properly, it was clear something was the matter. He looked grim-faced.

"They just found your missing steward."

We made our way to deck 5, where a white-faced David, from the pursers' desk, was waiting for us. The Chief Purser stood with him, looking anxiously towards a lifeboat.

The lifeboats were suspended from cranes and hung alongside this deck, the entrance to their covered cabins level with the railings for easy access in case of emergency. I was guessing this was a completely different sort of emergency than the type they were designed for. Two security guards had blocked off the deck and were fielding curious passengers, redirecting them on to the deck below and refusing politely to be drawn into conversation.

David turned to us. "After I spoke to you I thought I'd come and check out some of our secret spots," he said, his voice shaking slightly to match the trembling in his hands. "I know some of the stewards come here for a fag - we don't normally get many passengers up here because the lifeboats block the view." He ran a hand nervously through his hair.

The ship's doctor emerged from the last lifeboat, towards the prow of the ship, followed by Carter who looked grim. The head of security looked annoyed when he spotted me, Will and Joel waiting, and turned to protest to the Chief Purser. But she stopped him in his tracks.

"We all need to hear this, Mr Carter," she said firmly. "The Captain suggests you take advantage of Mr Carmichael's experience in these matters. And *I* suggest you do what the Captain says."

The doctor looked around at all of us before speaking. "Okay, before I go any further let me remind you that I'm not trained in forensic medicine. I'm not a scene of crime officer and I'm a lot more accustomed to dealing with live bodies than dead ones." We all nodded. "Having said that, I'm becoming more used to crime scenes and murder victims by the day. By the time we get to New York I'll be able to give CSI a run for their money."

"So what's the verdict, Doc?" asked Carter. The doctor smiled grimly.

"Well, he's definitely dead… Abdominal stab wound, right - here." He demonstrated. "Judging by lividity, swelling and discolouration I'd say he's been dead for around 3 days, maybe more, maybe less - difficult to tell with absolute certainty, due to the temperature inside the lifeboat. At least he died happy."

I frowned. "What makes you say that?"

He looked at David and Carter. "You didn't tell them?" David shook his head and Carter scowled at the very idea of volunteering any information to us. "He's stark bollock naked. And there are signs that he copped off before copping it." He held up a latex-gloved hand with a grimace. "Thank god for gloves."

"Ewww…" I said.

"So that ties in with no one seeing him since just after the murder," said Will. "Maybe he got worried when he found out about Louise's death, realising he'd got involved in something much worse than he'd thought, and arranged to meet this mysterious woman - "

"And she lured him up here for a bunk up and then did him in," I finished. Will nodded.

"But how could she have sex with him first?" asked the Chief Purser, with a disgusted look on her face. "And why?"

"To get him at his most vulnerable," I said. "He was young and fit, and presumably stronger than her. What better way to distract him?"

"Are his clothes still there?" asked Will. The doctor shook his head.

"No sign of them."

183

"And that ties in with what Karl said," I said. "Karl thought Rob had been back to the cabin, to drop off his dirty uniform and pick up a clean one. But that must have been our murderer."

The Chief Purser looked alarmed. "You mean the murderer's strutting around dressed as a member of the crew? But they'll have access to all areas of the ship - "

"They may not be using it, of course," said Will. "They may have just taken it to make it look like Rob was still alive."

"But they could have used it to get into Bella's cabin and steal her corkscrew without being noticed," said Joel. "And as a disguise when they killed Sylvia, in case anyone spotted them."

I felt a rush of gratitude for Joel, for still believing in me after everything we'd been through. And an equal rush of thankfulness to have Will by my side, helping me through this mess. Carter, of course, still had me pegged as the killer.

"None of this proves Ms Tyson didn't kill Ms Meyers," he said stubbornly. The Chief Purser shook her head.

"Haven't you read *any* of her books?" she asked. "If she was going to kill someone she'd have done it in a far less obvious way. Why would she use her own corkscrew, and her own belt in the second murder?"

"I'm not a big reader," said Carter. "I haven't read any of them. I'll admit it does sound pretty stupid, using her own belt - " *That's why he didn't say anything when I told him it was mine!* I thought triumphantly. *He knows it blows his case out of the water.*

But Will was frowning.

"Hang on - if you haven't read any of her books, how did you know that the corkscrew murder was in one of them?" he asked.

"I can't remember," said Carter, looking uncomfortable. We all stared at him. "Alright, I didn't come up with it myself, one of the passengers might have mentioned it to me - we're running a murder mystery cruise, there are a lot of your readers on this ship."

"Who told you about it?" I demanded. He shook his head.

"I can't tell you, you know that," he said. "Look at what happened to the last person who said something against you."

"Oh for God's sake - " I started, but Will put his hand on my arm.

"I know who it was," he said. "Who was the one who riled Sylvia up and made her suspect you?"

CHAPTER 26

Back at the poolside bar - I had a hankering for another one of those camp, fruity mocktails - we discussed Will's hunch. Joel looked unconvinced.

"Her? But she's a bloody airhead!"

"Think about it," said Will. "You weren't there, Joel, but all our amateur detectives, led by Zoé, had a meeting to discuss the case, and she sat there listing all the things that pointed towards Bella being the murderer."

"True…" I mulled it over, sucking on my straw. "But she was just saying what the police would possibly think."

"I know, but she did go on about it in great detail," he said. "She's managed to continually protest your innocence whilst making you sound completely guilty."

"I heard about that," said Joel. "I saw Harvey and Michael at breakfast and they were arguing about you. Michael said that it all pointed to you and I told him he was a twat."

"So Michael thinks I did it as well now," I said. "He'd better be careful, I might bump him off in some ridiculously obvious fashion too. Maybe I'll carve 'Bella woz ere' into his forehead, just to make sure they know it was me." I was so annoyed I accidentally sucked up a tiny bit of fruit and nearly choked on it.

"Okay, so we know Zoé has got a big mouth," said Will, patting me on the back before I succumbed to death by pineapple. "What else do we know about her? Who is she?"

I shrugged. "She's my number one fan, apparently. That's what she told me on the first night."

"Have you read 'Misery'?" asked Joel with a shudder.

"I have, I just hope she hasn't… What kind of a grudge could she have against me?"

Joel looked alarmed. "Bloody hell, is that what you think? That the murderer was actually after you?"

"Not after me as such," I said, "but trying to set me up. Look at how the bodies were left for me to find. We think someone's trying to frame me for murder."

"Shit…" Joel looked genuinely worried for me.

Despite the fact I could easily believe she was the one who had dobbed me in to Carter, mentioning the similarities between my book and the murder, I still couldn't believe that Zoé was guilty of anything other than having a loose tongue. As much as she could irritate me, she'd been nothing but supportive ever since Louise's murder. She worked in a book shop, for Christ's sake; she was basically a mild mannered librarian. What possible motive could she have for getting me into trouble?

I sighed. "Even if she did arouse Carter's suspicions about me, what does that prove? Only that she likes a good gossip - " I flushed as I remembered her loudly prattling on about Joel and Louise, and me being jealous - "and that she speaks before she thinks. Plus she's one of the few people we know was definitely in the Pearl during the pretend murder. Her phone went off, remember?"

"If it's someone with a grudge against you, you should talk to Susie," said Joel. I wondered if he had any idea of the names my faithful friend and agent had called him after his indiscretions. "She might have some idea of the people you've upset over the years…"

"Let's hope she kept a file," said Will, and he and Joel both sniggered. *Great*, I thought. The last thing I bloody wanted was the two of them becoming best buds.

"Oh you are sooo funny," I said moodily, watching the ice cubes glittering at the bottom of my glass as I stirred them with the straw.

"I've been taking lessons from you," said Will, grinning. I reached out and clipped him round the ear.

"Behave!"

"Sorry Mum." He tried to look contrite but it just came out smug. I put my hand out to slap him again and then stopped as inspiration struck me like a bolt of lightning. Will's smile evaporated instantly. "What is it? Your face just changed like *that*." He clicked his fingers. "And you didn't hit me…"

"It's Sarah," I said, still thinking it through but already convinced. It had to be her.

"Sarah?" repeated Joel, stunned. "Not *Sarah* Sarah?"

"How many other Sarahs are there?" I said. "Well, I mean there are loads, obviously - "

"Yeah, but *Sarah*? She's always got Doris with her. Unless you think the old biddy's in on it too. She's - "

"She's a would-be crime novelist who sent her work to my agent." I said. The two men looked at me, mouths open. "I spoke to her and Doris at the karaoke. Doris said she came on this cruise specifically to talk to me, and when I told her to send her book to Susie - " Joel opened his mouth to berate me but I shook my head - "I know, I know, never offer to help someone unless you know they can actually write - I was kind of on the back foot at the time, I'd just almost suffocated Doris - " Both men looked at me again, their mouths open even wider. I shook my head again.

"Doesn't matter - anyway, I told her to send it in and she said she already had… This is after Doris had said she wasn't getting anywhere."

Joel shuddered. "God, it's hard enough sending your work out there without having Doris playing the Voice of Doom when you do," he said. I nodded.

"What with the almost constant rejection you get when you're starting out, along with having to care for an elderly and very demanding parent - "

"It would be enough to drive anyone mad," said Will, thoughtfully. "But would she have had the opportunity to kill Louise and Sylvia? Doris seems to keep her on a short leash."

"That night my belt went missing - you know, when we got back to our cabin and I was sure someone had been in there - we saw Sarah in the corridor, didn't we?" I remembered her coming across us, forcing us to stop our saucy shenanigans; we hadn't really taken much notice of her, being somewhat out of breath and flushed with horniness, but she had been heading back to the dining room. "She could have been coming from our room then! She could have been in there and taken my belt - "

"Okay…but how did she get hold of our corkscrew, days before?" asked Will.

"I don't know, but how did *anyone* get hold of it?" I asked defiantly. "I know it sounds tenuous, but there's no one else on this ship who's even remotely connected to me, apart from you and Joel. I'm telling you, there's no one else it could be."

"Come to think of it, you might be right," said Joel. "I've seen her, wandering around the ship late at night on her own…"

"How come *you're* wandering around the ship late at night?" I asked.

"I haven't been sleeping very well," he said. I looked at him and he gave a small, self-conscious smile. "Bad life choices coming back to haunt me." He looked at me for a moment, aware of Will watching him, then looked away. "Anyway, the casino bar is open 24 hours so I go for a walk around the deck and then get a night cap. I've seen her a few times."

"Hmm…" Will still looked thoughtful. "You definitely need to talk to Susie."

But Susie was not an easy person to track down. I dialled her number and heard it go straight to voicemail. Where could she be? The woman practically had her phone welded to her hand; I'd known her to take calls on the toilet, at the hairdressers and even with her feet up in stirrups having an IUD fitted. My fevered imagination conjured up images of my late, lamented agent sprawled across her desk, her life snuffed out by the cloud of innocuous-looking white powder spilling from an envelope addressed to me, sent by a rejection-crazed aspiring author.

Or she might just be at the dentist. Even Susie couldn't talk with a drill in her mouth, although she'd give it a bloody good shot.

So instead I left a voicemail message, and texted her. And then sent an email, outlining the importance of checking into Sarah and getting back to me.

"And now we wait…" I said, but of course waiting patiently is not something that's ever come naturally to me. "Better get another mocktail. Maybe with a shot in it."

CHAPTER 27

"There you are!"

The soft Scottish burr next to me made me jump. Joel had gone for a walk around the ship to spy on our murder suspect, while Will had popped back to the cabin (using his own key card, for once) to call a colleague at Interpol, leaving me sitting on a bar stool gazing into the distance as I supped at another drink. I'd been so caught up in the whys, whens and hows of Sarah being our killer that I hadn't heard the Chief Purser approach.

"I've got something you might be interested in," she continued, placing an iPad on the table in front me.

"I've already got one of those," I said (to be fair I was on my second pretty strong non-mocktail and the sun was still barely over the yard arm, and as I never usually drink anything stronger than a well-brewed cup of tea in the day I was starting to feel the effects. The bar stool seemed to have developed a pronounced lean, although that could have just been me). The Chief Purser eyed my glass suspiciously but diplomatically didn't mention it.

"No," she said patiently, "it's what's *on* it that you'll want to see. Will, too."

On cue, Will arrived. "Who's taking my name in vain?"

"Talking about you, not to you," I said. Was I slurring? I felt like I was slurring. I ran my tongue over my lips and opened my mouth to try that again, but thought better of it. Will frowned and discreetly moved the glass away from me, signalling the bartender to bring us a bottle of water.

"What can we do for you?" Will poured me a glass of water as he addressed the Purser and I sipped at it obediently.

"Harry Carter told me there was no CCTV footage of the night of Ms Meyer's murder," she said. "But there was." Will and I looked at each other, dumbfounded. CCTV had never even occurred to me - if there were security cameras around they were well hidden - and from the look on Will's face, he hadn't thought of it either.

"Where's it from?" asked Will. "Too much to hope that it's from the corridor outside Louise's cabin…"

The Chief Purser smiled ruefully. "Yes, that *is* too much to hope for. This ship is basically a hotel, and like all hotels, we have to maintain a balance between discretion and security. For whatever reasons, our guests don't like to feel that they're being spied on, even if it's for their own safety. So there are no cameras in the cabins, of course, or the accommodation corridors. But there are cameras in all the public areas - the bars, the casino, and the dining rooms."

"Including the Pearl?" said Will. She nodded.

"But what good will CCTV footage from inside there be?" I pointed out. "The lights went out, remember? We won't be able to see anything."

"No, but we'll be able to see for certain who was there when the lights went out, and who was there when they came back on." Will turned to the Purser. "We now suspect that it wasn't Louise who made that last phone call. So the murder could have taken place just before or during lights out."

The Purser nodded. "David told me about your conversation. I asked Harry for the footage from that night days ago, and he said there wasn't any. But this morning, when I realised that we had a much wider crime window of opportunity, I asked him again."

"I can't believe he didn't volunteer it," said Will. I snorted.

"I bloody can," I said. "It's just one more thing that'll prove I didn't do it."

"We hope," said Will, and I immediately felt totally, horribly sober.

"Yeah, we hope..."

"So this time I made sure I asked him in front of the Captain." The Purser grinned again, and I realised that she disliked the head of security as much as we did. "It didn't go down well when Captain Butler realised Harry had been keeping information from me."

"So let's see it, then!" I reached out for the tablet but Will stopped me.

"Can we watch this inside the Pearl? That way we can work out where people were, from the footage." He looked around. "Quite apart from the fact that I think we should be keeping this amongst ourselves, it often helps if you can visualise the crime."

"Spoken like a true detective," I said, sliding off the bar stool and straight into his fortunately waiting arms. "Oopsy..."

The Pearl felt weird in the day time. The dining room did not have any windows or natural light, just masses of gilding, shiny metal and mirrors, all reflecting the ceiling lights - so it wasn't that it looked different in daylight; day time and night time were arbitrary here. But it just felt *wrong,* like seeing a drag queen without their make up on, or a nightclub at 3 o'clock in the afternoon, or a room you've lived in for years with no furniture. Or a body with no life left in it...

The Purser flicked on all the lights and we sat at table in the centre of the room. I thought back to that night and tried to remember where everyone had been, as the Purser scrolled through the footage.

"So where do you want to watch from?" she asked. I considered.

"What's the absolute earliest time Louise could have been murdered?" I asked.

"After she left and went back to her cabin," said Will promptly.

"Okay, then let's start with Zoé and Rob taking her out."

The Purser fast forwarded through the footage, which was surprisingly sharp, although it was on a fairly small screen and I suspected it would be horribly blurred if we tried to zoom in too much. There we all were, clad in our fancy dress - the Bonnie and Clyde outfits really suited us, I thought - all chatting, laughing, oblivious to what was about to happen.

In the corner of the screen, a tiny me guided an equally tiny but incredibly wasted Louise into a seat. The steward, Rob, stood nearby, looking around the room. Even on this small screen, it was clear to see that he was on edge; it seemed so obvious now that he was waiting for something to happen that I wondered how I hadn't spotted it at the time. But then you don't, do you? When you're at a bar or restaurant, how much notice do you take of the person waiting on you? What better way to become invisible than by putting on a uniform and serving drinks.

Zoé, who had been out of shot, scuttled across the screen heading straight towards me. We exchanged a few words, then she waved Rob over and I helped the two of them drape Louise's arms around their shoulders. I spoke to Zoé again - I remembered telling her to be discreet - and they walk-carried Louise away, out of the Pearl and back to her cabin. I shuddered. They were taking her to her death. Why hadn't I just let her pass out at the table? Why did I care if the mysterious photographer - who had thankfully gone quiet - took an embarrassing picture of her and shared it on Twitter? Because as much as I'd hated her, I didn't *hate* her. Not really. Will was right; I *had* enjoyed bitching at her on the Internet.

On screen I watched them leave, then turned back to the game of 'Who Am I?'. I joined Will, who was talking to Harvey and Michael. At one of the tables, Joel sat with Doris, Sarah and Sylvia, seemingly oblivious to the fact that all three women - who between them easily spanned ages 30-80 - were flirting outrageously with him. That much was clear to me, even at this distance. Sarah might have been too shy to talk to me, but she was having no trouble with Joel. But Joel wasn't really listening; his attention was elsewhere. On me.

I felt Will stiffen beside me. He'd noticed it too. My ex-husband could not take his eyes off me, his gaze following me as I wandered between the groups, now talking to the Chief Purser, now getting another drink and standing apart for a moment, watching Rob return, alone, and go behind the bar.

Joel took a deep breath and a swig of his drink, then headed over to me. He'd come to ask if I knew where Louise was, but it hadn't looked like he was missing her very much.

We chatted briefly, then he headed out of the Pearl.

I turned to Will. "How long had Louise been gone by this point? About 10 minutes?"

He looked at the time stamp at the bottom of the screen. "A bit less. Just under 9 minutes."

"So Zoé and Joel are both with her now. Is anyone else missing? Although of course the camera angle means there are a few areas of the room we can't see…"

We studied the screen, but all the other murder mystery players - apart from Heather and Karl, and we knew exactly where *they* were - were present. Joel and Zoé re-entered the Pearl, the door that led into it from the balcony of the Excelsior dining room swinging open for a moment right at the edge of the shot. Zoé made her way to the bar, fiddling with the wimple that covered her head, as it was looking decidedly lopsided. I wondered what those two had been up to, out in the corridor… Joel started towards me and Will then stopped, looking a bit lost.

"Well that doesn't help us much," I said. "The lights will be going out any second now - "

"Look!" said the Chief Purser, pointing to the top of the screen.

She tapped on the miniature version of herself, looking at her watch then up at the steward - Rob - behind the bar, raising her hand to signal lights out. And next to her, at the edge of the picture, the door swung open again as Sarah - who'd lost interest in the conversation at her table the minute Joel had left it - made her way out of the room.

CHAPTER 28

"So," said Will, as the Purser fast forwarded through the footage - the lights had gone out as Sarah left the room, and the screen was in darkness - "it looks like our new main suspect had the opportunity…"

"And she had motive," I said. Will raised his eyebrows. "She did!" I insisted. "She must've done! I told you, she's the only person on this ship with even a tenuous link to me - "

"Other than me and Joel," said Will, meaningfully. I groaned.

"Oh come on! It's not Joel. And I know it's not you." I took his hands. "I told you, Joel's not out to get me banged up. He's trying to clear my name."

"Hmm…" Will looked unconvinced. The Purser looked awkwardly between the two of us and stood up.

"I - I think I'll go and look at this over there, under the light…" she said diplomatically, and I smiled gratefully at her as she left us. I took Will's hand.

"Look, I know you don't like Joel - " he snorted. "Believe it or not, I don't particularly want the three of us to become best buddies and all hang out together after this cruise has ended, either. But you can't let your personal feelings towards him affect the investigation."

"I won't if you won't," he said. I felt a little guilty twinge; but the only personal feelings I had involving Joel were disgust at myself for still finding him attractive, despite myself. Will was the only man for me, surely he knew that?

"I'm not," I said firmly. "When it comes to arrogance Joel could win Olympic gold for Britain, and he does have a tendency to descend into full blown twattery after a few drinks, but he's no more a murderer than…" My voice trailed away and Will snorted again. Really, he had an enormous talent for contemptuous snorting, and to this day I've never heard anyone do it better.

"No more than me, you were going to say."

Busted. "Yeah, okay. But it's different with you. You were a soldier, you're in Intelligence. It's your job to protect people, which occasionally means getting your hands dirty."

Will gave a small but genuine smile. "That's a diplomatic way of putting it."

"It's true, though. You're trained to protect people. The only person Joel's ever protected is himself." I leaned over and kissed him. "You are worth ten of Joel. Maybe even eleven…"

He laughed. "As many as that? Wow. Okay."

The Purser returned, clutching the iPad and looking relieved that whatever was going on with us, was clearly over.

"So, I've got to the part where the lights come back on," she said. "But I have to go and do some work. I'll leave the detective stuff to you." She handed me the iPad. "If you need anything else, do let me know."

We watched her leave the room, then turned back to the footage. I hit Play. On screen the Pearl was suddenly illuminated, showing the body of the pretend-murdered steward sprawled across a table. Will pointed to the doorway. "Look!"

Sarah scurried in, looking around in confusion at the scene before her. Her face cleared as she realised the corpse was only play-acting, then she rushed over to Doris and handed her something.

Will and I exchanged looks.

"So she was out of the Pearl for the whole murder window," I said.

Will nodded. "I was wondering why anyone would set you up, rather than just murdering you, which must surely be easier." I shuddered. "But of course the murderer could also have had a grudge against Louise. Kind of a two-birds-with-one-corkscrew thing. If we're going with the rejection scenario as motive, surely one rejection wouldn't be enough? Maybe she approached Louise's agent and got turned down there as well. It's perfectly feasible she'd approach the agents of all her favourite crime writers."

"You could be right," I said. And then something occurred to me. "Joel's with the same agent…"

"Where is he now?"

"He said he was going to follow her around for a bit, maybe get close to her…" I looked at Will in alarm. "What if she tries to kill Joel next?"

Despite Joel not being his favourite person in the world, Will was concerned enough about his fate (and the possibility of yet another murder being blamed on me - let's face it, if there was one person I couldn't be blamed for wanting to see the back of, it would be Joel) to agree that we should go and look for him. We decided to split up, so I headed outside onto the deck and wandered around, enjoying the sunshine and the fresh air despite being on the trail of a suspected murderer and their potential 4th victim. What can I say? I'm not insensitive, I just like being on boats.

I ambled to the prow of the ship; by now, anyone wanting to recreate the scene out of Titanic (the *"I'm flying!"* bit, not the *holy crap we've hit an iceberg* bit - that would just be daft and against all sorts of Health and Safety regulations) had got it out of their system, and the only people out on deck were oldsters with no desire to be either Kate or Leo (or the iceberg, for that matter), light blankets tucked over their knees, doing crossword puzzles and drinking tea on the sun loungers. Which I had to admit was beginning to look more appealing than spending the entire cruise tripping over corpses and protesting my innocence.

I strolled casually, trying not to look like I was searching for someone, but there was no sign of either Sarah or Joel. I made my way to the back of the ship, towards the swimming pool and the poolside bar. Earlier - during my non-mocktail session - there had been a couple of diehard swimmers, ploughing up and down the pool in an attempt to mitigate the effects of the all-day buffet (or was I just projecting my own insecurities on to them?). But now the placid chlorinated water had turned into Kid Soup, a roiling cauldron of slightly sticky small children clinging onto brightly coloured inflatable unicorns and dolphins, screaming, while indulgent (or just too knackered to care) parents drank cafe lattes and pretended they were someone else's responsibility. It was a scene to gladden the heart of any infertile woman, I thought. Although it wasn't really.

I plumped myself down on a sun lounger, watching the children playing for a moment. I hadn't thought about my infertility for a long time - after my initial shock and grief, it felt pointless to dwell on it - but every so often it popped into my head. I wondered what sort of mum I would have made. Will would be a brilliant dad, I thought; but then, would I have even met him if Joel and I had been able to have kids? Would I have been enough for Joel, if we'd had a baby or two to seal the deal? Chances were he would still have been a cheating scumbag, only I might not have been so quick to chuck him out and make myself a single mum. No, as much as I had wanted children, much better to be childless and happy with Will, than miserable and sprogged up with Joel…

"Sorry, can I join you?"

I jumped and looked up in surprise. Sarah stood before me, looking at me anxiously. I felt a lurch of alarm; was she about to try and drown me in that sea of toddlers? But I just smiled.

"Of course. Don't mind me, I was miles away…" I wished, now that she'd found me, that I really was; and where the hell was Joel, if he was supposed to be keeping an eye on her?

Sarah sat on the sun lounger next to me, not lying back to relax but perching awkwardly on the edge. She fidgeted nervously. She didn't *look* homicidal, for what it was worth.

"What can I do for you?" I asked her. "I think you have something to say to me, don't you?" *Maybe a confession?*

She nodded. "I wanted to apologise for the other night, at karaoke. It just seemed a bit trivial, after finding poor Sylvia…"

"Apologise for what?"

"My mum, asking you to read my book - I was so embarrassed, I mean you don't just ask a bestselling author to read your novel when you're an aspiring writer like me - "

I held up my hand to stop her. "Oh that! It's fine. Everyone's mum is embarrassing at times, according to mine that's one of the perks of being a parent." She laughed. "And don't call yourself an aspiring writer. If you write, you're a writer. End of." She smiled at me gratefully and I felt myself warming to her. Surely she couldn't really be a murderer? I'd been so convinced earlier… And of course, she had been out of the room during the time of Louise's murder. I steeled myself, hiding it under a smile.

"So where *is* your mum? It must be hard on you, coming on a cruise and spending the whole time looking after her. The elderly can be very demanding."

Sarah smiled and shook her head. "Oh no, not really. I don't see her much generally, I'm so busy with work and writing and everything - I did offer to move in and look after her, but she refused. She wanted me to have a social life, not spend all my free time looking after her." Her face softened and I realised that we'd got it completely wrong about her being downtrodden and in thrall to the indomitable Doris. "She insisted on getting a carer - she does need a lot of looking after - which is great, but it makes me feel a bit guilty. So when we go on holiday together I make sure the carer stays at home, so I can devote myself to her. It's lovely spending some proper time with her, even if it does get a bit tiring for both of us."

"Aw, that's so nice!" I said, touched. "You must really love her."

She looked at me, almost in surprise. "Of course I do! She's my mum…"

We watched the children in a slightly awkward silence for a while, then she turned to me again.

"I also wanted to explain about what Mum said - about me not talking to you? Well that was her idea as well. I don't want you to think I'm some kind of stalker! She doesn't really understand how writing and publishing works. When we were talking about a holiday, I suggested a cruise because she can't really get around much now. By the time I visited her again, she'd booked this one because of you being here for the murder mystery. She thought I could come along and pump you and the other writers for information on getting my book published, which was sweet of her if completely misguided and embarrassing…" I laughed and she smiled again.

"And you sent your book to Slater Douglas?" I was starting to lose faith in my theory, but if she really had been rejected by my agency…

"Among others," she said. "I haven't heard back from them yet, but it does say on their website that it could take 3-6 months, maybe more, to hear back. And it's not been that long yet."

"Still, the rejections can get you down…" I was just about ready to give up on my theory; I really couldn't see this woman murdering anybody.

She nodded. "Yes, I've already had plenty. But someone turned down JK Rowling and the Beatles, remember?"

I laughed. "Yes, they did. And Star Wars. And probably 99% of everything else that's now a huge success."

"Exactly. It's hard, but I'm trying not to take it to heart."

We sat in silence again for a moment, a rather more companionable one this time. I fished into my bag and brought out the iPad that the Chief Purser had left with me.

"Can I show you something?" I said. She looked surprised but nodded.

"Of course."

I brought up the CCTV footage from the Pearl.

"Will and I have been trying to work out when Louise was killed," I said. "The other two deaths - "

"*Two* deaths?" She looked genuinely shocked, and I remembered that the steward's death was not common knowledge. Another mark against her as our murderer.

"Yes. We have reason to believe that one of the stewards was helping the murderer, only they obviously decided they couldn't trust him and shut him up permanently." She gulped. She really did look surprised; although of course it could have been surprise that the body had been found, as no one had mentioned it. She could have been confident that Rob wouldn't be found until after we'd reached New York.

She could just be completely innocent. I continued.

"With the other two deaths we've got so little to go on. We've concentrated on Louise's murder, as we think it's highly likely that the murderer had contact with her prior to her death."

"You think it was one of the murder mystery players?" Sarah narrowed her eyes, thinking. "That does make sense. We've kind of kept to ourselves as a group, haven't we? I don't know who else would have even known she was on the boat."

"Exactly! So we've managed to narrow down the murderer's window of opportunity to the same time as the pretend murder in the Pearl that night."

"What time was that?" she asked. "I didn't see the murder, I wasn't there…"

I held out the iPad and showed her the footage. She watched herself on the small screen, entering the Pearl as the 'corpse' was discovered and looking alarmed, then hurrying over to her mother.

"Where had you been?" I asked.

"My mum had forgotten her pills and I went back to the cabin to get them…" She looked at me, her face clouding. "Wait, you don't think I did it? Just because I was out of the room?" She shook her head angrily. "Is that why you were asking me about Mum? Trying to see if I was some downtrodden, repressed weirdo who had suddenly snapped and stabbed a bloody irritating woman with a corkscrew?"

"No - no, of course not," I said, unconvincingly. She looked furious.

"No? How many other people have you had this chat with?"

I sighed. "Just you. You're the only one who was out of the room at the time. All the other suspects were in the Pearl."

"Well it wasn't bloody me!" She stood up. "You might write a good murder but you're no detective."

"I know," I said, "but like you I'm a suspect, and an innocent one, and I am desperate to find out who really did it."

She calmed down but still looked a bit peeved. Well, I had just accused her of being a serial killer, so I suppose it was fair enough. I gave a small laugh.

"I bet you're wishing you hadn't apologised to me now," I said.

CHAPTER 29

So it was looking like Sarah hadn't had a grudge against me (and Susie) after all, but chances were she had one against me now. Ho hum.

I sat back in the sun lounger and wondered what I'd missed. Sarah was right, I was rubbish at being a detective. The murders in my books were always at the very least logical, but in real life, murders can be impulsive, spur of the moment and very, very messy, both literally and metaphorically. Had Louise's death been planned before the murderer had even set foot on the ship? The use of a date rape drug (which seemed likely, but we still didn't know for sure) pointed to a certain level of planning; but then very few people had known that she was going to be on the ship, seeing as she was a last minute replacement for another writer. Maybe they'd chosen her at random. But then they'd apparently left her for me to find. Or maybe they hadn't; maybe we'd been overthinking it, maybe they'd been in a hurry and they just hadn't shut the door behind them properly. Maybe I needed another cocktail…

No, that wouldn't help. Well, it would help me not care, but it wouldn't improve my powers of deduction. Maybe I should get an opium habit like Sherlock Holmes? But my limited experience with drugs (not opium or anything nasty like that, I should probably point out) had sharpened my dancing skills, rather than my mental faculties. Or I *thought* they had sharpened my dancing skills; in reality I'd probably looked like a baboon going through a mental health crisis.

Focus, Bella! Honestly, when I'm having trouble seeing the full picture I tend to go off at a tangent.

The full picture... I face-palmed (internally - there were other people nearby). We still hadn't watched all the footage from the Pearl, distracted as we were by our fear of Joel's impending demise. We needed to watch the whole thing, from the beginning.

I sent Will a quick text message - *S is not our killer. Back to the drawing board! Am by the pool* - then scrolled backwards through the footage and began to watch.

Dear Reader, let me tell you that watching people eat their dinner is pretty boring... what with that and the alcohol I'd had earlier, I'd just started to doze off when Will appeared.

"Do you want a blanket, dear?" he asked, grinning. I swiped quickly at my mouth - I have a tendency to dribble in my sleep - and sat up.

"Cheeky sod." I picked up the iPad, which had slipped unheeded from my hands onto the floor, and stopped the footage. He sat on the lounger next to me, leaning in to kiss me tenderly on the lips. I reached round to touch his cheek and pulled him in closer for another one.

"Do you think they'd notice if we got jiggy right here?" I murmured. He laughed.

"Hmm, I could just lie back and let you ride me like a polo pony..."

"A polo pony? Oh my god you are so posh." He opened his mouth to protest but I stopped him with another kiss. "Don't get me wrong, I like it. It's very sexy..."

A buttoned-up middle aged woman holding the hand of a wet, ice-cream faced toddler *ahem*'d in our direction as she passed, the sticky child staring at us in deep interest. I pulled away from Will and smiled sheepishly at her, but I got the impression she was less scandalised by our behaviour than envious of us having the opportunity to snog on a sun lounger like a couple of horny teenagers.

"So…" Will became businesslike. "How come Sarah's no longer a suspect?"

I filled him in on our conversation, cringing as I recalled my heavy-handed attempt to question Sarah. He noticed.

"Hey, you're a detective now, Mrs Carmichael," he said. "You're not out to make friends, you're out to find the truth."

"I'm not doing a very good job of either, am I?" I said.

"At least we're managing to rule out people."

"Yeah but I'm *too* good at that. I've ruled out just about everyone. Are we sure it wasn't me?"

Will smiled. "I don't know why you're worried about it, this is my job and even I haven't got very far…"

I held up the iPad. "We need to finish watching the footage - all of it, from start to finish. *Something* has got to jump out at us, some clue…"

So with seagulls shrieking and wheeling through the sky above us, we watched. We watched as everyone trooped in wearing their fancy dress. Louise and Joel made their grand entrance again. We moved between the tables again, talking to the other diners, laughing. Rob came in and chatted with Karl, who had been paying a lot of attention to Heather on the other side of the bar. As we watched she wrote something down on a beer mat and slipped it across the counter to him, then slid off her bar stool and walked away to rejoin Sylvia. Smiling, Karl discreetly pocketed the beer mat and went to clear a table.

We watched as Rob took over bar duties, mixing drinks for the waiters during courses, and then for the diners as they wandered up to the bar in the less formal part of the evening. If he really was there to meet someone, were they already in the Pearl? There was no sign of him acknowledging anybody. I watched him closely, but -

"There!" I jabbed my finger at the screen, stopping the footage.

"What?" Will looked surprised.

"I think Rob just did something to that drink…" I rewound the footage, and sure enough behind the bar the late steward poured a glass of something - the camera was too far away and at too difficult an angle to see it clearly - and paused to look around surreptitiously. His hand disappeared into his trouser pocket, then hovered briefly over the rim of the glass - then away. He paused again, maybe to let whatever it was dissolve. Then he turned and placed the glass, which looked to contain white wine, onto the bar counter. Next came a glass of red wine and an orange juice.

"Oh my god," said Will. On screen, my husband turned away from his conversation and picked up all three drinks, balancing the glasses precariously between his hands, and walked over to the table where I sat with Zoé, Sylvia and Heather.

"Rob spiked *my* drink, not Louise's…" I couldn't quite believe it. Despite knowing that someone had been deliberately trying to frame me for murder, it hadn't occurred to me that maybe I had actually been their first choice of victim. I watched as, at the table, we continued our discussion - if I remembered rightly, we'd been talking about carefully planned murders versus spontaneous ones, and which was more likely to get you caught. I remembered Will saying that the problem with planning everything down to the last detail was that the people involved don't always behave the way you expect. And I hadn't. I hadn't drunk that drink. I'd reached that stage of the evening where I was starting to feel a little worse for wear and had decided to stick with water for the rest of the night…

I watched as a fascinated Zoé, listening to Will with her mouth open and an air of sheer concentration on her face, picked up my glass and went to take a sip. I held my breath, even though I knew that she hadn't drunk any of it. On screen Zoé suddenly noticed what she was doing and shook her head, passing the drink to me and picking up her own orange juice. It could so easily have been Zoé murdered in my place! For a long time after that my glass of wine just sat on the table, all through dessert. I went to the bar and got a glass of water, and we did our usual wandering between tables, chatting. And then it happened. Louise bowled over to our now-empty table and reached for my glass - it seemed like any glass would have done - but mine just happened to contain adulterated white wine.

And no one spared her a second glance. If the mysterious woman who we'd all but forgotten about, convinced as we had been that it was Sarah - if she was in the Pearl keeping an eye on her cunning plan as it went down the toilet, she was very good at being discreet and non-reactive. There was no sign of anyone thinking *bugger* as Louise necked the spiked wine, no reaction to her fairly rapidly becoming legless. I seemed to be the only one who noticed her stumbling around; even her date for the night, Joel, was unaware. He was too busy watching me.

No, there *was* one person who'd noticed; Rob. I could see his puzzled look as he watched me, no doubt wondering when I was going to start showing the effects of the drug; then his alarm at Louise's state, the realisation that something had gone wrong clearly apparent now that I was looking for it. As Louise got increasingly unsteady on her feet he came out from behind the bar, lurking, waiting for something to happen. He looked very much on edge.

We watched as Karl and Heather left the Pearl within two minutes of each other, having carefully avoided each other beforehand but for one surreptitious nod from Heather as she headed for the door. Nearby, I steered an apparently wasted Louise into a chair before she fell over and spoke to her, looking around for help. Zoé - who had wandered out of camera shot a few minutes before, standing on the periphery of a group of chattering murder mystery players - scurried over and, after we exchanged a few words, waved Rob over. They carefully hoisted Louise up and quickly walked her out of the room. And everyone else was so busy chatting, the drinks flowing freely, that few of them even registered them leave.

Back on deck, Will's phone beeped. I stopped the footage as he swiped at the screen, squinting; he'd left his glasses behind in the cabin again. He frowned.

"What is it?" I asked.

"I don't know," he said, squinting harder. "I asked Carmen in the London office to do some digging on a few of our fellow passengers, and she's sent me a report. I can't get the attachment to open on here…"

"Where are your glasses? Do you want me to do it?"

He shook his head. "No, I need to see it on a big screen. I'll nip back to the cabin and look at it on the laptop. Are you coming?"

"I'll stay here," I said. The fresh air was helping to clear my head, which felt fuzzy not just from alcohol but from the realisation that I had been more of a target than I'd previously realised. "I'll watch the rest of this."

"If you can stay awake," said Will, grinning. He gave me a kiss on the cheek and left.

I rubbed my eyes, stretched, and hit Play again.

I tried not to notice the way Joel's eyes followed me around the room, or the way he took a deep breath, as if summoning his courage, before approaching me. One of the many other things that had been a

211

surprise on this cruise was finding out that he apparently still had feelings for me. I say 'apparently', because the way he'd behaved towards the end of our marriage, and then in the Press afterwards, hadn't pointed to him having any particular regrets other than getting caught and not being able to enjoy my money any more. Ooh, that sounded bitter. But it was true. Had that been the only reason he was with me? I'd been so infatuated with him and, I dunno, ridiculously *grateful* that someone so young and hot and cool had fancied me, that I think maybe deep down I'd never really accepted that he loved me. I think I'd always been waiting for him to find someone equally young and sexy. Had I done him a disservice? Had he been a lot more genuine in his affection for me? But then he had cheated on me. Would he have done that if I'd been able to have children with him?

Did any of this bloody matter now? My relationship with Will was just about the best thing that had ever happened to me. I could stop writing and never have another best or even mediocre seller now, and I wouldn't care. I loved that man as an equal, with every fibre of my being, and I knew he felt the same about me and always would. And if that sounds soppy and pathetic and completely Mills and Boon, you know what? I don't care. I hope you feel that way about someone some day.

I rolled my eyes at myself (internally again - there were still other people around). *For god's sake Bella, you're supposed to be looking for a murderer, not analysing your feelings about your bastard unfaithful ex-husband!* But I felt uncomfortable referring to him as that now. He *was* trying to help clear my name after all, and he'd apologised for his behaviour, sort of.

On screen Joel and I talked, and I told him where Louise was and sent him on his way. I rewound the footage and watched it again, this time completely ignoring the two of us - who I knew weren't guilty of murder - and concentrating on everyone else. There *must* be something, someone acting guilty, or looking at the door, wondering what to do about their cunning plan that had gone so horribly awry that the wrong victim had been carted off. No. Rob came back after a few minutes and resumed his place behind the bar, smiling at the diners as he poured drinks and looking tense as they turned their backs. He was not a happy bunny.

Joel and Zoé came back, the timid bookseller looking flushed as her companion held the door open for her; very few women (and not that many men) could withstand a blast of the Joel Quigley charm when it was aimed at them, and he seemed to have recovered sufficiently from our conversation beforehand to chat easily to her. Flirting came as naturally to him as breathing, but Zoé wouldn't have known that. And then Sarah left the Pearl, off to get her mother's medication, and out went the lights…

I stared at the darkened screen for a few seconds; I couldn't see a thing. Just as I went to fast forward, a flash of light appeared suddenly and disappeared just as quickly. I remembered that night; I'd thought at the time that maybe someone had opened the door and slipped out, but it was on the other side of the room so I'd dismissed it - in as much as I'd even thought about it, after everything that had happened afterwards. I rewound and watched it again; it was so brief, and the sudden brightness in the pitch dark made it difficult to make anything out. What was it?

I let the footage carry on. No more flashes of light, except for a tiny but insistent flash at the bottom of the screen, which I realised was Zoé's phone ringing. The screen lit up as the phone rang - I heard that awful ring tone in my head again, and smiled as I remembered how loud and inappropriate it had been, and how it had completely ruined the atmosphere - then after a few seconds, it stopped. The screen went dark again. Poor Zoé, she was so mortified that it had taken a couple of rings before she'd been able to turn it off.

"Hello! I've been looking for you everywhere!" Talk of the devil, Zoé stood at the foot of my sun lounger, smiling. I smiled back. "What are you doing?"

"Just relaxing, getting some air," I said, turning off the iPad. She looked at the tablet in my hand, an unasked question on her face. I hesitated for a moment; but she'd been in the Pearl, I'd just seen the evidence of that. What could be the harm in telling her? She was my greatest supporter on this ship *after my two lovers - ooh, imagine a Will and Joel sandwich BELLA STOP IT!* Thanking god she couldn't hear my internal monologue (and call a psychiatrist), I held the iPad up. "I've been going over the CCTV footage from the Pearl, from the night Louise died."

She looked surprised. "There was a camera in there?" I nodded. "Why didn't Mr Carter tell you before?"

"Because he was - still is - convinced it was me whodunnit. I only got it this morning."

"Has anyone else seen it?"

"I don't think so. The Chief Purser gave it to me and Will to watch. I haven't got to the end yet."

"Right…" She gave me a look, and I knew she was itching to ask if she could watch it too. I knew she would love to be the one who proved my innocence. Bless her.

"I was just thinking about going to the Pearl to watch the rest of it," I said. "There's something on here that's a bit weird and I want to have a look at the room again." I thought maybe I could work out where that flash of light had come from, if I had a look around the dining room. I smiled at her. "Wanna come and be my Dr Watson?"

CHAPTER 30

The answer to that question was, of course, an enthusiastic 'yes', so the two of us made our way to the Pearl. I thought briefly of texting Will to tell him where I was, but Zoé chattered away constantly and it felt a bit rude to pull out my phone while she was in full flow.

Will and I had left the door to the Pearl unlocked, so I led the way in and sat down at a table, Zoé still warbling on about something or other (I'm ashamed to admit that I tuned her out after a while; sweet as she was, she was given to brainless prattling). I nodded in response to her comment to make it look like I was listening (don't ask me what she said though, because I wasn't), surreptitiously slipped my phone out of my pocket and typed in a quick text to Will, telling him where I was.

Zoé breathlessly plumped herself down next to me and leaned over to look at the iPad, which I'd lain on the table in front of me.

"So what's this weird thing you want to have a look at?" she asked enthusiastically. There was something about her that made me think of an excitable puppy.

I looked up at the ceiling. "We're right under the security camera," I said, pointing upwards. "So this is as close to the camera angle as we can get."

I scrolled back to the bits where the lights had gone out and pressed Play. There was the flash again. I looked at Zoé, who just stared blankly at me.

"What do you think that is?" I said. She shrugged. "I thought at the time it was the door opening, but then I realised that the door's on the other side of the room. That's why I wanted to come and have a look around now."

I stood up and let my gaze travel in the direction the flash had come from. The end of the bar was on that side of the room, blocking everything else from view. I got up and walked around it. The wall behind the bar was painted black, and with the rich decor in the rest of the room it kind of made this area invisible. The door into the Pearl's kitchen was back here, but more to the centre of the room; so the sudden burst of light had not come from there. But as I got closer to the wall I noticed an outline, and a small handle, wooden, painted black; another door. I pulled.

Inside was a large storeroom, full of pots and pans, tinned goods, spices, flour - all the pantry essentials. It was cool but brightly lit, the large windows along one side of the room painted out. I remembered Will telling me about the cabin that had stood between Louise's room and the Pearl, which had been turned into a storeroom; this was it. Maybe the killer had come in here and slipped through the connecting door into her cabin?

Convinced that I had a lead at last, I searched for the connecting door. It took me some time to find it, as it was blocked by a rack of metal shelves, covered in oven trays. I pushed them aside, frustrated, and found the door handle. It was firmly locked and, by the look of it, the door opened into this room, rather than the room next door; or would've done, had there not been a bloody great rack of metal shelving in the way. So that was yet another dead end. There was no way the murderer could've come in here, slipped through the door and done the deed, and then got back to the Pearl. Even if they had been able to, the lights weren't out for that long, so it was really pushing it for time.

I sighed in frustration.

"Not what you were hoping for?" I jumped; Zoé was right next to me, and I'd almost forgotten she was there.

"No," I said, "unless…" I looked around for the door out into the corridor; but that too was blocked, by a tower of drink crates. Had this been a bar on land, there would have been the possibility that these had just been delivered, meaning the doorway might have been clear a few nights ago; but we were in the middle of the Atlantic - everything in this room would have been put there in Southampton, and wouldn't be moved again until we reached New York, tomorrow morning.

I turned and made my way out of the storeroom, pausing at the door. On the wall, just inside the room, was a telephone. It was an odd place to have a phone, I thought. But then it had been a cabin, so the cabling would already have been there; and it was probably handy for the chef when he was putting an order for supplies in.

It also meant that Louise's final phone call - made by the murderer - could have been made here…

Mind whirling, I went back into the Pearl followed by Zoé. We sat at the table again and I opened up the footage once more.

"This is so frustrating," I said, and she patted my hand comfortingly.

"I know."

"I need to prove someone else did it," I said, and she nodded again. "What if the police don't believe me? What if they blame me?"

"It is annoying when the wrong person gets the credit for something," she said soothingly, although I thought 'credit' was a slightly weird choice of word. I reached for the iPad again and scrolled back to the beginning of lights out.

There was the flash of light - I was certain it was someone going into the storeroom - and then the illuminated phone screen at the bottom, as Zoé's phone rang for a good 10 seconds before shutting off.

Something stirred in my mind. I replayed it.

The phone screen lit up - and then it just went dark. Surely if Zoé had picked it up, I would see it move on the footage? It would look like the phone was floating upwards, as she picked it up and declined the call to turn the ringing off.

The phone stayed on the desk. There wasn't even a shadowy figure or hand reaching out to turn it off, obscuring the screen. It just stopped ringing. *Or the person calling had rung off, after letting it ring just long enough for everyone in the room to hear it.*

Zoé had kept her phone under her nun's habit costume; that was where she had pulled it from earlier, and then replaced it.

Zoé had said she had gone behind the bar when the lights went out, for an assignation with Rob, and that her phone had ended up on the floor when she fumbled trying to turn it off.

So why was her phone on the table? She hadn't picked it up to turn it off - if she really was behind the bar snogging Rob, she couldn't have done.

There was a phone in the storeroom. Someone had gone in there. Someone had rung Zoé and given her an alibi for the time of the murder.

I had assumed she'd been in the room because I'd heard her phone go off. *But I hadn't seen her*. I hadn't even really seen where she'd come from when the lights had come back on.

All this time I'd ruled her out because of that phone call…

Zoé was watching me, an unfamiliar expression on her face. She no longer looked like an over-excited puppy, and her IQ seemed to have gone up a couple of notches. *Zoé's played me like a fool,* I thought. I'd been pre-disposed to, if not like her, at least think kindly of her, because

218

she was my number one fan and because she was apparently going through a traumatic marriage breakdown, just like I had.

I am a bloody idiot.

"Oh dear," she sighed. "I was hoping you wouldn't work it out." She chuckled. "I was hoping to write the book and send it to you in prison, when it was too late. Believe it or not, I was hoping not to kill you."

My mouth suddenly felt very dry. I swallowed hard. "Well that's one thing we've got in common, then," I said. "I'm hoping you don't kill me as well."

"Ah, but I think it's too late for that," she said regretfully. She almost sounded sincere. I went to stand up, but then stopped as I felt something sharp pressed into my side. I looked down to see a very sharp carving knife, pressed against my kidneys.

"Bloody hell!" I said. "You say you were hoping not to have to kill me but you still came prepared."

She shook her head. "I just got it out of the store cupboard," she said. *Bollocks. Note to self: when on the trail of a serial killer, avoid big cupboards full of potential weapons.* It was a rookie mistake, but it was also possibly my last one.

But Will was on his way. If I could just keep her talking long enough for him to get here… On cue, my phone rang. I looked at her.

"If that's Will and I don't answer, he'll know something's wrong," I said. She stared at me thoughtfully.

"Okay, take it out and see who it is."

I took out my phone and placed it on the table. "It's my agent."

Her eyes narrowed. "Susie Slater? Answer it." I went to pick the call up but she stopped me. "Put it on speakerphone and don't try anything. Just tell her everything's fine."

I answered the call. "Hi Susie." My voice sounded funny, kind of like I was being held at knifepoint by a mad woman. She was sure to know something was up.

"Oh my god!" said Susie, speaking in her normal slightly rushed you-are-NOT-going-to-believe-this voice. "I just got your message. Sorry, Guy took me to this Buddhist retreat place, did I tell you he's thinking of taking up meditation? Anyway we went for a look round and you would NOT believe it, they don't let you take your mobile phone in with you! We had to leave ours in a box by the entrance. That put Guy off, I can tell you. Anyway - "

"Yeah, I'm fine thanks for asking," I said, somewhat aggrieved that she hadn't asked how I was. *I'm stuck on a boat with a serial killer and I'm being set up for their murders, and you are NOT going to believe this but being framed is currently not the worst thing I'm facing.*

"Sorry, darling, how are you? Anyway I looked into this Sarah woman and actually, you really wouldn't believe it but I'm in the middle of reading her book and it's really good! If you see her tell her I'll be ringing for a chat."

"That's great…" I said. I was trying to recall a conversation we'd had a while ago, inspired by something daft I'd seen on Twitter. You've been kidnapped and your captors are listening in to your phone call, so you can't tell anyone - what would you say that was so out of character that the person on the other end of the phone knew you were in trouble? We'd had a good laugh at that. I could remember what I'd come up with, but I wasn't sure I could introduce the phrase, *'Actually I think Boris Johnson is a misunderstood genius and not at all twattish'* without it sounding suspicious.

Susie hadn't noticed my uncharacteristic lack of conversation and carried on.

"I did come up with someone else, though. Do you remember, after we brought out Dead in Venice, that woman who contacted me and said you'd stolen the idea from her?"

I looked at Zoé and I immediately knew who that woman was.

"Oh yeah, I remember her," I said deliberately. "She was a bloody nutcase."

Zoé opened her mouth to speak, but remembered the phone in time. *Damn.*

"Well I have to confess I did rather downplay the situation," said Susie. "You'd been through such a lot, and you were just finding happiness again with Will, I didn't want anything to spoil it…"

"What happened?" I asked, looking unwaveringly at Zoé, who was starting to look flushed and angry.

"She was convinced you'd read a manuscript she'd sent in," said Susie. "Ludicrous of course, I'd never pass someone else's story onto you."

"No, you never have done that." Zoé was looking very flustered. Good.

"Anyway, I explained all this but she was insistent and threatened to take you to court for plagiarism." I shook my head slowly, my eyes still locked on Zoé's, as Susie spoke. "She was a bloody pest. I pointed out the expense of a court case, the unlikelihood of her winning - even if it was true, which it wasn't, these things are almost impossible to prove - but she kept sending us letters. Guy was quite concerned at one point. In the end we had to get Geoffrey - " Geoffrey Maddox was the company's solicitor - "to send her a strongly worded letter, threatening her with the police. It did the trick."

"Did it now."

"Well, yes, we thought so. But you think she's connected with this terrible business there? Do you think she's on the boat?"

Zoé reached out and disconnected the call.

"Yes," I said. "I think she's on the boat…"

CHAPTER 31

Zoé picked up the phone and tapped on the text messages. *Bugger.* She spotted the message I'd sent to Will.

"So you planned to keep me talking until he turned up to save you, did you?" she said. I shrugged.

"Maybe. Possibly. I don't know - "

"And you're *still* trying to keep me talking until he gets here." She rolled her eyes. "I'm not stupid. Get up." She prodded me with the knife and I stood up. She followed suit, turning briefly to pick up the iPad, which was still playing the CCTV footage. "Let's go for a little walk."

"Fine by me," I said. How far did she think we were going to get on a ship full of people, without someone spotting the carving knife in my side?

But when we left the Pearl, walking through the Excelsior dining room towards the lifts, other than a few staff getting ready for the evening's dinner service there was hardly anyone about. I realised that it must be around 5 o'clock, and many of the guests would be having a lie down, before scrubbing up for the night's festivities; as it was our last night at sea, there was to be a big gala dinner and dance, all black ties and fancy frocks.

We stepped into a lift and Zoé pressed the button for deck 5. *Someone else must get in* I thought, but they didn't.

We got out and Zoé prodded me through a doorway and out onto the deck. The life boats, including the last resting place of Rob the steward, lay ahead of us.

"Returning to the scene of the crime," I said. "Or one of them, anyway. Why did you kill Rob? Was he going to dob you in?"

"Shut up." She pushed me along the deck, past the lifeboats until we reached the end of the metal passageway. After a calm and sunny morning, the wind had picked up and was whipping the sea into peaks and troughs. The ship was heavy enough and had a stabilising mechanism that meant it could plough through some pretty big seas, but we still staggered a little as the waves parted briefly and then came together again to thrust the boat upwards.

She pushed me against the thin metal railing. Passengers tended not to come this far along the deck, the purser David had told us, because the life boats blocked the view. Not that there was much of a view when you were mid-Atlantic; just sea, sea and more sea. We were close to our journey's end now though, and if you squinted your eyes there was the suggestion - no more than a faint haze - of land on the horizon. If you came out here in a few hours' time, when it was dark, the lights of New York would just be beginning to twinkle in the distance.

But I might not be here in a few hours' time.

"So you're going to kill me, then?" I asked, with an attempt at nonchalance. I'm not sure it fooled either of us. "What are you going to do? Stab me then leave me a in lifeboat, or push me off the deck? Or had you not planned that far ahead? Tell me, was killing Louise part of your plan?"

She rolled her eyes. "Do you really think I'm going to stand here and tell you how I planned everything?" she asked. "The murderer *always* does that in your novels, it's so tedious how everything gets tied up in a neat little bow at the end."

"It's called 'giving your readers what they want'," I said sarcastically. "They want a resolution. I'm assuming you've had less success with doing that than I have."

She glared at me furiously. "Only because you stole my idea - "

I snorted. Not Will-level contemptuous snorting, but getting there. "I don't need to steal anyone's ideas, I've got plenty of my own."

"I sent you my manuscript! Your agent - that bitch - said she hadn't passed it onto you, but six months later what comes out? Your book, with too many similarities to mine to be a coincidence."

I laughed incredulously. "You stupid tart, that was based on a real life case that happened when I was staying in Venice. I didn't have to make much up and I certainly didn't copy anyone."

"Your agent tried to fob me off with that excuse, then she got her lawyer to send me a threatening letter and I knew she was running scared. I knew I couldn't leave it at that. This has ruined my whole life - my marriage - my husband left me, he said I was becoming obsessed - "

"Well I think he might have had a point, don't you, you daft bint?"

She was silent for a moment, fuming, but I thought I could see a hint of confusion and doubt. I pounced on it.

"You tried to drug me, didn't you? You roped Rob into it somehow. I saw him put something in my wine that night, only I didn't drink it, Louise did. So how did you end up murdering her?"

"She was bloody annoying," hissed Zoé, and I could hardly disagree. But being annoyed and being homicidal were rather different things.

"You took her back to her cabin, you didn't have to kill her - "

"But I did!" she said defensively. "That idiot Rob blurted it out in front of her - I wasn't sure how much she'd remember - "

"I don't understand why you tried to drug me in the first place," I said. I had to keep her talking.

"It wasn't meant to knock you out, like it did with Louise," she said, and there was a definite sense now that she was panicking; she really *hadn't* planned any of this. "It was meant to be a truth drug, but it was too strong. Maybe I gave Rob too much…"

"What was supposed to happen?"

"You were supposed to drink it, and then I would either ask you why you copied my book right there, in front of everyone, or if it was too obvious that I'd drugged you I would get Rob to help me carry you back to your cabin, and then film you on my phone confessing to stealing my idea."

"Why would Rob help you?" I asked. "Was he a friend of yours?"

"No," said Zoé. "Not at all. He wasn't a very nice person. I heard him talking to that other steward - Karl? - out here on my first night, about stealing from the passengers. My cabin isn't a fancy one like yours, it's just there - " she pointed to a porthole just along the deck. "One of the cheap ones. The cheapest room on the ship, because the life boats block the view. I was going to carry out my plan alone, but I thought it would be easier for him to spike your drink. So I came out here when Karl left him and told him that I was going to make a very rich woman pay for wronging me, and that I would be coming into a lot of money."

"And the promise of that was enough to get him on side?"

She shrugged. "That and a blowjob."

I looked her, shaking my head. "You are one very sick puppy."

"It's not like you're a bloody nun, is it? The way you're leading Will and Joel on…"

226

A light bulb came on in my head. "Those photos on Twitter - they were you, weren't they? You were trying to make me look bad before getting me to confess."

"The first photos weren't," she said. "But they gave me the idea of taking the 'guilty' picture of you."

"So when did you stab Louise? You can't have had time when the lights went out." Zoé had said she wasn't going to stand there and tell me everything, but I was hoping she'd forgotten that. If there's one thing that I've found to be true in real life investigations (I've read police reports and occasionally been allowed to watch interrogations) as well as in crime novels, it's that when the murderer is cornered or nearing the end of the line, they really do like to tell you what they've done; whether it's to unburden themselves or show how clever they've been, I don't know.

"I got Louise back to her cabin and sent Rob away before he blurted out anything else. She threw up on me, stupid bitch, so I took off my nun's costume and went to wash it off in the bathroom. When I went back into the bedroom she was struggling to sit up and she said she'd tell you what I'd done. I was so angry with her for taking your drink and ruining everything, then bloody puking on me, that I just grabbed the corkscrew and stuck it in her neck." She ran a hand through her hair, and I could see that her fingers were trembling. "*That* sobered her up. She tried to get up and ended up on the floor."

"But Joel came to the cabin - "

She laughed scornfully. "Joel's bloody useless, isn't he? I mean he's hot, I can see why you'd want him, but he's not long term partner material. He stuck his head round the door but he obviously didn't really want to get involved. I was just coming out of the bathroom - I had to look in the mirror to get my wimple straight - and he was right there. If he'd come any further in he'd have seen her lying on the floor. I told him she was throwing up and 'spoke' to her in the bathroom. I pretended to hear her reply and Joel, desperate as he was not to have to deal with her, thought he heard her too."

"And all the time you were doing that, she was bleeding to death at your feet."

"Yes."

"But you must've been covered in her blood?"

"I was." She looked down at her hands. "My hands and face, my chest… I wiped the bits that showed on her bedding, then just put the nun's habit back on."

I looked at her in horror. "So you spent the rest of the night sitting in the Pearl, covered in Louise's blood under your costume?"

"I didn't know what else to do!" she said, almost pleadingly. Well she could plead as much as she wanted to, I was never going to have any sympathy for someone who had already killed three people and was eyeing up a fourth - all over a sodding book.

"So when did you decide to frame me?" I asked, and she sniggered. She was clearly barking mad. I wasn't sure if she'd been mental before getting on the ship or if murdering Louise had driven her around the bend.

"I thought it would be poetic justice if you got the credit for my work *again*," she said. "I knew I couldn't be the last one to see her alive, so I decided to ring the purser's desk - I knew there was a phone in the store room because Rob and I had had a - what do you call it?"

"Shag?"

"An assignation in there earlier."

"I was right, a shag. How unhygienic. And then you rang your own phone to give yourself an alibi, knowing that everyone had heard that stupid ring tone."

She smirked. "I know, how brilliant was that? I love that song. I was annoyed when my husband rang me earlier - I suppose he was trying to make sure I didn't do anything stupid - "

"That worked well," I humphed. She ignored me.

"He didn't realise he was helping to give me an alibi. Which makes it all the sweeter…"

CHAPTER 32

As Zoé smiled and looked irritatingly pleased with herself, I leant against the railing and let my hand drop to my side. I felt the reassuring shape of my own mobile phone in my pocket and prayed I hadn't inadvertently knocked it. I couldn't believe that I'd managed to slip it into my trousers as we left the Pearl without her noticing, but then she'd been distracted by the iPad and by the thought that Will was on his way, hurrying to get away before he arrived.

"So you killed Louise," I said, "and you gave yourself a brilliant alibi. You were never even on my list of suspects because I just assumed you were in the Pearl when the phone call was made. And then when Joel turned up - to carry on as if nothing had happened - to tell him she was asleep and then just leave her there, dying - you're a psychopath!"

Zoé shrugged. "Whatever. At least I'm not a plagiarist."

I gritted my teeth. "I didn't steal your bloody story! And anyway, I think murdering three people trumps plagiarism, don't you? Which leads me to ask - why *did* you murder Sylvia? Up to that point I was looking good for it, but you planted my belt on her and that was just too obvious. Harry Carter was convinced it was me, but even he started to have doubts after that." I looked at her. "And how did you get hold of my belt? And my corkscrew?"

"Don't you remember?" She smirked at me, and *then* I remembered. I groaned.

"You came to see me in my cabin the morning afterwards," I said. "Checking up on me, being a good friend… You took the corkscrew then, didn't you?"

She nodded. "I hadn't planned to, but it was there on the table. I saw it was a fancy one like Louise's, and I knew mine wasn't like that, so I was hoping it would narrow the field of suspects down a bit. And there was a key card on the side, so I took that too, just in case it came in handy. And of course, it did."

"You came in a couple of nights later and took my kimono belt," I said. "I knew someone had been in there. And you put the key card back so we wouldn't notice it was missing."

"I couldn't believe you hadn't already," she said. "Really, so careless leaving it lying around like that, anyone could've picked it up."

"Anyone did," I said shortly. "But poor Sylvia…"

"It was a toss up between her and Heather," said Zoé. "Heather was winding me up. She was so convinced of your innocence and she wouldn't shut up about it, but I could see Sylvia wasn't sure. When I started listing all the evidence against you, the cracks really started appearing - even Michael half-thinks you did it now. I wanted to shut Heather up, but I thought it would make more sense for you to murder Sylvia, so she had to go. I told her I'd discovered something that proved you'd done it, but I was too scared to go to the Captain or Harry Carter in case they told you about it. I asked her to meet me in the Gatsby, because I knew you wouldn't be there and it would be quiet."

"You were taking a big risk, though," I said, and she smirked again.

"Oh but I never went to the Gatsby," she said. "An unknown steward went there instead…"

"Of course - you'd already bumped off Rob to keep him quiet, and you went to his cabin and took his uniform."

"The stewards have got caps as well, although most of them only wear them during the welcome aboard party," she said. "I took that as well and tucked my hair up inside it. I walked straight past Harvey and Michael and they didn't even notice me. No one looks at you once you put a uniform on. All the stewards blend in with each other, don't they? That's how I got your corkscrew into Louise's room too."

"So you waited for Sylvia and suffocated her with a plastic bag. That must've taken some doing."

"I'm stronger than I look." Zoé almost looked proud of herself. Mad bitch.

"When did you kill Rob?"

"That night, after the murder - "

"Which one?"

"You know which one. Louise's. He was already panicking about slipping her the drug, and I knew that once he heard she'd died - well, I had to get to him quick, before he had a chance to confess to the Captain."

"So you lured him up here, to the life boats where you'd first met him, for a shag before dispatching him. Classy."

"He was stronger than Sylvia, wasn't he? I had to get him to let his guard down. If it's any consolation, he wasn't a very nice person and he died happy."

"You really are completely bloody bonkers. You feel absolutely no guilt about any of this, do you?" I could see on her face that she really didn't grasp what she'd done. In her eyes, she'd been totally justified - because I'd stolen her idea.

Let me be honest here: all writers worry at some point in their career about having inadvertently stolen an idea. I don't mean we read someone's unpublished manuscript and go, *'oh yeah, I'll have a bit of that!'*, more that, like everyone else, we watch stuff on the telly and read other books and go to movies, and some stuff just kind of sticks. Add to that the fact that there are only so many plots to go around, so many character archetypes, so many locations and settings and, I dunno, names - at some point there's going to be that nagging little voice that asks (quietly but insistently) where that idea came from. Sometimes I've come up with something that I think is so cool it worries me, because I think I can't possibly have invented something that good.

If Zoé had been talking about any other book of mine than the one I'd written about my time in Venice, when I'd met Will, I might have had one of those moments of worry; because who can honestly say, hand on heart, that they've never been influenced by someone else's work to some degree? But that book came straight from my own experience and I knew, without a shadow of a doubt, that any similarities between her work and mine were just a coincidence.

Besides which, she had just confessed, quite proudly, to murdering three people...

"So what happens now?" I asked.

"You die."

"Yeah, I guessed that bit." I rolled my eyes. "I meant, let's assume you've just killed me, what happens now? Do you really expect to get away with it?"

"I don't see why not." She smiled. I was looking forward to wiping that smug (if somewhat insane) look off her face. "Like you said, I'm not a suspect. I was never even on anyone's radar."

"Hmm, I dunno. Will thought there was something weird about you." I laughed. "Understatement or what? 'Weird'! I should bloody say so." She looked angry but I spoke again before she could say anything. "No, what I really mean is, how do you expect to get away when you've just done exactly what you said you wouldn't do and told me everything?"

"Yeah, well that won't be a problem when you're dead, will it?" She took a step towards me, drawing her arm back ready to thrust the knife in. I sent up a silent cry for help: *please be there...*

I pulled out my mobile phone and held it up. "It might still be a teeny bit of a problem, seeing as we've just been broadcasting live on Facebook." I risked a glance at the phone screen and was relieved to see that I actually *had* hit the Facebook live icon as I'd stuffed it in my pocket, and not the Amazon app instead, which would have been both embarrassing and possibly fatal. And I might have inadvertently bought something I didn't want, and you know what some Amazon sellers are like when it comes to refunds...

"What?!" Zoé shrieked in horror and made a grab for the phone, dropping the knife. I let her take it, gazing over her shoulder as she stared at it.

"Ooh, look how many 'likes' we've got!" I said. "I do have a lot of followers. Let's read some of the comments - "

Zoé gave what could only be described as a howl of rage and threw herself at me, hitting me with her full bodyweight - which, next to mine, was a bit puny, but still heavy enough to knock all the air out of me as I hit the metal railing. She pulled back and drew back her arm to hit me -

"Oh no you don't!" Will grabbed her arm and she howled again, as Joel took hold of her other arm. I looked up to see them standing behind her and felt relief wash over me.

"About bloody time!" I said, then swayed a bit as I realised how close a call I'd just had. Will let go of Zoé, handing her over to Joel, and took me in his arms; I wasn't sure if he was hugging me or holding me up, but at that moment I needed both so I wasn't fussed either way.

"Are you okay?" Will held me tight, his face buried in my hair, and I heard him take a deep, shuddery breath. Evidently it had been a bit close for him, too.

"Sorry we took a while, we had to make sure she confessed to everything," said Joel. "It was a bit hard to hear what she was saying - "

Will must have felt me freeze because he squeezed me and said, "It's alright, we got enough. She won't be going anywhere."

Suddenly Zoé stamped down hard on Joel's foot. Joel must've relaxed his grip slightly as he spoke to me, because the next thing we knew she'd freed herself and flown at me and Will. Will whirled me around, out of her way, but she had too much momentum to stop. Zoé screamed as she hit the railing, which was quite low here, and went straight over the top.

"Oh my god!" I rushed to the railing and looked over, expecting to see her thrashing about in the water below - that was certainly what she'd had planned for my body - but this deck was narrower than the one below, leaving room for the lifeboats to hang and then be winched out over the water during an evacuation. Zoé landed on the metal deck beneath us with a loud thud, which knocked her out cold.

"Is she dead?" cried Joel, looking down on her twisted body. A groan escaped her.

"No, but that's got to hurt," said Will. We all shared a look.

"Shame," I said.

CHAPTER 33

So Zoé, the previously air headed but harmless bookseller turned psychotic murderer, lived. The ship's doctor was called, and she was loaded onto a stretcher and taken away to where Harry Carter was waiting for her.

Meanwhile Will, Joel and I went to get a stiff drink.

"You took your time," I said to Will. "I was hoping you'd find me before we left the Pearl."

He smiled. "Sorry. Better late than never. If I'd known you were with Zoé though I'd have warned you." He looked at my confused face. "The email Carmen sent me - I'd asked her to dig up some back ground on a few of our fellow passengers. Zoé, Peter and Lauren - " He stopped abruptly, glancing at Joel. Joel noticed and shrugged.

"I'd probably have done the same in your position," he said. "Did you find anything interesting?"

"About you? Not a thing." Will grinned at him. "I didn't have much to go on with Zoé, just this feeling. I got Carmen to check up on her job. You remember she said she'd won her place on the cruise, for being top salesperson in a bookstore chain?" I nodded. "She said it was Montgomery's Books, but when Carmen checked she discovered they'd let her go last year after an incident."

"An incident?" I asked. Will nodded.

"That's all they would tell her. 'An incident'. She had to buy her own ticket. Why would she lie about that? It made me wonder what else she was hiding."

"Susie rang me - "

"She rang me too," said Will, and Joel nodded.

"Yeah, and me. I didn't even know she still had my number."

"She rang me and said you'd abruptly put the phone down on her, and that you'd sounded a bit funny," said Will. "And then she told me about this woman who was accusing you of plagiarism…"

I gulped at my drink, the warmth of the alcohol helping to calm the trembling in my fingers, although I suspected it would take a few more to stop it completely.

"When I grabbed the phone I wanted to call you, but I only had a couple of seconds while that mad cow's attention was elsewhere. I clicked the Facebook icon by accident as I picked it up, so the easiest and quickest thing to do was hit the live video button and hope the phone would pick up what we were saying."

"You could have been a bit more blatant when you said you'd returned to the scene of the crime," said Joel. "There have been quite a few crime scenes."

"How did you know I was on Facebook?" I said. "I was hoping you'd get a notification or something."

Joel nodded and I was surprised. He looked defensive. "I never got round to unfriending you."

"You know I don't really do social media," said Will. "But Susie saw it and rang me again straight away. Joel came and found me, and then we followed your trail."

"And you saved me. Both of you. My heroes!" I raised my glass to them both, and knocked back what was left of my drink. Joel grinned and followed suit, then so did Will, more hesitantly.

The Captain came and found us, and the Chief Purser, and by then the news was out all over the ship. Heather came and cried on me for a bit, relieved to have found out who had killed her best friend, and I think relieved that she hadn't been wrong about me. Harvey and Michael came and hugged me, Michael slightly shamefaced, although I told him I would have had doubts about me in his place too. I wouldn't have, but it didn't hurt to be magnanimous.

I looked at Will across the by-now crowded bar and gave him my 'rescue me' look - it had come in handy a few times, when we'd been at book events and I'd been accosted by over-enthusiastic fans. I'm an extroverted introvert; I do like socialising, but I get to a certain point and it's all just too much.

It had been a long day…

Will shouldered his way through the crowd and took my hand, pulling me gently to my feet and slipping an arm around my waist.

"I think Bella needs a lie down now," he said, looking around. "She's been through a lot."

The crowd looked a bit disappointed - they hadn't all had the chance to hear me recount my adventures first hand - but they made understanding noises and stood aside to let me through.

We got back to our cabin. It felt like it had been a very long time since we'd got up that morning, and there had been points where I hadn't been sure I'd ever see this room again.

Will kissed me gently, and held me as I cried small but exhausted tears. This trip had been emotional, and I was glad it was coming to an end tomorrow. Then we undressed and made slow, tender love until we fell asleep in each other's arms.

I woke the next morning fizzing with excitement. We were nearing New York, one of my favourite cities (in small doses) in the world! And I'd solved three murders, cleared my name, *and* survived an attack by an insane ex-bookseller. I leapt out of bed, filled with a kind of mad, manic energy; I felt ready for anything, but settled for putting the kettle on.

Will however had different ideas, and was still fast asleep. Even the boiling kettle and the scent of that first cup of tea of the day wafted under his nostrils couldn't make him keep his eyes open.

"Bella..." he groaned, rolling over. "It's too early..."

"No it's not!" I cried, bouncing on the bed in what really must have been an irritating manner. "It's - okay it's 7.30 and we don't dock for hours yet, but we might be able to see land by now!"

"Go and stand on the balcony." His words were muffled by the pillow.

"I already did. We're on the wrong side to get a decent view until we're closer." I leaned over and nuzzled the back of his neck. "Ooh you're so sexy when you're asleep..."

"Stop treating me as a sex object..." he moaned.

"You don't really mean that," I said, and he rolled over to look at me.

"Of course I don't really mean that," he said. "But I'm tired. How are you not tired after yesterday?"

I fidgeted. "I think it's *because* of yesterday."

He stared at me for a moment, then smiled. "I get it. But I'm still half asleep..."

"It's okay," I said, leaning in to kiss him on the lips. "You sleep. I need to go and burn off some energy. I'll go for a walk on deck. Back later."

I kissed him again, then threw on leggings and a hoody and left him lying there.

Out on deck the wind blew away the last vestiges of sleep and left me feeling even more awake and alert. I had the horrible feeling that I was still running on the adrenaline of the previous day, and that at some point I would crash, but that was later. Right now I wanted to get my first glimpse of the Big Apple from the sea.

I strode along the deck and round a corner, and nearly knocked Joel off his feet. He put his hands out to stop both of us falling over.

"Steady on, Bell!" He laughed. "Now that's the Bella I remember. Bella the whirlwind."

"Sorry, I just woke up this morning feeling like I need to go for a run or something."

"A run? You? Do you want me to call the doctor?"

I slapped him. "Alright, you cheeky sod! I did say 'or something'." He raised an eyebrow and I slapped him again.

"What was that one for?"

"I know what you and your raised eyebrows mean." I glared at him, then laughed.

"You know me so well, Bella," he said, smiling, and my tummy did that big stupid flippy thing. *Pack it in, you daft tart!*

"I know you too well, Joel," I said.

"Coffee?"

"Oh god no. Tea."

We walked to one of the many coffee shops. There were a few other early risers in for their breakfast, but the party last night had apparently been a big one and most people were having a lie in.

"Good party last night?" I asked.

"I don't know. I didn't stay for long after you left."

"No? Who was the lucky lady?" I smirked but he actually looked a bit hurt.

"I'm not *that* bad," he said.

"Hmm, you kind of are..."

He laughed. "I was. Not any more." He fixed me with an intense, serious gaze, and I felt my knicker elastic start to weaken a little...

"Bell…"

"Joel."

"You know what I'm going to ask you."

"Oh of course! Here you go." I pushed the sugar bowl across the table to him and he sighed.

"You're not going to make this easy for me, are you?" he asked.

"Hell no." He opened his mouth to speak and I reached over to touch his hand. "Don't, Joel. I'm happy. We're friends again - "

"Are we?"

"Sort of. I didn't think I could ever forgive you, but… Actually I don't entirely forgive you, but I just don't care as much any more." I smiled at him. "Let's just leave it at that, yeah?"

But Joel being Joel, he wouldn't. I moved my hand away but he grabbed it with both of his.

"Bella, I love you. I was wrong to treat you the way I did - "

"Why *did* you treat me the way you did?" He looked down at the table, but I reached out with my free hand to touch his cheek briefly. He looked up again in surprise and I jerked my hand away. "I'm not trying to punish you, I just want to know why. And I want *you* to know why."

He let go of me and sat back. "I don't know… I just had this image, the bad boy of crime writing, didn't I? Women like a bad boy." He grinned at me then, a hint of the old arrogant Joel charm surfacing. "Some women, anyway… They just threw themselves at me."

"I know they did, Joel. But you didn't have to catch them."

"No, I know. I just - I felt a bit useless. *You* made me feel useless - " He saw the look on my face and spoke quickly. "Not on purpose, I know. But your career was doing so much better than mine. I couldn't write, I couldn't even get you pregnant…"

The word hung in the air between us. It hurt. But at least I knew now that it had hurt both of us.

"You twat, that wasn't your fault, was it? It was both of us." I looked at him properly, for the first time in ages, without swooning or wanting to kill him, and was struck by how sad he looked. I didn't think it would last, but it reminded me that Joel - for so long referred to as my bastard unfaithful ex-husband - did actually have feelings. He had a heart, and once it had been mine. The question was, did I want it back?

"Let's try again," he said, hopefully. "You've made your peace with not having kids, I mean you and Will won't be having them will you?" Okay now he was starting to annoy me again. But to his credit he realised that. "Forget I said that. I didn't mean it like that. I just meant…" He sat back in his chair and sighed again. I'd never heard so much sighing or evidence of regret come from this man. "I miss you, Bell."

I felt the tears pricking at my eyes. He missed me.

"You shouldn't have left me," I said.

"To be fair, you threw me out."

"I might have packed your bags, but every time you slept with someone else you left me a little bit more."

"I'll never cheat on you again, I swear! Please, Bella - "

I looked at him silently. He stopped, hastily swiping at his eyes.

"Do you know, after we spilt up I used to wake up every morning and roll over to kiss you good morning, and it would physically hurt me that you weren't there," I said. He looked away so he wouldn't have to meet my gaze. "Did you feel like that?"

"I didn't, not straight away," he said. "That might not be what you want to hear, but I'm being honest. I thought I was fine being single, hooking up every now and then with Louise, or there were other women… None of them meant anything, not the way you did. I was lonely and I didn't realise it. And then I came here and saw you and Will together, and it just reminded me of what I'd lost - "

242

"Thrown away," I corrected him. He nodded ruefully.

"You're right," he said. "But I can make it up to you! I can - "

"You can't," I said. "And not because you hurt me too badly and I still hate you or anything like that. Because you didn't - I mean, you did at the time but I got over it - and I don't. Hate you, that is. But I don't want you to make it up to me. I love Will. I trust him with my heart and my life. I told you that. Will and I have been through things that would've torn you and me apart straight away."

"But I love you!"

"No you don't. You just said it yourself. You're lonely. You don't want me, you want what we almost had, what me and Will *do* have. You want to be in love again. That's good. It's better than just wanting to jump the bones of anything in a skirt." I patted his hand. "It means you're growing up, Joel."

He still looked sad, but he managed a smile. "Noooo! Do I really have to grow up?"

"I'm afraid so. A little bit, anyway." I leaned in and whispered to him. "You don't have to go as far as buying a cardigan or getting a funeral insurance policy, though."

He reached out and took my hand, and I let him hold it for a little while. Then I pulled away.

"Better not," I said, "the phantom Twitter photographer might take a picture."

He laughed. "I didn't tell you, did I? I found out who it was. I've got a friend who works at the newspaper that leaked it. It was Peter Maguire."

I was amazed. "The skinny dude who's so white he looks like he's wearing a doctor's coat but isn't?"

243

"Yeah, him. Apparently he's trying to raise funds for his next film project. My contact said he was well pissed off when they only gave him a hundred quid for both photos."

"Well I never…" I shook my head. "You did realise I wasn't jealous, didn't you?"

"I knew you weren't," he said, and we both knew that I had been, a little bit.

CHAPTER 34

I made my way back to the cabin. New York was really near now, and I wanted to stand on the balcony of our cabin with my gorgeous husband and watch it get closer.

Will was up and dressed. He looked pleased when I entered.

"I was just going to come and find you," he said. "You've been gone ages."

"Yeah, sorry about that," I said. "I ran into Joel."

He was immediately on his guard. "Oh, right, What did he want?"

"He asked me to take him back."

Will looked away, busying himself with packing the last of his things into the suitcase.

"I hope you told him to get lost," he said, with a surprising lack of confidence.

"No, I didn't," I said, and saw his shoulders sag immediately. I ploughed straight on. "Because that would mean that I hate him, which I don't. I have no strong feelings towards him either way. All my strong feelings are currently reserved for you and only you."

He turned to me, hesitantly. "Are you sure? I mean, he's younger than I am, and cooler, and more successful, with better hair…"

"Oh god you're right, what have I done?" I laughed and grabbed him, pulling him in for a long, deep kiss. "You know what, you and I have got to stop comparing ourselves to other people. I think for a while there I was jealous of Louise - "

"You what?" Now Will looked flabbergasted.

"Honestly, I think I was. She was young and tall and slim, not as attractive as me of course and a terrible writer… But she had this reputation for being fierce and gritty and serious, all the things I'm not."

"I'm glad you're not," said Will. "That sounds awful!"

I laughed. "It does actually, doesn't it? You and I are bloody awesome. Together we're magnificent! I will never let anyone come between us, and I will never, *ever*, want anyone other than you. You do know that, don't you?"

He grinned slyly. "Hmm, I don't know," he said. "Prove it."

So I did.

Thanks and Acknowledgments

This is the trickiest bit of any book to write, because there are so many people I want to thank - for their help, for their encouragement or for inspiring me - and I want to strike a balance between an abrupt 'yeah, thanks' and the type of embarrassingly long Oscar-acceptance speech that has the floor manager making winding-up motions, followed by throat cutting ones. And of course now I'm making it unnecessarily long by explaining myself. Ho hum.

So to cut to the chase: thank you to the wonderful women and fellow (massively talented) writers who have been my biggest cheerleaders and who continue to push me, stop me quitting and occasionally feed me chocolate. **Carmen Radtke** and **Jade Bokhari**, you are always there cheering me on and I would not have done any of this without you. And then of course there are my Renegade Sisterhood of Writers, **Sandy Barker**, **Andie Newton** and **Nina Kaye**. Thank you for the encouragement and the laughs! And last but definitely not least is my agent, lovely **Lina Langlee**, who has never given up on me, even when I have. Writing can be a lonely business, but not with these six wonder women behind me!

And of course I really must thank my lovely family, husband **Dominic** and son **Lucas**, who have been there with mugs of tea, hugs and the odd box of tissues to keep me going. I love you!

About the Author

Fiona Leitch is a writer with a chequered past. She's written for a football magazine and a motoring agency, despite knowing nothing about either football or cars. She's acted in TV commercials, played keyboards in a band, and organised illegal raves. She loves travel, food and writing romcoms and cosy mysteries, and is represented by Lina Langlee at the North Literary Agency.

Printed in Great Britain
by Amazon

48950019R00142